SECRET PUCK

REBECCA JENSHAK

ALSO BY
REBECCA JENSHAK

Smart Jocks Series

The Catch

The Assist

The Fadeaway

The Tip-Off

The Fake

Standalone Novels

Sweet Spot

Electric Blue Love

Jilted Jock

If Not For Love

PLAYLIST

"Forever" by FLETCHER
"Wow" by Zara Larsson
"I'm Not Alright" by Loud Luxury and Bryce Vine
"Savage Remix" by Megan Thee Stallion feat. Beyoncé
"Break My Heart" by Dua Lipa
"DNF" by Preme feat. Drake and Future
"Be Kind" by Marshmello feat. Halsey
"Sick and Tired" by iann dior feat. Machine Gun Kelly
"Fantasy" by Mariah Carey
"Paradise" by Bazzi
"Say So" by Dojo Cat feat. Nicki Minaj
"Boyfriend" by Selena Gomez
"24" by Arizona Zervas
"ROCKSTAR" by DaBaby feat. Roddy Ricch
"Turn Down for What" by DJ Snake, Lil Jon
"Emotionally Scarred" by Lil Baby
"Find My Way" by DaBaby
"Celebration Station" by Lil Uzi Vert
"Young & Alive" by Bazzi
"Kings & Queens" by Ava Max
"X" by Jonas Brothers feat KAROL G
"Teenager in Love" by Madison Beer
"Wishing Well" by Juice WRLD
"Love Somebody" by Lauv
"LMK" by Lil XXEL
"You Be Killin Em" by Fabolous
"The Fix" by Nelly feat. Jeremih
"ily" by Surf Mesa feat. Emilee
"Baby Girl" by Bryce Vine feat. Jeremih
"Fantasy Remix" by Mariah Carey feat. ODB

AUGUST

Chapter One

GINNY

What are you doing here?" I ask my brother through a small crack in the door.

He leans his large frame against it, widening the gap and keeping me from closing it on him. "I'm checking on my favorite sister."

"I'm your only sister."

He pushes a big shoulder against it, and I give up on trying to keep him out. Crossing the small dorm room in three steps, I resume my position on the bed.

"Have you left the dorm at all this weekend?" He follows me and takes a seat at the end of my bed. "Hey, Ava."

My roommate Ava's on the phone with her boyfriend Trent, but waves and blushes when Adam acknowledges her.

"I'm enjoying my last days of summer vacation," I tell him as I pull my hair down from the messy bun and attempt to make it look like I haven't been rocking this same hairstyle for three days. It's the day before classes start and the only things going on around campus are parties and new student activities—neither of which have sounded appealing enough to get dressed and leave my room.

He picks up the package of cheese and peanut butter crackers I'd been devouring when he knocked. "This looks like the opposite of fun. And you bailed on my party last night."

"A party with a bunch of your teammates… yeah, no thanks."

"You can't sit in here moping forever. Bryan did you a favor. Long-distance relationships in college suck. Next to no one survives them. Plus, the guy was a tool anyway. Don't let it ruin college. College is awesome."

My heart cracks a little more at the reminder that my ex-boyfriend, who should be with me at Valley starting our freshman year together, decided at the last minute to go to Idaho instead.

It wasn't entirely his fault. He got the offer after they'd lost their second-string quarterback to an injury. Bryan became their new second-string and I was cut from his roster altogether.

Adam nudges my arm with his elbow. "Come on. Let's grab lunch, or come over and hang at the apartment, meet my roommates. *You don't need no man. There's plenty of fish in the sea.* What kind of pep talk are you feeling?"

I smile. "Of course you think there's plenty of fish in the sea. You have a new girlfriend every semester."

"Exactly. I speak from experience."

I don't think it'll be that easy for me. My brother is a hockey player, tall and muscular, and I guess objectively he's attractive. He certainly has no problem finding girlfriends if that's any indication. He has perfect hair; I'll give him that. I've had hair envy my whole life. Where my dirty blonde hair is stuck somewhere between straight and curly, his is lighter, thick, and the longish strands hang perfectly at the nape of his neck.

"How about lunch?" he asks.

It's tempting, really. If anyone can make me feel better, it's Adam, but I'm not sure I want to feel better yet.

Being single is a wonderful and liberating thing. "Single and ready to mingle." "I'm every woman." "Put your hands up." "Truth hurts". There are so many songs about it, I can't even list them all. But the thing about the single girl anthem... it's usually born out of a lot of tears from the last heartbreak.

The girl power and celebration of singledom only comes after you've cried your eyes out and burned every item that belonged to the last man who did you wrong.

I'm still somewhere between the two, but I catch Adam's drift—it's probably time to re-enter the land of the living.

I let out a cleansing sigh. "Tomorrow. Breakfast tomorrow, I promise. I need to help Ava get our room organized." I glance over to the boxes stacked on top of my desk that I still haven't unpacked.

Adam doesn't look convinced.

"I said I promise."

He holds his pinky out and I roll my eyes but link it with mine.

"I'll swing by on my way to the dining hall. You've got an eight o'clock, yeah?"

I nod and groan. I am so not a morning person. "Yeah, but you don't."

"Preseason workouts this week and next at six. I'll be heading over to eat around that time anyway."

"Six o'clock in the morning?"

"Yeah. In the morning." The deep chuckle that follows makes me smile. He stands and ruffles my already messy hair.

"Stop it." I swat at his hand. He knows I hate it when he treats

11

me like I'm twelve. In his mind, a three-year age gap makes him *so* much wiser.

"Be ready at quarter `til," he says as he moves to the door. "I'd hate to have to bang on the door and wake up the entire hall."

"God, you're obnoxious," I say, but he's already gone.

I get up and shower, hoping it washes away some of the lingering sadness along with the cracker crumbs. Back in my room, I look around it with fresh eyes and cringe. Ava's side is organized and decorated with bright colors and then there's my side. Even I can admit it looks a little depressing. Okay, a lot. White concrete walls, gray bed frame, and desk. The only color is my pale-yellow comforter.

After I'm dressed, I finally unpack. I didn't bring a lot of personal items because so many of them reminded me of Bryan. I fill the closet with my clothes and shoes, organize all of my school stuff on the desk, and I tape up a few pictures of my family and friends from high school on the wall.

Standing back, I survey the results. It's a start, and I feel a little more ready to face the world tomorrow. I flip on the small bedside light and crawl under the covers to sleep. I pick up my phone out of habit. Nothing good ever happens from scrolling your phone after midnight.

All of my friends from high school are posting selfies and tours of their new college dorms. There's Bryan, handsome as ever, in blue and orange. The college campus is in the background and he's lined up beside a group of big guys I assume are other football players based on their size. They hold beers and smile looking at the camera. He's obviously having no problem enjoying college without me.

That same handsome face I've known my whole life. We were neighbors, childhood friends, and then high school sweethearts. I close my eyes and the last conversation I had with him replays in my mind.

"I don't understand. What do you mean you're not going to Valley? We're supposed to leave in three days." We lie on my bed and I'm still in that post-sex high, so it takes me a few seconds to realize he's serious.

His heavy weight on top of me suddenly feels claustrophobic. "I got a call from the coach at Boise State. One of their incoming freshmen got into a car accident. He's out all year, maybe longer."

"But we've been planning on going to college together for two years, and Idaho is like... a long way from Arizona. How is this going to work?"

He hesitates and runs a hand over his jaw while he studies me with an embarrassed look on his face.

"Oh my god. You're not just telling me you're going to Boise; you're ending this?" I motion between us.

"I don't think it would be fair to either of us to go to college with unrealistic expectations. You said it yourself, Idaho is a long way from Arizona. When we come back for holidays or summer vacations, we can pick up where we left off. You'll always be my perfect girl, Ginny." His gaze drops from my face to my cleavage and continues doing a long sweep of my naked body. The least a guy can do is avoid staring at your boobs while he breaks up with you. Or pull out. *"But, I think we should give ourselves the freedom to explore and have fun while we're apart."*

"Why would you break up with the perfect girl? That doesn't make any sense," I mutter quietly to the room, swiping a rogue tear. I didn't give him the satisfaction of seeing me cry then and I'm not going to let him ruin my first day of college tomorrow.

I force a smile as I reimagine all the amazing things college will bring without Bryan. For starters, I don't have to do anything I don't want to. I can be absolutely selfish with my time. Truthfully, I have no idea what that looks like anymore, but I'm ready to find out.

I put in my earbuds, hit play, and fall asleep with Beyoncé on repeat.

THE NEXT MORNING, AVA AND I GET READY FOR CLASSES. SHE'S got the TV hooked up and *Vampire Diaries* season one, episode one playing. Feels right somehow. The first season of everything starting today.

Our room finally looks like two excited freshmen live here. Ava's side is a little more personalized, photos of her and Trent, her boyfriend, take up most of the wall above her bed.

My roommate is in a serious relationship with her high school boyfriend, who is going to college upstate. It was something else we'd shared when we first connected over the summer, being in serious relationships. They don't seem concerned about the distance, although it's not nearly as far as Idaho.

Ava's been on the phone or texting him the better part of the last week since we moved in. She's nice and I think we'll be great roommates. I guess since she's in a relationship, at least I won't have to worry about her bringing random guys back to the dorm. Because I'll be starting college single and not exactly thrilled about the opposite sex, it'll be nice not to worry about that.

"Do you want to come to breakfast with us?" I ask as I'm preparing to leave.

"No thanks." She shakes her head, making her short, black hair toss around her heart-shaped face. "I'm going to video chat with Trent on our way to our first classes."

A little pang of jealousy hits me, but I push it aside and head downstairs to meet Adam. Excited energy floats in the air. Blue and yellow banners hang on the front of the dorms welcoming us to the new school year.

Students are already out in droves heading off to classes, backpacks strapped to their shoulders, coffees in hand. They walk mostly in groups to their destinations; those who don't have earbuds in or stare down at their phones.

The Valley campus is truly beautiful. When we dropped Adam off before his freshman year and I got a look at the campus for the first time, I knew that it's where I wanted to go to college too. The buildings are mostly old and historic looking, green grass makes it feel a little less like the desert, and there's a huge fountain in the middle of campus.

"Ginny," Adam calls out, catching me by surprise while I'm lost people watching.

"Hey." I turn to see him and his friend and teammate Rhett with him.

"You remember Rauthruss?" Adam asks and runs a hand through his still-damp hair. Even wet it looks better than mine.

Rhett grins and steps forward with his hands shoved in his pockets. "Hey, Ginny. Good to see you again. Welcome to Valley."

Rhett Rauthruss is a giant man-boy. He's tall and built. His legs are like tree trunks. Seriously, his thighs could crush my head.

But he's got this baby face and pouty mouth that keeps him from looking too intimidating. He's also got a really great Minnesota accent that I absolutely love.

He and Adam have been teammates and roommates since their freshmen year, so I've met him a few times over the years and he came home with Adam once last semester for a weekend.

"Hey, Rhett, good to see you too."

He grins a little shyly.

"Are we ready?" Adam asks. "I'm starving."

My dorm doesn't have its own dining hall, so we cross the street to Freddy Dorm to eat. I follow Adam and Rhett inside, and we fall into the long line of people entering the dining hall, scanning their student ID cards as they go.

The smell of burned toast hangs in the air as we shuffle inside the busy dining room. Rhett heads off at a near jog for food, but Adam hangs back with me. "Grab food and then meet us at the big table in the right corner. You can't miss us."

With that, he rushes off too.

I do a lap while I check out the food options. Five or six different stations are set up with varying breakfast foods ranging from yogurt to omelets and everything in between.

I decide on waffles, get at the end of the line, and pick up a tray. The guy in front of me drums his fingers on the back of his tray impatiently. His fingers are long and strong-looking… somehow just really attractive. I let my gaze move up to his forearms and appreciate them in the same way. Tan and toned. The gray T-shirt he's wearing hugs his back and the short sleeves are snug against his biceps. Muscular but not too beefy.

When it's finally his turn, he sets the tray down and grabs a plate. With his profile to me, I take in his straight nose and sharp cheekbones. Dark, messy hair that I have the ridiculous urge to run my fingers through, sticks up on his head.

I think maybe I spent too many days in my dorm room crying over Bryan. I'm flat out gawking at this point, but it's a little hard not to. This guy is attractive without even getting a front view. He has this whole look about him that feels like he didn't bother glancing in the mirror this morning. Actually now that I think about it, it's a little frustrating that I spent twenty minutes taming my hair while he rolled out of bed and managed to look like that.

Damn. Welcome to Valley, Ginny.

He proceeds to fill his plate with four waffles. These aren't the size of the small, frozen waffles that you pop in the toaster, they are huge, bigger than my head waffles. He grabs a second plate and fills that one with bacon and eggs farther down the line. He glances between his plates and the food still left on the warmers ahead like he might not be finished.

I chuckle and he glances back at me. My breath hitches when his blue eyes meet mine. Not blue, a thousand shades of blue. He gives me a sheepish smile.

"Can you hand me another plate?" His deep voice washes over me, vibrating my insides. He's a lot to take in, but I do, not able to stop myself. His hair isn't only dark brown, it has hints of lighter strands too. It's like no part of him could decide on being one thing and instead he's made up of varying shades and depths.

He has an athletic build, tall but not towering over me like Bryan did. My ex was six foot four, which made him a great height to see over a mass of bodies on the football field, but not so great for kissing without standing on my tiptoes. I'm standing here wondering if I could kiss this guy flat-footed.

Aaand he asked me a question.

"Are you serious?"

He doesn't bat an eye, so I grab another plate and hand it to him.

"Thanks."

I fill my plate with one waffle like a reasonable human and continue to scoot down the line behind him. He's added four pieces of toast and a handful of grape jelly packets to the third plate, and he's *still* eyeing the food ahead of us.

"Are you feeding a family of bears?"

One side of his mouth pulls up. "Just one very hungry dude."

We reach the end of the line and he slows like he's waiting for me. He eyes my tray. "Barely four hundred calories on that plate. How are you going to make it to lunch?"

"Somehow I think I'll manage."

We start walking, both in the same direction.

"Are you following me?" I ask when we've walked shoulder to shoulder for three steps.

"No. I think you're following me." We reach the table where Adam and Rhett are seated with a group of guys.

"Yo, Heath!" one of the guys calls to him.

It takes a couple of seconds for my brain to catch up.

"You're a hockey player?" I frown while I try to place him. I've only met a few of Adam's teammates, but I've been to several games, so I'm surprised I don't recognize him.

His brows pull together studying me, maybe trying to place me as well. "Not a fan of hockey? I think you're at the wrong table then."

Adam stands and puts a protective arm around my shoulders. "She's not a fan of any men at the moment."

Kill me now.

I stare down at my white tennis shoes as Adam introduces me. "Guys, this is my baby sister, Ginny. It's her first day."

The group offers their hellos and grunts of acknowledgment. They've all got several plates of food in front of them like Heath and are shoveling it in like they haven't eaten in days.

I take a seat and so does Heath, across from me.

"Did you come to the games last year?" he asks as he pours syrup over his waffles.

"Yeah, a couple. Why?"

"I don't recall seeing you."

This makes me laugh. In a crowd of cheering fans, how could he possibly remember? "I don't recall seeing you either."

He leans across the table with a cocky smirk. "I was the one doing all the scoring."

Chapter Two

GINNY

I eat my breakfast, staying mostly quiet while the guys talk back and forth. They complain about the workout this morning and talk up the season. I've gotten good over the years at tuning out hockey talk.

I catch Heath staring at me an uncomfortable number of times. Uncomfortable because I only know he's staring at me because I'm staring at him too.

Oh, and he eats every one of the giant waffles, plus the rest of his food.

"Where's your first class?" Adam asks me as we're finishing up.

"Umm… the humanities building, I think."

He nods and sits back in his chair. "You know where it's at? Want me to walk you?"

I resist rolling my eyes. "Yes. I'll be fine."

"Humanities building?" Heath asks. "I'm walking that way."

Standing, I put on my backpack and then pick up my tray. "I've got it, really." I glance at my brother. "See you later." And then I give a little wave with my free hand to the rest of the table.

As I'm dropping my empty tray, Heath steps up beside me. "Adam Scott's sister... I don't see the resemblance."

"Thank you... I think?"

He's still following me when we get to the exit. "There's really no need. I know where I'm going."

"Okay." He shrugs one shoulder. "See you around, Ginny Scott."

The way he says my name is taunting and playful and has my tummy doing weird, excited things.

"Hopefully not if I want there to be any food left to eat," I say before he can leave.

I should walk away now, but there's a bizarre chemistry between us and something about him makes me feel the best I have in days. We stand a foot apart, grinning at one another and forcing people to go around us.

He snaps out of it first. "Better get here early for lunch then. That's when I get in my big meal for the day."

"Your big meal?" I can't help but laugh.

"That was nothing. I burned those calories before you woke up this morning."

"Presumptuous, much? Maybe I'm a runner or a soccer player."

His gaze sweeps over me slowly and I hold my breath. "Are you?"

"N-no."

He laughs and takes a step away. "Noon. That's what time I eat lunch, in case you want to get here early or join me."

He gives me his back before I come up with a witty response. I can't decide if that was flirty banter or him really asking me to have lunch with him, but I figure it's best not to dissect it too much and not to show up at noon. I might be ready to sing all the single girl anthem songs, but I am not ready to start planning my schedule around cute boys. No matter how very, *very* cute they are. The only thing I've made any sense of from my breakup with Bryan is that I need to figure out who I am and what I want, make my own friends. Over the two years Bryan and I dated I grew farther and farther apart from my other friends. To the point, I really don't have any good girlfriends to call up and cry on their shoulder.

This is my fresh start.

I find English Composition easy enough. It's a big class in a room with long rows of seats, many of which are already taken.

I take a spot in the middle trying not to appear too eager or too much like a slacker. I don't mind English, but I'm not a fan of being called on in class either.

After English I have algebra and I'm not quite as confident about where the building for it is located. The Valley campus is pretty big, and the number of people walking around makes it hard to get my bearings. I slip my thumbs around the straps of my backpack and fall into the crowd of students, hoping I look like I fit in and don't have FRESHMAN stamped on my forehead.

I'm backtracking to find Moreno Hall when my front pocket vibrates. I pull out my phone and move off the sidewalk onto the grass, so I don't get trampled.

Adam: Get lost yet?

I glance up at the building that is most definitely not Moreno Hall.

Me: Of course not, but say I was looking for Moreno Hall...

Adam: Hang a left just past the engineering building, it's on the corner—big fancy-ass looking building, can't miss it.

A minute later he follows up.

Adam: Find it?

Me: I would have found it on my own eventually.

Adam: I'm sure.

Hurriedly, I pocket my phone and head to Moreno Hall.

By the end of the day, I'm exhausted but even more excited about the semester. All of my classes seemed okay, I met a few girls on our hall, and Ava and I spent the late afternoon walking around campus and soaking in all the first-day excitement.

I don't even think about Bryan until we get back to the dorm and I'm lying on my bed listening to Ava and Trent share first-day stories. I consider texting him for all of a millisecond. I don't hate him. Maybe I should. It'd probably be easier to get over him that way, but despite the awful way he ended things, I don't totally blame him for taking a great opportunity. And I'm working on not blaming him for not even wanting to try to make it work. Of course, I don't text him. Mostly because I don't think I can handle hearing how awesome everything is on his end. Not when the most notable part of my day was watching a table of jocks devour food like they hadn't eaten in months.

Over the next few days, I don't have any more hockey team run-ins. Which might be in part because Ava and I stock up on noodles and have lunch in our room most days and when I do go to the dining hall, I avoid the back table. My brother's teammates all seemed nice, but I'm not interested in continually being referred to as Adam Scott's baby sister.

Adam texts me every day to check in and invites me over to his place to hang out. I finally give in and agree to dinner Thursday night.

"Are you going to the dorm social tonight?" Ava asks that afternoon as we're hanging out in the room. I'm watching a new makeup tutorial, and she's letting me practice on her. I know a lot of people like to use themselves as a model, but I've never been one for wearing much makeup. Putting it on other people, though, makes me insanely happy.

"Can't. I'm having dinner with my brother. Tomorrow night? I've heard several fraternities are having parties."

"Trent is coming to town this weekend. I meant to ask how you felt about him staying in the dorm? If it makes you uncomfortable, we'll get a hotel."

"He's coming to visit already?"

She grins wide and the raspberry red color I've put on her lips looks fantastic. "Yeah, we've worked it out so we can visit each other almost every weekend this semester."

I hadn't given much thought to what we'd do when he was visiting. I grab a gloss and she parts her lips to let me coat them with a little shine. "He should stay here, of course."

"Cool. Thank you. Trent was stressing about coming up with the money for a hotel. The only one in town that's reasonably priced looks like it also rents by the hour." She pulls her mouth down into a grimace. "But it'll be fun. You'll like him."

"I'm excited to meet him. What are you guys going to do?"

"I'm not sure. Maybe the football game, maybe skipping it to make out." She blushes.

I nod, suddenly imagining a weekend of trying to ignore the sex sounds coming from the other side of the room.

Adam picks me up after he's done with classes for the day. I smile when his familiar Jeep comes into view. He stops at the curb outside of my dorm and I hop in.

"How's the first week?" he asks as he drives toward his apartment.

"Good. I think I'm finally getting a feel for the campus. It's sort of confusing—all the old buildings look the same. And what's up with the floor numbering in Emerson?"

He chuckles lightly. "How long did it take you to figure out there are two second floors?"

"Long enough that I was late to class."

"You'll have it memorized in no time and then you'll be laughing at the newbies getting lost."

"You're laughing at us?"

"Of course, we are." He winks.

"I think I might need to find a group or join something." I didn't do a lot of extracurricular activities in high school. I hung out with friends, I attended sporting activities and was always happy to cheer on my school, but there wasn't anything I cared about enough to dedicate my hours before or after school.

"Why's that?" Adam asks as he pulls into the parking lot of the apartment complex.

"Everyone here seems to be into something except me. The girls on my hall are great and I've met a few people in class, but they've all got a clique of people interested in the same things. The girls rushing sororities, the jocks, the nerds... I swear it's worse than high school."

25

He nods. "I guess that's true. I never thought about it before."

"That's because you came to college already in one of those cliques and with an instant group of friends."

"What about your roommate?"

"Ava's great, but she has a boyfriend at another college. I get the feeling she'll be spending a lot of her weekends visiting him or him visiting us." I scrunch up my nose. "He's staying with us this weekend."

"Did you find somewhere else to crash?"

"No. Why? It's my room too."

"Ginny, trust me, you need to find someone on your floor who'll let you stay in their room this weekend. Your dorm room is tiny, and they're going to be naked and going at it—that sounds hella uncomfortable for everyone. Unless you're into that sort of thing." Now he scrunches up his face. "Don't tell me if you are. I'd like to continue to believe my baby sister is asexual."

I snort laugh, but then everything he's saying hits me. "You're right. I can't stay there."

He nods. "There's always someone leaving on the weekends. Ask around and see who's heading out of town and will let you crash in their room."

"This is a thing. Seriously?"

"I lived in a suite, so it wasn't that big of a deal. I'd just crash on the couch in the living room."

"Ugh. I should have been a jock. Then I would have a ready-made clique and I wouldn't be getting kicked out of my own room."

"You're welcome to stay at my place."

"I'll figure it out." I appreciate him, but there has to be another option.

Adam's apartment isn't far from campus and if the number of vehicles with Valley University bumper stickers and license plate holders is indicative of how many students live here, then I'd say it's a lot.

He leads me up the stairs to the second-floor unit.

"Where is everyone?" I ask as we walk into the quiet living room.

"Campus or the gym." He drops his backpack on the couch. "We have preseason workouts twice a day this week. I'm gonna change real quick." He heads into one of the bedrooms off the living room.

"Where do you want to eat?" he calls through the open door.

"I don't care. Wherever you want."

I walk around the apartment scoping out my brother's living arrangements. There are three bedrooms, Adam's and then two on the opposite side of the unit. In the middle is an open concept area that has a kitchen, dining, and living room.

The place isn't that big but it's a pretty nice setup and feels huge by comparison to my tiny dorm room.

In the living room there's a matching couch and chair in a light brown leather. A coffee table, its top made of old hockey sticks, sits in front of the couch. The only artwork on the walls are a few jerseys and a hockey poster of the Bruins—Adam's favorite team.

The entire apartment is cleaner than I would have expected. A few empty Gatorade bottles on the kitchen counter, a football and a hockey stick—which I can't help but note is a random combination of sporting goods—lying in the middle of the floor in the living room, and a couple of stray articles of clothing on the backs of the chairs at the dining room table.

Adam reappears as I'm looking inside their empty refrigerator. "Where's all your food?"

"We haven't gone shopping yet."

"What do you eat?"

He fills a glass with tap water and chugs it before responding. "We mostly eat on campus or we go out. We have a small kitchen in the locker room too that is re-stocked every few days."

"Can I use your bathroom before we go?" I head toward the one that is near his bedroom.

"Use the other one." He points to the bathroom on the opposite side of the apartment. "The light is out in mine. I need to get new bulbs."

"How do you see to shower or pee?" I ask.

"I leave the door open."

Boys are weird.

INSTEAD OF GOING TO A RESTAURANT, ADAM AND I GO THROUGH a drive through and eat in his Jeep while he takes me all around Valley showing me Frat Row and some of the popular college bars and restaurants.

"Have you heard from Mom and Dad?" he asks. "Are they back from their trip?"

"They get back tomorrow, I think." Our parents went on some fancy, romantic vacation to Mexico. Initially I'd been bummed that they weren't going to be able to drop me off at college, but I'm glad they missed seeing me all sad and teary. The day Adam and I arrived on campus, I dropped my things in my room and then fell onto my new bed and sobbed. Poor Ava must have thought I was nuts.

"I'm really glad you're here," I admit.

He grins. "Me too. I get to spend the last year of college with my baby sister."

"You have to stop calling me that. I'm not a baby."

His mouth pulls into a wider smile. "Come over this weekend and crash at my place. You'll avoid listening to your roomie's sex sounds, and I'll introduce you to everyone. People are always coming and going from our apartment. It'll be good to meet more people here. Hell, maybe I'll throw a party."

"You never let me come to your parties in high school and now you're practically begging me. I find this quite redeeming even though now I don't actually want to go. Back then I would have killed to hang with you and your friends."

"High school was different. No one here cares if you're a freshman or senior or if you go to college at all. Plus, I want to see that you're settled. I know the shit with Bryan was rough."

I groan and Adam laughs.

"Only one condition. Promise me that you won't get wasted and make an ass of yourself in front of my teammates. I'm captain this year, and I need them to respect me."

"I promise," I say as I roll my eyes and toss a fry in his direction.

Chapter Three

HEATH

"Carry me. My legs are dunzo." Maverick leans his sweaty, heavy frame against me.

"Get the fuck off. I'm barely standing on my own." I wobble and take a seat in my stall.

The first week of hell training is done and we survived... mostly. Coach Meyers likes to start out the year with a shit ton of conditioning and weight training. We won't even be allowed to step on the ice for another two weeks.

My buddy falls into the seat next to me and pulls a T-shirt over his head. "Wanna grab a drink at Prickly Pear?"

"I can't. Scott's called a house meeting," I say, annoyed and loud enough so Adam can hear me.

"Four-thirty. Don't be late," Adam says sternly. The rest of the guys are scared of him, being our team captain and all, but I know better. He's all talk. I push his buttons on a regular basis and I'm still standing despite him having a good three inches and fifteen pounds on me.

Maverick and I stop for alcohol to restock for the weekend.

When we get back to the apartment, we settle into the couch for our house meeting.

I've only lived here for a month and this is the second meeting Adam has called. It looks to be a long year. At least I have Mav for entertainment. He lives downstairs in a single apartment, but he spends way more time here than his own place.

His French bulldog, Charli, lies at his feet, staring up at him with adoring eyes. Charli is pretty much the only one who looks at Maverick like that. He's a total jokester and softie, but his size and tattoos intimidate most people.

Adam and Rauthruss wander out of their respective rooms. Rauthruss grabs a wooden chair from the dining table and Adam takes a seat in our leather recliner. He eyes the bottle in Maverick's hand. "Dude, really?"

"Ah, ah, ah," Mav tsks. "You can't speak until you have the bottle. New house rule." He hands it to Adam with a smirk. "Take a shot, captain, my captain."

"You don't even live here." Adam takes a long swallow of the MD 20/20 anyway and grimaces. "That shit's nasty. I haven't had Mad Dog since high school."

"Ironically, that's the last time I got called to a family meeting, too," Mav points out, taking the bottle back.

"Yeah, well feel free to leave since, again, you don't live here, but this won't take long. Three things." He holds up his fingers like he's talking to children. I glance over at Mav as he runs a hand along his tattooed chest where he's spilled on himself and a trail of alcohol trickles down to his shorts. Okay, maybe we're more like overgrown toddlers than functioning men. Maverick and I like to have fun, so sue us. We show up on the ice where it matters.

"Number one," Adam goes right into it. "We looked like shit out there this week."

Mav holds up a finger, takes a drink, and then speaks. "We're not even on the ice yet. Give it time."

Adam starts to respond, but not before Mav hands him the bottle and he begrudgingly takes another sip. "No, it's my last year and I'm not taking any chances by waiting for ice time. I think we should invite the guys over."

"Party. Good call," I say and find the bottle thrust into my side.

As I'm taking a drink, Adam shakes his head. "No, not a party. Well, okay, a party, but no girls. Just the team."

"You want us to spend our nights with a bunch of sweaty guys now too?" We're already spending long days in conditioning together. The only thing that got me through the week was the promise of a weekend of fun. "I'm not sure more time together is the answer."

"Girls," Mav says. "The answer is always girls. Let's get the freshmen laid."

"That's actually not a bad plan," Rauthruss speaks up for the first time. The bottle is passed to him and he fingers the label as he finishes. "Maybe they just need to let off a little steam."

Adam frowns and the vein in his forehead becomes noticeable—never a good sign. "We party all the time. The guys don't need our help finding chicks. This is about coming together as a team."

"You're going to go all weekend without your latest girlfriend?" Mav asks Adam pointedly.

Adam always has a girlfriend. I can't remember the current one's name. Hannah? Holly? I don't understand why he doesn't stay single. It isn't like he, or any of us for that matter, need the relationship label to get laid. But, no, Adam Scott is the full boyfriend experience. He doesn't only hook up or go on a few dates. He wastes months on these girls, going all in with dates and sleepovers… just not for more than six months or so at a time. He's an odd duck.

Rauthruss too. He's been dating the same girl since high school and she lives in freaking Nebraska. Why have a girlfriend you never see? The only perk of having a girlfriend is getting laid on a regular basis, right? I'm really asking; I have no idea.

"Maria and I broke up," he says with a shrug. "And it's just for tonight."

Maria. Wow, definitely off there.

"What happened to Heather?" Mav asks.

Ah, yes, Heather! My memory isn't failing me yet.

"They broke up in May. Keep up." Rauthruss reaches out for the Mad Dog again, but Maverick holds it up and shakes the empty bottle. Fuck, we went through that fast.

"Fine. Party tonight. No girls," Mav says and looks to me. I'm the last holdout. "It's one night, man."

"What are the other two things on the agenda. We'll circle back," I say with a smile and Mav chuckles.

"Nice. Circling back. I think my dad used that the last time we talked."

His dad is a big executive—suit and tie, phone permanently attached to his ear. Rich as sin, but kind of a prick, so we have a bit of fun at his expense with our corporate speak, or jargon, if you will.

Adam interrupts our joking, which to be fair is probably the only way to get us back on track. "Number two. Heath, you have to walk your dates out the door. Like personally see that they make it outside." He looks to Rhett who's turning a nice shade of red.

Mav gasps dramatically with a hand to his chest. Charli at his feet lifts her head to check on her owner. "Heath would never. He's a true gentleman."

"It was one time and I did walk her out." I glance at my flushed roommate. The memory of him all bed head and in his boxers kicking out a half-naked Kimberly still makes me smile. "I just didn't lock the door behind her. How was I supposed to know she was going to come back and try to work her way around the apartment?"

I mean, seriously... is it my fault that she broke into our place and slipped into bed with the guy? Apparently nothing is sexier or more challenging for a girl than a guy in a real committed relationship. And Rauthruss is as loyal as they come even though he barely sees his woman. It drives girls crazy. Seriously, he could have any chick he wanted. He might be onto something, not that I have any plans to try his method. Mine's working just fine.

Maverick sets the empty bottle on the coffee table and heaves a sigh. "Are there any items on your list that don't revolve around our dicks?"

No one speaks. Adam raises his brows and keeps his sharp stare on me.

"Agreed. I will walk them out." I'm almost positive I can remember to do that. Definitely can tonight since I'll be spending it with my hand apparently.

"Next item on the agenda," Mav prompts.

Adam looks a little nervous, pausing before he speaks. This can't be good.

"My sister is crashing here this weekend, so best behavior." He stands.

"What the hell? What happened to no chicks?" I ask.

"She's my sister, not the same thing."

"Depends. Is she hot?" Mav asks, totally serious, which makes the vein in Adam's head protrude.

Yes, yes she is. I keep that to myself. I'm not scared of Scott, but I'm not an idiot. If he knew my unfiltered thoughts on his little sister, I'd be neutered in my sleep. Nah, actually, he'd probably do it when I was wide awake. Can't really blame him. Ginny Scott is sexy as hell and all my thoughts about her are dirty.

Long, blonde hair, light brown eyes, and her legs... those long legs are the things dreams are made of.

"Best behavior." Adam pulls his phone out and walks toward his room.

"Meeting adjourned then, eh?" Mav says and then looks to me. "I'm gonna need a copy of the minutes on my desk by end of business."

"I'm right on top of that, sir," I say and give him the middle finger.

"What the hell are we going to do tonight?" Mav looks seriously defeated as he runs a hand through his dark hair.

"Halo?" Rauthruss lifts an Xbox controller.

"Why the fuck not." He pets Charli and grabs the controller with the other hand.

I get up and take a step toward my room. "I'm going to shower and touch base with myself."

Mav cackles. "Not as good as circling back, but good wordplay. Mariah or Ariana for inspiration music?"

"It's definitely a Mariah kind of day," I decide.

Mav hums as I walk by. "'Santa Baby' or 'Heartbreaker'?"

I shake my head. "'Fantasy.' Always 'Fantasy.'"

LATER, I CLOSE MY DOOR SO I CAN HEAR NATHAN ON THE PHONE over the noise in the living room. A few guys have already made it over. I hope Scott's right, and this is what we need. He might be a pain in the ass, but he's not wrong about us needing to play better together. It's his last year, so I get the extra pressure to make it the best before he's done.

He's not interested in playing professionally, so this really is it for him.

"How does it feel to be back?"

"Not as good as it would feel to be practicing with the Coyotes right now," I say as I take a seat at my desk.

He snickers. "Soon enough."

"Eh," I grunt. I've never been much for living in the future. Even now that it's set. I signed with Arizona's professional team over the summer. Three more years at Valley and then I'll get paid to play hockey. It still hasn't really sunk in. "How's everything in Florida?"

"Good. Busy. Between the team and all the wedding plans, it's gotten nuts. Did you get the save the date?"

"I did." I pick up the thick paper invitation on my desk. "June, huh? You really think you can continue to not screw this up for another ten months?"

"God, I hope so. I don't know what I'll do if she wises up before then," he says in a teasing voice. I can hear his fiancée Chloe in the background taunting him back but can't make out her words.

"Tell her I said hey and thanks for the giant box of stuff. This one's got Chloe written all over it. A gift card to The Olive Garden?"

Nathan speaks away from the phone, "Busted. Totally called you out on The Olive Garden gift card."

"Take a nice girl to dinner," Chloe yells.

"You hear that?" my brother asks.

"Yeah, I got it."

They've been sending me packages every month since my freshman year. Each one is different and contains shit ranging from razors, body wash, homemade oatmeal raisin cookies (my favorite), to new clothes and cologne. And then there's the gift cards. Each month, a hundred dollars or more from random places.

Since I refuse to take money outright from Nathan, they find creative ways to be generous. I don't really need it. I have a full-ride scholarship for hockey and a part-time job that helps with anything else. But that's Nathan, always trying to take care of me.

"All right, well I won't keep you. Chloe and I are headed to the beach. Stay out of trouble."

I groan and tilt my head back.

With a chuckle, Nathan says, "I'm proud of you, but what kind of big bro would I be if I didn't remind you not to screw up? You've got more than ever on the line."

"Oh, I don't know, the cool kind maybe?"

"Have fun. I'll call you next week. Let me know if you need anything. Oh, and call Mom. She said she hasn't heard from you in two weeks."

"Been busy."

"Mhmm, weak excuse. Later, Heath."

"Bye, Heath," Chloe says in the background.

"Bye, guys, talk to you later."

Chapter Four

GINNY

Trent arrives late Friday afternoon and Ava is brimming with excitement. She introduces me and then recaps a list of facts about the guy. Facts she's already told me several times. I feel like I know him better than I know Ava at this point; she's told me *that much* about him. Maybe a little too much.

"I'm going to show him around campus and then we're going to the football game. Do you want to come with us?" She's practically beaming with happiness and I have a twinge of sadness that this could be me and Bryan if he weren't in freaking Idaho.

She leans into his side and Trent wraps an arm around her waist. His fingers slip under the hem of her T-shirt and he kisses her forehead.

It's obvious how much they've missed one another by the touchy-feely display in front of me, and I'm starting to understand just how imperative it is I get the hell out of here. I haven't even been able to bring myself to watch porn since Bryan broke up with me. I certainly can't handle a full-on romantic display with a side of orgasms.

"No, thanks. You two enjoy. My brother is having people over, so I'm going to go hang with them. You two will have the place all to yourself tonight. It was really nice to meet you, Trent."

I shower and get ready, hesitant to head over to Adam's before the party gets going. I appreciate that he always looks out for me, but I want to find my own friends at Valley, too, and if I run over there every time I need an escape, I'm going to spend the next year as Adam Scott's little sister instead of Ginny Scott. So tonight, I need to find some friends.

I text Adam to make sure he's there before driving over.

Adam: Yep. Just hanging out at the house. You coming over? I warned the guys to be on their best behavior.

Me: Yes, but please don't make it weird. I know you and your friends are disgusting. You don't need to warn them like I'm some sort of delicate flower.

I ignore the rest of his messages that pop up, telling me he's only looking out for me or whatever. Having an older, overbearing brother is a real pain sometimes.

The apartment is easy enough to find and I carry my backpack with a change of clothes and toothbrush up to the second-floor door and knock.

"You must be Little Scott." A guy with a shit ton of tattoos on full display thanks to his bare chest greets me with a goofy smile. "I'm Johnny Maverick."

"Ginny."

He pulls the door wide and I enter. A bunch of guys I don't recognize are standing around the apartment. For real, it's like I just entered the men's locker room with the way they all stop what they're doing and stare at me.

Adam's head pops up from the kitchen and he hustles forward. "Did you find it okay?"

"Yeah. I have this thing called maps on my phone."

I spot Rhett in the living room and he lifts a controller in greeting. "Hey, Ginny. Good to see you again."

I wave awkwardly. They're all still staring.

Adam shuts the door and I follow him into the living room. He points to the guy who answered the door. "You met Maverick. Ignore any and everything he says."

He scoffs. "I am hilarious and awesome."

"That's Liam, Jordan, and Tiny."

"Hey," they say in unison.

"Want something to eat or drink?" my brother asks and goes back to the kitchen.

"I'm okay for now." There's an empty seat next to Maverick, so I head for it and sit down.

"Where is Payne?" one of the guys asks him.

"Still showering and jerking it to Mariah, probably." Maverick stills, looks to me, and clears his throat. "Shit, sorry."

I laugh and wave him off. "Good for him. And Mariah."

"I like you." Maverick puts his arm around me on the back of the couch, but it's in a friendly way that doesn't feel like he's hitting on me.

"Hands off," Adam's deep voice bellows from the kitchen.

Maverick rolls his eyes and I'm glad he's not so easily intimidated by my brother. It was a real issue in high school before Adam graduated. He would look at guys the wrong way for talking to me and they'd scamper off too afraid of him.

He stands and looks down at me. "You need a drink? A smoke?"

"Yeah, I think I might need a drink after all."

The party, or what's arrived of it, moves outside on the deck off the kitchen of the apartment. It's nice out. Still hot like August nights always are in Arizona, but a nice breeze and the cold drink in my hand helps. Even Adam seems to relax as the guys kick back with their beers. It's still just the guys on the team, but it's early.

"I'm going to get another drink." I head inside to the bathroom and have to use the flashlight on my phone to see anything. Why my brother hasn't changed the light bulb is beyond me.

I can't really see much in the mirror, enough to make out my French braid is mostly still intact. In the kitchen, I rummage through the refrigerator looking for something besides beer, but it's that or Wild Turkey. Definitely no.

As I turn, movement catches my eye and I jump in surprise. "You scared me."

He grins, hand gliding through the wet hair sticking up on his head like he ran a towel through it and said fuck it. He looks me over carefully. I'm frozen, my tongue feels heavy or too wide for my mouth or something.

"Hey, Ginny."

"Hi." I look around dumbfounded. I'd expected to run into him, but not half-naked. "Do you live here?"

"Well, I don't usually walk around in my boxers at other dude's houses." He looks to the ceiling and a smirk pulls at his lips. "Well, not often."

I'd been actively avoiding the wall of nakedness in front of me, but now that he's acknowledged it, I can't look away.

The only thing he wears are a pair of gray boxer briefs that hug his huge thighs and—oh my god, Ginny, do not look at his crotch. Shit, too late. I tear my gaze away from the bulge and up to his abs. Forget a boring six-pack, Heath has ridges and lines that wrap around his midsection. I follow the line to his chest and biceps. It shouldn't be possible for someone to look this good naked.

And oh my God, stop looking already!

Adam comes through the door before I can make words come out of my mouth.

"Payne, fucking finally. We thought you drowned in there." Adam tosses his empty in the trash and grabs another beer, his face hardening as he gets a good look at him. "Dude, what the hell? Put some clothes on in front of my sister."

"Relax, I didn't know she was here yet." Heath's tone is agitated, rightfully so.

"Pants, dude. Now."

"Adam," I admonish.

"And no hitting on my baby sister." His demeanor relaxes slightly, and he punches Heath playfully in the arm, although it seems a little harder than necessary.

"Are you coming back outside?" Adam asks me, pausing at the door that leads to the deck.

"I'll be right there," I assure him.

Heath brushes by me, the heat of his body licking flames up my arm and grabs two beers from the fridge. He hands one to me. "So, I hear you're sleeping with me this weekend."

"Umm…what?"

"I hear you're sleeping at our place this weekend." He leans a hip against the counter and pops the top off the beer.

"Right. Yeah. My roommate's boyfriend is in town for the

43

weekend."

"Lucky for us."

"I doubt you guys will even know I'm here."

"One chick among twenty-seven guys? Plus, it's you. You're kind of hard to miss." His eyes drop to my mouth.

"One chick? Please. Actually, I'm surprised there aren't girls over already. Are you hiding an orgy in your room?"

He laughs. It's a deep, playful tone that lights up my insides. "I wish." He pushes off the counter. "Your brother has banned girls from the apartment tonight."

"What? Why?" That doesn't sound like Adam.

"Team building or some shit. Just you and the team, Ginny Scott."

"No. Absolutely not. Adam said he was going to introduce me to people, not hang with his bros."

With a light chuckle, he lifts his beer and takes a drink making me realize I haven't touched mine.

"I'm going to kill him."

"Well, that I want to see. I better get dressed." He winks and heads down the hall on the opposite side of the apartment from Adam's room. I'm finally able to take a breath again. Holy mother of all that is good, he's a lot.

I head outside and take a seat next to Adam. "No girls? What the hell? I thought you wanted to introduce me to people."

He looks conflicted on how to respond. "I will. I am." He motions around the party.

"People besides your teammates, Adam." I flail my hands around. "Girls."

"Yeah, let's get some girls over here," someone says and Adam scowls at them over my head and then drops his gaze back to me.

"Please?" I ask quieter. "I'm sure your teammates are great, but I don't want to hang with a bunch of dudes all weekend."

"Shit, Ginny, I didn't even think about Bryan and what it might be like to be around a bunch of guys…" He rubs at the back of his neck. "All right, yeah, let's have a real party."

That wasn't exactly what I'd meant by not wanting to hang out with a bunch of dudes, but if it gets girls over here, I will keep my mouth shut and let him think it's my sad, I hate all of mankind broken heart speaking.

"On it," Maverick says and pulls out his phone.

Chapter Five

HEATH

A knock brings my attention to the door and Scott's head peeks in. "Hey, I'm going to run to the store to get more alcohol. You need anything?"

"Are you sure I'm allowed out of my room?" I ask. I still haven't bothered to get dressed. I sat down at my desk to check in with work and got distracted.

"Sorry, man, I'm a little protective of her. She's been through a lot."

I nod and open my top desk drawer and pull out the stack of gift cards. "Where are you going?"

"Dude, what all you got there?" He laughs and walks closer.

"Gift cards to pretty much every place you can think of."

His eyes widen. "You're coming with me. Bring your stash."

I don't know what his sister said to him, but in an hour's time, our place has become packed with guys *and girls. Good work, Ginny.*

Adam and I head out and make several stops getting booze and food. When we're on our way back, I finally decide to broach the subject on my mind.

"Soooo… your sister's smoking hot."

I'm messing with him, sort of. She is smoking hot, but I'm only sharing this information to get a rise out of him. As predicted, he pins me with a hard stare. I meet it and smile, letting him know I'm not intimidated.

"Off-limits, Payne."

"Relax, I'm giving you shit. I don't do the whole girlfriend thing like you. We've only talked a few times. She's nice."

"She is. I worry about her. She doesn't know a lot of people at Valley yet and I want to introduce her to everyone, but she's off-limits. Friend zone only, man. I know how you are."

Ouch. I'm a perfect gentleman, thank you very much. Just because I don't date the same girl for months at a time, doesn't mean I treat them any worse.

"Is there some sort of big brother gene that makes you all giant overprotective assholes?"

"I'm serious. She just got out of a relationship and she doesn't need another guy screwing her over."

We pull up to the apartment and grab the bags to carry inside. Before we enter the apartment, Adam stops and regards me seriously. "You'll help me keep an eye on her? Make sure the rest of the guys don't mess with her?"

"She doesn't need a babysitter, man, and I'm no nanny."

His mouth pulls into a thin line and I cave, some part of me understanding his concern. I can't imagine having a little sister around my teammates and friends.

"I will keep an eye out, but I'm not going to lord over her like some sort of protector. Normal, friendly, keep an eye out, not whatever you've got going on there." I lift one of my arms bringing the grocery bags with it and motion to him and his moody intensity.

"Good enough, I guess."

I barely get the beer to the fridge before people are grabbing for it. I take two and spot the object of my and Adam's conversation sitting on the couch watching Maverick and Rauthruss play Halo.

"Hey," I say as I take a seat next to her and hold out a beer. Her hair is in an elaborate looking braid, the end hanging over one shoulder.

She takes the can hesitantly. "Thanks."

"Where's mine?" Maverick teases.

"In the fridge."

He holds a hand to his chest and pretends to be appalled.

"When you're as hot as Ginny, I'll start being your beer bitch, too."

She rolls her eyes as she pops the tab on her beer, but there's a faint blush to her cheeks.

"Genevieve," Adam calls from the kitchen and lifts a beer in a silent offering. She holds up the one I gave her so he can see she's already got one.

"Genevieve?" Mav asks. "I thought your name was Ginny."

"Ginny is short for Genevieve."

"That's rad. Why would you ever go by anything else?" He says her name again slowly. "Genevieve."

"Adam couldn't pronounce it when I was born."

Mav and Rauthruss bust up laughing.

"He was three," she adds, sticking up for him.

Rauthruss wins, like he always does, and Mav looks to me. "I'm done getting my ass kicked. Do you want to play?"

Nodding, I hold a hand up and he tosses the controller to me.

I nudge Ginny. "What do you say?"

Rauthruss holds his out to her and she takes it.

"Have you played before?"

"I grew up with Adam. What do you think?" She sits forward and places her beer on the coffee table and straightens her shoulders. She's taking this seriously, looking determined and sexy as hell.

I set out with the goal of taking it easy on her, but Ginny doesn't need it. A few of the guys on the team crowd around to cheer her on and voice their hope of me getting my ass kicked. I win, just barely, and everyone boos.

"Thanks a lot, guys. Real team spirit."

"Do over," she demands.

I'm not confident I can pull off a victory twice, so I hesitate. We lean forward and grab our beers at the same time. I take a long drink while she sips and then grimaces.

"What was that face?" I stare at her cute little mouth and pink lips wet from the beer.

"Do you actually like the taste of beer?" she asks.

"I wouldn't drink it otherwise. Why didn't you say something?"

"I'm trying to learn to like it. It seems to be what everyone drinks here." She takes a longer drink as if to prove her point.

"Be right back."

I find Jordan and trade a twenty-dollar gift card for a twelve-pack of his hard seltzers. Two more people have taken over the game, so I motion for Ginny to follow me and lead her out to the deck.

"Try this."

"Thank you." She takes it and I lean back against the railing. There are a lot of people out here, but no one is paying us any attention except her brother. Big brother radar, I guess. Dude needs to chill.

I turn so his big-headed scowl isn't in my peripheral. There's no pleasing the guy. He wanted me to look out for her. I am, yet he still seems displeased. "I don't remember seeing you last year. You were really at our games?"

"A few of them." This time when she takes a drink, she smiles. "Much better." She plays with the end of her braid. "I was at the Colorado game and Arizona State and whoever you guys played for Parent's Night."

I think back to that game for a second. "Western Michigan."

"Right." Her smile lifts higher.

"I can't believe I didn't see you." Her phone is stuck in the front pocket of her jeans and I nod toward it. "Let me see your phone."

She hands it over without question and I program my number in it and send myself a text so I have hers.

"A lot of people come to the games. Plus, it wasn't like I was sitting on the bench with the team. Do you guys notice anyone in the crowd?"

"We notice hot girls." Maverick butts into the conversation and puts an arm around her shoulders. "You're hot, Little Scott."

She blushes and I hand her phone back.

Mav holds on to her and takes a step away from me. "I'm stealing her. Ginny here has a lot of people dying to meet her and you're hogging her, Payne."

"I do?" Ginny asks, sounding a little hopeful.

"Oh yeah." Mav nods. "Come on. You need a tour guide."

"Okay, yeah, that'd be great." She glances at me. "You probably want to hang out with your friends anyway." She lifts her seltzer.

"Thanks for this."

"Anytime, Genevieve." I wink and tug the end of her braid.

She follows Mav, and I head inside, grab another beer, and take a seat back on the couch next to Rauthruss's giant frame. "I've got winner."

Chapter Six

GINNY

True to his word, Maverick introduces me to everyone. He has a shirt on now, but the tattoos that cover both arms, all the way down to his fingers, are still visible. And I can spot a hint of his chest ink peeking out of the top of his T-shirt.

He leads me to where Liam and Jordan are standing. Liam and Maverick look like polar opposites. Where Johnny Maverick is dark-haired and covered in tattoos, Liam is blond and clean cut. He's even wearing a polo shirt. Even though I met him earlier, this time when Maverick introduces me, Liam extends a hand for me to shake. "Ginny, really nice to meet you."

"Same." His politeness catches me by surprise, but I slip my hand into his giant palm and squeeze.

"Roadrunner?" Jordan asks, holding a blue shot glass out to me. I take it and sniff. "What's a Roadrunner?"

"It's like a Blue Kamikaze," he says and continues passing out shots.

I don't bother asking what a Blue Kamikaze is. My experience with alcohol is pretty limited. My high school bestie always grabbed a bottle of white wine from her parents' wine refrigerator and we'd drink that when we went to parties or had sleepovers. I never paid much attention to the label—none of it was great, but it was better than beer.

Jordan lifts his and the rest of us mimic the movement. I watch the others drink first. No one grimaces, so I take a sip. It's good, sweet. I smile and then drain the rest of the glass.

"We're off to meet more people," Mav tells them, pulling me away. He stops every couple of steps to make introductions and share the bottle of Mad Dog he's carrying. He's funny and kind of ridiculous, saying whatever pops into his head. Or maybe not, but if he's holding back at all—I don't want to think about the thoughts left unsaid.

"Total douche," he says after we're done talking to one guy that I think he said was a neighbor.

I laugh. "Then why did you introduce me to him?"

"Gotta know which ones to stay away from."

The next time he stops, it's in front of a girl standing by herself, her face hidden behind her phone. "Dakota, baby, I missed you all summer."

"You missed having someone to bum laundry detergent and junk food from." She looks up and over the device at Maverick. She's pretty. Big, ice-blue eyes and strawberry blonde hair that hangs in loose waves around her shoulders. She looks sweet, but the playful glare she gives Maverick makes me believe she could cut a bitch with words alone. That gaze slides to me and softens. "Hey."

"Dakota lives in the apartment next door. I'm her favorite neighbor." He tips his head to me. "This is Scott's little sister,

Ginny."

"Hey there." I wave three fingers around my drink.

"Where's Reagan?" Maverick asks. Then to me, "Her roommate. The nicer of the two."

Dakota flips him off. "She'll be here. She was still getting ready. Ginny, you're a freshman?"

"Did the seltzer give it away?"

She lifts her cup. "We've got a better variety at our place if you want something else. These guys only know cheap beer and hard liquor."

"Thank you. That's really nice."

"Of course."

Dakota's phone pings, and she smiles at the screen. "Wardrobe emergency. I should go make sure Reagan's not buried under a pile of dresses. Do you want to come with me and scan our booze?"

Maverick nods his approval and smiles like a proud parent who's set up their kid on a successful playdate. "You two have fun. Don't tell her any lies about us, Dakota."

"Lies would be less incriminating."

Dakota lets us into her apartment across the breezeway from the guys.

"Help!" a muffled voice calls from one of the bedrooms. A girl with hair the color of honey pulled up in curlers rushes out wearing a silky robe. "I don't know what to wear."

Dakota laughs. "This is Ginny. Ginny, that's my neurotic but lovable roommate, Reagan."

"Hey," she says, breathless, cheeks pink.

"Green's a good color on you," I tell her and motion to the emerald color of her robe.

"She's right. Put on that green dress with the crisscross back."

Reagan smiles, deep dimples popping out. "Oh, right. I forgot about that one." She disappears back into the room.

Dakota moves to the kitchen and I hang in the living room looking around.

"I like your apartment." It's decorated with lots of black and white with pops of dark pink. Old Hollywood movie posters and cute furniture. It's a smaller version of my brother's, but same basic setup with bedrooms on either side of the living area.

"Thanks," she says, and I join her in the kitchen area. "Pick your poison." A wide selection of alcohol is spread out on their kitchen counter. Wine—red and white, hard lemonade, vodka, Captain Morgan, and a bunch of mixers. I settle on half a cup of white wine. After all the mixing, I'm a little nervous to drink too much.

"So, you're Adam Scott's little sister?" she asks with a smirk once we both have a fresh drink.

"I am. Yeah. You know him?"

"Everyone knows him. He's Adam Scott."

Reagan reappears in green with her hair down, looking like she walked out of a salon. If I could make that sort of transformation in five minutes, I'd probably get dolled up more often.

"Do we have a winner?" Dakota asks.

Reagan holds her arms out to her sides. "I think so."

"You look great." I glance down at my jeans and tank top. I'm underdressed by comparison. Dakota's in a skirt and T-shirt with tennis shoes, but her makeup and jewelry give it all a much more put-together look than my casual outfit. "Do you guys always dress up like this for parties?"

Dakota responds first. "This is my basic uniform, but that one" —she nods toward her roommate— "has her eye on a boy."

Reagan makes a face at her but smiles.

"Oooooh. Someone at the party?" I ask. "One of the hockey guys?"

"Yeah." She takes a seat next to me.

"She won't say which one. I've got money on Liam. He's got that nice guy vibe, but something about him screams that he's probably not afraid to get down and dirty in the sheets." Dakota pours white wine into a cup and hands it to Reagan.

"Liam? Really?" Reagan asks with a shake of her head. "He's not my type. And I'm not saying who because I don't want to jinx it."

"Well, he'd be a fool to turn you down," I tell her honestly. Reagan is the kind of pretty that you wish only existed on the pages of a magazine or on TV.

She takes the drink and sighs. "I'm nervous, which is ridiculous, right? Who gets nervous about going to a party where their crush is? It's like junior high all over except without the zits and braces. Thank god. I've been trying to talk to this guy for… a long time. I get all weird and shy around him. Well, shier than normal."

"You're going to knock his socks off. Trust me." Dakota says. "And if not, you get to come home to me."

"Have you guys been roommates for a long time?" I ask. It's easy to see how close they are. They tease, but it's with a smile and none of the catty, fake compliments that some girls do to one another.

"Since our freshmen year in the dorms," Reagan answers. "Dakota was all fast-talking and no-nonsense, and I think I spent half of first semester completely terrified of her."

Dakota laughs. "It's true. She said maybe three full sentences until she saw me crying over *The Notebook*."

"She was *sobbing*."

"Those old people get me every time."

They smile at one another and then Reagan adds, "We moved out as soon as we could last year."

Even though Reagan and Dakota are two years older than me, we fall into an easy camaraderie. They tell me more about their time in the dorms together and they ask me about Ava and how my first week went.

When we finally fall silent, my cheeks hurt from smiling.

"I can see it," Dakota says looking me over closely. "You've got the same eyes and smile."

This makes Reagan look between us and when her brown eyes land on me, they narrow as she studies me. "Same eyes and smile as who?"

"Ginny is Adam's sister."

"Adam Scott?" she asks, eyes widening through thick, black lashes.

Man, it really pains me that even someone as beautiful as Reagan has this reaction about my brother. At least my high school friends hid their fascination with him better.

"That's the one." My phone buzzes in my front pocket and I pull it out. "That's him, checking in. He's a total pain in the ass." I type back a response letting him know I'm next door.

"Everyone ready?" Dakota asks.

Reagan and I nod.

Dakota leads the way. "Let's do this."

Hanging out with Dakota and Reagan is fun. They know everyone, and after the initial shock of finding out I was Adam's little sister, they haven't made me feel like the other Scott.

Speaking of the popular Scott, when I finally spot him, he's in the corner with his arm wrapped around a girl I haven't met. He leans down and whispers in her ear and she giggles and tips her mouth up to let him kiss her. Gross. Seeing my brother in action—really not cool.

"What do women see in him?" I huff. "I mean, honestly?" I turn to Reagan and Dakota.

"Dude, your brother's hot." Dakota shrugs. "Sorry."

I scrunch up my face and walk toward him. He comes up for air when I clear my throat.

"Ginny." He pulls the girl tighter to his side and then nods to Dakota and Reagan. "I see you two met my sister."

"Yeah, she's way cooler than you. What happened?" Dakota deadpans.

"Tough crowd." Adam tilts his head to the girl still clinging to him. "Guys, this is Taryn."

"Hey." Her red lips pull up into a big smile. "Your brother's told me so much about you."

"Oh really?" I ask, surprised since he's never mentioned her, but I smile because I'm not an asshole, and it isn't her problem my brother jumps from girl to girl. "Well, it's nice to meet you." I give Reagan and Dakota a *save me* look, which they interpret quickly and make excuses for us.

"How does he already have a new girlfriend?"

Neither of them answers, not that I expected them to.

"It's the hot thing," Dakota says. "And the hockey thing."

"We should hang out tomorrow," Reagan offers.

"Are you coming to the pool party?" Dakota asks.

"What pool party?"

"Oh yeah, you should definitely come." Reagan smiles. I freaking love her dimples. "It's at The White House. It's a big, back to school party they have every year. Everyone will be there."

"I'm in." And just like that, I'm pretty sure I've made two new friends here.

Chapter Seven

GINNY

The next morning, I'm sitting outside on the deck FaceTiming with Reagan and Dakota recapping last night. I had so much fun and I'm excited to hang out with them again today.

Adam comes out, shirtless, hair matted from sleep, and a giant bottle of Gatorade in hand. "Morning."

"Hey."

He takes a seat next to me with a big, tired sigh and glances to the phone in my hand with a smile. Which reminds me...

"Reagan, what happened with that guy last night?"

"Oh, nothing." She bites at the corner of her lip, making one dimple dot her cheek. "It was stupid. He's dating someone else. I didn't realize until last night. Moving on."

"How is that possible? You're gorgeous. Did you tell him you were into him?"

She shakes her head.

I angle the phone so she can see Adam. "Would you tell her that she needs to tell this guy so he can break up with his girlfriend to date her?"

He chuckles and Reagan's eyes go wide. "Oh my god, Ginny. Adam, you absolutely do not need to—"

"She's right." He nods and smiles at my new friend. "Guy must be crazy."

"See. Told you."

She covers her face with her hands like she's embarrassed.

"I'm going to hang with Adam for a bit."

"Hurry up and get over here," Dakota says, popping her head in front of the screen for a second.

"I'll be over soon," I promise.

"Looks like you made some friends," Adam says as I hang up the phone.

"I did. Thanks for letting me crash in your room last night."

"No problem. The couch wasn't too bad."

"That might have had something to do with the girl that was on it with you."

"Probably so," he agrees. "Do you girls want to ride over to the party together?"

"Sure, sounds good." I stand and stretch. "See you later."

I knock at Dakota and Reagan's and then open the door. "Hello?"

"In my room," Reagan calls.

Dakota sits on the bed and Reagan tosses two giant handfuls of swimsuits onto the comforter.

"I pulled all my suits for you to choose from," Reagan says.

I didn't bring a bathing suit from the dorm, so I'm thankful she's letting me borrow one but holy crap. "That is a lot of options."

She nods happily.

I shower and pull my hair into a braid. I go for a low-cut pink one-piece suit and my own cut-off shorts and sandals.

I'm waiting on Dakota and Reagan's couch while they finish getting ready when I get a text.

Hottest guy on campus: Did you leave without saying goodbye? <sad face>

Me: Who is this and how did you get this number?

Hottest guy on campus: Name is self-explanatory.

It is self-explanatory, sadly. I met dozens of people last night, but Heath is the only one I can recall with any detail. There's a hotness about Heath that goes beyond types and is more universal truth.

Hottest guy on campus: Back at the dorm?

Me: No, actually I'm next door waiting for Dakota and Reagan so we can leave for the pool party. Are you going?

Hottest guy on campus: Depends. Are you going to be there in a bikini?

I glance down at my very covered midsection.

Me: Guess you'll have to come to find out.

Despite Heath's texts that sound anxious to see me, he isn't around when Dakota, Reagan, and I meet Adam and Rhett in the parking lot to catch a ride over.

We pile into Adam's Jeep and drive the few blocks to the pool party. Adam parks along the street and points. "That's Ray Fieldhouse. The student fitness facility is inside, and a lot of the teams have private workout rooms there, too."

"Where's the rink from here?" I ask, trying to get my bearings. The Valley U campus is big and I'm still not sure where everything is.

"Couple of blocks west," Rhett answers.

I sling my beach bag over my shoulder and follow the guys up the sidewalk. "Whose house is this?" I ask once we get to our destination. I was expecting an apartment with a community pool or an old house with a tiny yard and pool. This is none of that.

"This is The White House," Adam remarks. "Guys from the basketball team live here."

We walk around to the back of the giant white house, aptly named, to the pool party going on outside. The pool itself takes up half the large yard and the other side is grassy with a volleyball net set up. There are people everywhere. *Everywhere.* The scene looks like something straight out of a spring break video. Music pumping loudly, girls lounging on rafts, guys chilling with beers in hand, a coed volleyball game.

Even in my tiny shorts and my cleavage pushed up to my ears, I'm grossly overdressed. And where does one stow a bag in a place like this? Something tells me I'm not going to need any of the things I packed: sunscreen, towels, bottled water, three pairs of sunglasses.

On the plus side, there are entirely too many people in the back yard of The White House to feel uncomfortable or self-conscious about my giant bag. My thoughts only stray as far as my next step.

We squeeze through behind Adam and Rhett's large frames to the keg. I'm introduced to more guys from the hockey team, some I recognize from last night.

"Tiny?" I can't help but ask of the guy who is anything but. "Your name is Tiny?"

Tiny, I find out once I have a beer in hand, is a nickname because Tony Waklsinski is the shortest player on the team. And I guess in comparison with Adam, who's at least five inches taller, I can sort of see it. I know how sensitive boys are about inches.

Maverick finds us and joins the circle. Today he's wearing a brightly colored Hawaiian shirt left open to reveal his chiseled abs and tattoos. He lifts the bottle of Mad Dog in his hand. "Shot?"

The other girls pass, but I'm feeling adventurous, so I take it and tip it back, letting some of the sweet liquid slide down my throat. I grimace; it's so sickly sweet that I chase it with beer, which doesn't really help since I'm not a fan of it either.

"All right. Let's not get my baby sister shitfaced." Adam takes the bottle and takes a drink three times as big as mine as if he's trying to drink it all so I won't.

"Anyone seen Payne? He's supposed to be bringing reinforcements." Maverick reaches for the nearly empty bottle and gives it a shake.

"No clue," Adam says. "Thought he was with you."

When Taryn shows up with her friends, that feels like my cue to leave.

"Mingle?" I ask Dakota and Reagan.

We make a circle around the party and head inside to check out the drink selection. "This is not what I thought of when you guys said pool party."

"It's more bikini party unless you're brave enough to get in the pool," Reagan says.

"What's wrong with the pool?"

"Going into the pool is the equivalent of posting an *I'm here to get laid* sign on your forehead," Dakota says. "Which if you're into that, it's totally fine, but don't say I didn't warn you." She holds up the vodka in invitation. "Drink?"

After we swap out our beer for vodka and tonic, we head back outside.

We sit on lounge chairs on the patio near a mister and watch the people in the pool. Some love matches (or rather, hookups) are being made while other people are being hilariously blown off.

Dakota drills me with twenty questions while we people watch. Now that we've spent a little time together, she holds nothing back, but somehow the way she pries is endearing.

"So, no boyfriend?" Reagan asks, leaning forward with her elbows on her knees.

"No," I say with a scowl.

Dakota laughs. "Oooh, there's a story."

"Not a good one."

Water drips onto my toes and I look up to see Maverick leaning over and shaking his head on us.

"Bad dog," Dakota scolds him.

I'm laughing as I dodge him continuing to get us wet when my gaze falls to a guy approaching from behind him.

"Ah, there he is," Maverick says, taking a seat next to me. "Payne, where the hell have you been?"

"Been around." His dark blue eyes land on me. He's got a twelve-pack of hard seltzer under one arm and my stomach flips. He pulls a bottle of Mad Dog out of his pocket and hands it to Maverick.

"Trade you." He motions with his head and Maverick stands,

giving up his seat and taking the bottle.

He smells like soap and sun and wild dreams. Dreams you shouldn't allow because they're so out of reach, but you can't help but want. Dreams you don't speak of, but that live in the darkest corner of your mind.

"Swim anyone?" Maverick asks.

I shake my head as does Reagan.

"Oh, why not." Dakota stands, looks to me and shrugs with a smirk

"I'm going to find the bathroom. Do you want to come?" Reagan asks me, then glances between me and Heath.

"I'm good."

Heath opens the case and holds out a can. "Drink?"

As I wrap my hands around the cold can, he holds tight and leans in. "You look good. Do you want to skip this party and go make out?"

I laugh, but heat rushes to my core at the thought. "Pass."

"You wanna not skip this party and just make out right here?"

"Definitely pass." I pull the drink from his hand and pop the top. After I've taken a long drink, I ask, "Does that usually work for you?"

"Honestly?"

I nod.

"Every time."

I roll my eyes. "What is wrong with women?"

"I'm really good at making out." His stare darts to my mouth. I have no doubt.

"You and I are going to be just friends."

"Friends?" His brows raise. "I don't have girl friends."

"You do now."

Chapter Eight

HEATH

Looks like the Scotts are on the same page, anyway. Friends? With Ginny?

I can't stop staring at her lips. That's not a thing friends do, I don't think.

When Reagan comes back from the bathroom, I'm disappointed at the prospect of sharing Ginny, but Reagan takes off her coverup and tosses it on the lounge chair. "I'm going in the pool. Anyone want to join me?"

"Really?" Ginny asks and she and Reagan share some sort of look I can't decipher.

"Only live once. Coming?"

Ginny shakes her head and Reagan heads to the pool

"You know it's a pool party, right?" I ask when it's just the two of us again.

She gives me an annoyed look and motions to her chest, covered by the swimsuit, but uh, I might get lost a little too long staring at her chest. Also, not something a friend does.

"Something against swimming?"

"No, I love to swim. But…" She pauses. "Dakota said the pool was where people go to find hookups."

I try real hard to keep from smiling too big. Sweet, innocent Ginny's not looking for a casual hookup. I could have guessed that. It shouldn't make me happy because it also means I won't be hooking up with her, but for some reason, I'm glad that no one else will be either.

"What do *you* want to do?" I ask her. "We've got people watching which we're perfectly positioned for now, we could play one of the many party games—flip cup, beer pong—all the usuals, there's volleyball, I'm still offering up making out in case you want to rethink that one, or we can go to the pool and I'll swat the swarms of boys away so you can swim without being harassed."

She rolls her eyes. "Swarms?"

"I mean, look at you. Yeah, *swarms.*"

"And you're going to be my protector?"

"Totally self-serving," I tell her honestly.

"How's that?"

"I like spending time with you."

She glances to the pool, and I can see the longing there.

"Come on." I stand and take off my T-shirt. Her eyes flit over my chest and abs before she gets up and carefully removes her shorts and sandals.

The light pink suit she's wearing dips low in the front and cuts up on her hips. Ginny's thin and her frame is small, but her boobs did not get the memo because they're disproportionately bigger. Thank fuck for disproportions.

We enter the pool at the shallow end. A lot of people are swimming or hanging out near the edge, but I manage to snag a floatie for her.

She leans her upper body onto it and we go to the middle of the pool. The water comes up to my armpits and I dip down so it covers my shoulders and I'm at eye level with Ginny. Her gaze darts around taking it all in, but I see the exact second that she relaxes into the blue floatie and decides to be in the moment with me.

I grab a hold of the floatie and let my legs drift underneath me. Music pumps through the speakers and I close my eyes behind my sunglasses soaking it in. Good tunes and a bunch of people hanging out, talking and laughing. Not a bad way to spend a Saturday. Not bad at all.

"You look pretty comfortable in here," she says. I open my eyes to see her skim her fingers across the water. "This your typical hang out?"

"Are you trying to ask if I use the pool to find my hookups?"

"Do you?"

"Don't knock it `til you try it."

She laughs, her lips pulling wide and flashing her straight white teeth. "Maybe I will. Anyone you suggest?" She lifts her head and glances around the pool.

"Just say the word." I find myself staring at her lips again. They're full, the lower one so plump I want to trace it with my thumb and my tongue, and they're this perfect pink color.

"I'm not dating for a while. Boys suck."

"Why is it when girls get their heart broken, they go off men entirely? A guy gets his heart kicked in and he moves on to the next. Chicks aren't like that."

"Well, women are smarter. It takes you guys longer for your

small brains to catch up and be brokenhearted."

A chuckle escapes from my lips and she smiles.

"I got out of a relationship right before I came to Valley."

"Might have heard something about that."

"Ugh. Really? Adam told you about Bryan?"

"Not by name, but he did mention that you'd recently gotten out of something. He's worried about you, wants me to look out for you."

Her mouth gapes and her shoulders tense. "Is that why you're…"

"No. Fuck no." Her hair is in another braid today and I finger the end and tug it gently. "I thought we established that I like hanging out with you."

"Same." Her body melts back into the raft and those perfect pink lips pull apart. "How'd you and my brother become roommates? I get the hockey connection, but you don't seem like the best of friends."

"Cheap rent," I tell her honestly. "I wanted to move out of the dorms but couldn't afford a place on my own. Your brother and I are cool. We're not the best of friends, as you said, but we get each other. He's a good captain."

It's hot out and there's really no escape from the sun in the middle of the pool, so we get out when Ginny's shoulders start to burn. Inside the house, we find Adam and his new girlfriend sitting with Maverick and a brunette he introduces as Maddie. Rauthruss is there too with his phone in hand, no doubt texting his girlfriend.

"Little Scott," Maverick greets her as we take a seat. She bristles at the name, which I totally get. Since Nathan went to Valley too, I've often been called Baby Payne and that shit gets old really quick.

"She has a name, man," I tell him.

His brows raise slightly, but he nods. "Yeah, I know, just messing around."

"Do you want something to drink?" I ask her and stand. She nods and I head outside to where we left our stuff.

Dakota and Reagan are sitting in the lounge chairs we abandoned.

"Where's Ginny?" Reagan asks.

I grab the alcohol and all our clothing. "Everyone's inside." I motion with my head and they follow.

"Got a crush on Ginny?" Dakota asks with a tease to her voice.

"It's not like that."

"What is it like?" she presses as we walk toward the house.

"She's cool."

"Cool? So you don't want to sleep with her?"

Of-fucking-course I want to sleep with her. She's beautiful and fun and if I had standards… she'd exceed them.

"She's Scott's sister."

She nods in understanding. "He would kill you. Better get your shit on lock then. It's written all over your handsome face."

Inside, Liam has slid into my spot and a few others have crowded around the table. When Ginny sees me approaching with her things, she stands. "Oh, thank you."

I take her seat while she pulls on her shorts and steps into her sandals. The end of her braid swings forward into my face. Back and forth all hypnotic-like. Reminds me of that movie *Office Space* and I'm going deeper and deeper, way down into Ginny.

When she's ready to sit, I crowd Liam and make room for her

on half the seat. As she settles in, I wrap an arm around her to keep her from falling off.

She smiles at me all sun-kissed skin and smelling like chlorine and something twists in my gut.

"Heath."

My name being called draws my attention to a group of girls walking up to the table.

"Hey, Kimberly. How are you?"

"Good, good." She glances around the table, stopping on Rauthruss for a few seconds longer than the others. He gets real busy staring at his phone. I don't get it. I get loyalty. I respect him for that, but if he wants a girlfriend, why not find one he can actually see... and fuck?

Kimberly's stare finally finds its way back to me. "What have you been up to? You didn't call."

Ginny giggles quietly next to me and I squeeze her waist playfully as I answer. "School, hockey... the usual."

"Well, let's hang out later."

I give her a noncommittal head bob. "See ya."

"Friend of yours?" Ginny asks with a smirk when she's gone.

"Never seen her before in my life." I wink and she giggles again.

Her face is soft and sincere when she pulls away. "Go, you don't need to keep an eye out for me just because my brother asked you to. I'm good."

"I thought I told you—"

"I know what you said, but it's a party and... we're friends." Her insinuation is clear. She and I aren't happening. "Go." She shoves at my shoulder playfully.

I stand, though I don't know why. I don't want to hang out with

Kimberly. "All right, you know where to find me." I tug her braid one last time and head off to the pool.

Chapter Nine

GINNY

The more I drink and the darker the sky gets, the more relaxed I feel. We moved back outside now that it's cooled off. I can feel the slight burn on my skin from earlier and the breeze makes goose bumps dot my arm.

Adam and Taryn are sharing a lounge chair next to me and Reagan. Dakota and Maverick are both in the pool. Maverick's tossing a beach ball back and forth with the girl he's been hanging out with all afternoon and Dakota's full-on making out with some guy Reagan tells me is a basketball player.

Liam sits on the ground between us. He's attached himself to my side. I can't tell if he's hitting on me or if he's another one of the guys Adam's asked to keep an eye out for me. His approach is much more subtle than Heath's, and dammit if I don't prefer Heath's cocky, playfulness to Liam's politeness.

I find him in the pool. He's leaning against the side and the girl I all but pushed him into hanging out with is next to him. She's facing him, her back to me, but I have a clear view of Heath.

He smiles and holds a beer in one hand. They're not touching, at least that I can tell, but they're standing close. He laughs and his stare moves past her to me. It isn't the first time he's caught me staring in the last hour.

I know he's all wrong for me. Dakota and Reagan have filled me in on all the guys and what they said about Heath is exactly what I expected. He hooks up, he's all for the fun, but he doesn't date, and he's never had a girlfriend that they're aware of.

The reasons to not hook up with him are many, not the least of which is him being my brother's roommate and teammate. And if I'm totally honest, I'm not one hundred percent over Bryan. I think it's mostly turned into anger at the way he ended things and missing the idea of what I thought college would look like. We were supposed to be doing all of this together, but if we had, I wouldn't have met Dakota and Reagan and I already can't imagine that.

"You're staring," Reagan says, nudging me with an elbow.

"I know. It's pathetic. She's beautiful. Do you know her?"

"No, not really. I've seen her around."

"With Heath?"

She nods. "If it's any consolation, I don't think it's serious. I think it's lack of options and similar goals."

"Is the goal not going home alone?"

She laughs. "Yeah, pretty much. And Heath's a hot commodity, especially now that he's been drafted."

"Drafted, like to the NHL?" It clicks before she answers. "I remember Adam saying something about one of his teammates being drafted, but I didn't realize it was Heath."

"Heath and Maverick both already signed with teams." Standing, she slips into her shoes. "Come on, I see Rhett playing flip cup."

I take one last look at Heath and our eyes catch again. I tear my gaze away first this time and stand. "Let's do it."

"College is awesome. A-W-E-S-O-M-E awesome."

Reagan and Dakota's laughter is a hazy sound as they help me into Adam's bed.

"I put a glass of water on the nightstand and your phone on the desk. Do you want help getting changed or at least out of those shoes?" I think it's Reagan who asks.

My eyes are shut, and their voices are surprisingly similar.

"No, it's fine. This way I'll be ready to go to classes in the morning. No getting ready. Voi, voile, I mean voila!"

"Tomorrow is Sunday, sweetie."

"How did you get so drunk?" Dakota asks. I can tell it's definitely her this time, the little snort laugh she does gives her away.

"I'm not drunk. Just tipsy and tired."

"Now I see the family resemblance. You're as stubborn as your brother. Last time Adam got drunk, he swore he was fine until he fell down the stairs on the way to the bar."

I'm too tired to laugh, but the image in my head of my bossy and always in control brother tumbling down a flight of stairs is hilarious.

"Okay. Night, Ginny. Sleep tight."

Their footsteps retreat and one of them flips the overhead light off before the door shuts.

"Wait," I call, not loudly enough. I groan and sit up, prying open my eyelids. A small strip of light underneath the door is the only thing saving me from total darkness. I get up and look for my phone, but I can't see anything. I flip the light on and take a deep breath. I still don't see my phone, but now I need to pee.

I stumble out into the empty living room. Rhett came back at the same time as we did, but he must have gone to bed. I hurry into the bathroom and close the door, then fumble with the light switch.

Only nothing happens. Damn Adam and his inability to change a freaking light bulb. It's really dark in here and my pulse quickens. I find the door handle, turn and yank, but nothing happens. It's a standard turn lock, but no matter which way I turn, it doesn't seem to do anything and my breathing gets more erratic with each failed attempt.

Oh my god, this can't be happening. I close my eyes to try to trick myself into believing it isn't as dark as it is, but I'm already panicking too much to fool myself.

I bang on the door. "Little help in here."

I wait for a few seconds before I try again, this time louder. Rhett's room is all the way across the apartment, and I have no idea if anyone else is home. I didn't see Heath when we left, and Mav was going to catch a ride with Adam and Taryn. "Help!"

I slide down onto the floor before my legs can give out and continue banging with both fists. I try counting to focus on something else. One. Two. I'm fine. Everything is fine. Three. Four. Someone will come home any second now.

My hands fall to my lap and I suck in deep breaths. All the

fuzzy edges from the alcohol are gone and I'm entirely too sober and aware that I'm trapped in a very dark, small room.

Hot tears roll down my face. I yell as loud as I can through the crying. "Help!"

"Ginny?" Heath's voice on the other side of the door makes me cry harder. "Are you okay?"

"I can't get the door open."

The handle rattles. "It's locked."

"I know. It's too d-dark to see, but I can't get it open either way I turn it. Could you get Adam?"

"Ginny, I'm going to kick the door open, but I need you to move back out of the way. Maybe step into the shower."

"O-okay." I crawl on my hands and knees and sit inside the tub, hugging my knees.

"Are you away from the door?"

"Y-yes."

A second later the cheap wood door slams in and against the wall and the light from the living room pours in. Heath stands in the doorway frozen as he takes me in, then rushes toward me. "Are you all right?"

I nod even as I shiver and hug my knees tighter. He's quiet and I'm all too aware of my ragged breaths filling the silence between us. I close my eyes and concentrate on taking slow and even breaths. One, two, three…

"Everything okay?" Rhett asks in that heavy Minnesota accent.

I'm so embarrassed. I wonder if it's possible to never see any of Adam's teammates ever again.

"Can you get her a glass of water?" Heath asks Rhett.

My eyes fly open as my space is invaded and Heath climbs into the tub in front of me. He doesn't exactly fit, and his long legs are bent and flank me on either side. His hands raise to my shoulders and he strokes me gently. "Deep breaths in through your nose."

Yep, epic proportions of embarrassment.

"Here ya go." Rhett reappears with water in a big green plastic cup.

Heath takes it and thanks him, while I smile awkwardly.

"Uh, you guys good?" Rhett shifts uncomfortably. "Should I call Adam? I think he went with Maverick and Taryn on a taco run."

Heath's fingers continue to stroke my arms and back. "I've got her."

That's all the convincing Rhett needs to get the heck out of my bubble of crazy.

"I'm fine. Really. You can go now," I say, chest still rising and falling too fast. "Go back to the girl in your bed."

"You're not fine. You're having a panic attack. And there's no one in my bed. I left right after you." He hands me the cup of water. "Try to take a sip or two. Sometimes forcing your brain to do something else helps."

I do as he instructs, and the cool liquid does seem to help a tiny bit. Enough that I can better appreciate the man in front of me. He's shirtless, his ab muscles defined even as he sits. Blue basketball shorts hang on his hips, but his bare calves press against my back.

When I finally feel the sharp edges of my fear dissipate, I finish the water and let out a long, cleansing breath. "I'm sorry."

"For what?" A ghost of a smile tugs at the corner of his mouth. His arms wrap around me again and he rubs my back softly.

"For getting myself locked in and for that." I point toward the busted door. The trim hangs away from the wall where the lock pushed it away from the frame.

"That's nothing. Don't even worry about it. Are you feeling better?"

I nod. "I want to go to bed."

"Okay." He moves his legs and groans. "I think I might be stuck."

Standing, I offer him my hand. He smiles goofily as he places his calloused palm in mine, and I attempt to help him up. Somehow, we manage to get him upright and he's so close my breathing picks up all over again, but for a completely different reason.

He notices and his brows furrow. "Are you sure you're okay?"

"I'll be fine."

"This kind of thing happen before?" he asks and then adds, "When you've been drinking."

I nod, refusing to meet his concerned blue eyes. "I just need some sleep." And to wake up and pretend this never happened.

As gracefully as one can in this situation, I step out of the tub and glance at the burned-out light bulb over the vanity. "How many hockey players does it take to change a lightbulb?"

He follows me out of the bathroom. I walk to Adam's open bedroom and face him. "Well, this was humiliating and awful. Pretend it never happened?"

His lips twist into a playful smile and he reaches out and squeezes my hand. "Night, Ginny."

In Adam's room I flip the overhead light on and shut the door. And then I climb into bed and somehow sleep through the night.

When I wake up, Adam is on the couch sleeping with Taryn

curled up next to him. The rest of the house is quiet. I tiptoe to the bathroom and reach for the light before I remember. Except this time, the bathroom floods with light and the doorframe is fixed.

It turns out it only takes one hockey player to change a light bulb, and I have a very good idea which one it was.

Chapter Ten

HEATH

I'm lying in bed fully dressed when Maverick sticks his head in my room. "Time to stop touching yourself and go get fondled by the elderly instead."

I sit up and swing my legs onto the floor.

"Was that Mariah I heard while I was playing Xbox with Rauthruss?" he questions, dark eyebrows raised and a playful smile on his lips.

"It's weird when you listen in, man."

"Just looking out for you."

"How thoughtful."

We meet the rest of the team at the assisted living home. Coach's mom lives here. As such, this is where a good portion of our community service hours are done. At least once a semester, he drags us out here. Today we're doing some outdoor landscaping. Manual labor shit that sucks balls, but in truth, I enjoy it more than going inside the place.

It smells like old people, which makes sense, but I don't need reminders that we are all going to die and, if we are lucky, get to stink up the world on our way out. I learned that lesson the hard way when my dad died at forty-one. He didn't even get a chance to enjoy that mothball and shit stench. He'd gone out looking fit and healthy and smelling like Acqua di Gio. I was fourteen and thought he was invincible.

Desert Rose is a massive place. So many residents that I have to wonder if there are any old people left in Valley who aren't living here. The grounds are well cared for, flowers and shrubs trimmed to make Mother Nature look like a Monet painting.

We're probably more of a hindrance than a help to the crew since they clearly have it under control, but the old people enjoy watching us work hard. The old men come to sit outside in lawn chairs and regale us with tales of their youth, sleight-of-hand reminders at the end of every tale to enjoy being young and stupid.

Done and done.

Scott and I are spreading rock with rakes along a pathway to a gazebo. I'm tired and a little hungover. It's hot work, no reprieve from the sun blasting down on us.

"Rhett said Ginny got locked in the bathroom last night," he says, breaking the silence.

I'm really not sure how much to say. She was in a full-blown panic, but I don't want to freak out Adam. However, it sounds like Rauthruss filled him in.

"Yeah, she got in there with no light and couldn't get the door open to get out."

"Oh shit." He stops raking and stares at me with wide eyes. "Ginny's got a thing with the dark. She okay?"

"It took a few minutes to calm her down, but she seemed all right when she went to bed. I put a fresh bulb in, just in case." She was gone this morning before I woke up and she hasn't answered my texts.

"That must be why she left so early this morning. I'll check on her after we're done here. Thanks, man, I appreciate you looking out for her."

I swallow thickly and nod. His request to look out for her wasn't even a factor in it or really any of the times I've hung out with her. I like her. I like being with her. She makes me be in the moment more deeply. I'm not looking for hookups or to get drunk, I want to sit beside her, pull her hair, and tease her. Basically, I'm five again. I was thankful that I was there last night when she needed me. Last semester me wouldn't have been. He'd have been wasted or with a girl.

I take my shirt off and tuck it in my back pocket. It's so damn hot out. It's nice not to have the material sticking to my sweaty back, but now I can practically feel the sun turning my back into a barbeque grill.

Adam looks past me. "The old women at six o'clock are not so subtly undressing you with their eyes."

I pause and lean against the rake. Sure enough, three ladies with snow-white hair are walking toward us in monochromatic cotton ensembles and thick Dr. Scholl's sole-type shoes.

"Take it off. Scott, give the ladies something to live another day for," I taunt him. "I get it if you don't want them comparing our bodies and finding you lacking."

"Good morning, ladies," he says as they approach. He stands straight, lifts the hem of his shirt, and wipes his face. The ladies pause, taking in his abs, and when he drops the material, he tosses me a smirk. Fucker.

"You boys are doing a wonderful job." The one in the middle drops her gaze. As she brings it back to my face, I wink.

"Just trying to make this place as beautiful as you," Mav appears out of nowhere. The guy has a freaky ability to find the center of attention.

I hand him my rake. "I'm going for water. Make yourself useful."

I take my empty water bottle inside to the water fountain and fill it. Burt's in his usual spot sitting in front of the TV watching CSI or ESPN. I only know his name because someone is always yelling at him. He's a grumpy old prick, always sitting alone, and always pissing someone off. He's beating the remote on the arm of the chair, cursing under his breath. No one pays him any attention. A nurse walks by and sighs. I can't really blame her for not rushing to his aid. I've only been here a few times and even I'm tired of his shit.

"Goddamn remote." He tosses it across the room and it skips along the white tile floor, coming to a stop in my path back outside.

I lean down and pick it up and walk it over to him. He frowns as I hold it out.

"Trouble with the remote?"

"Trouble with everything," he grumbles as he punches at the buttons with his thumb.

"Maybe it's the batteries."

"Already changed them out, twice, to be sure they weren't dicking me around. That Sharon's got it out for me." He twists his body in his chair and hollers over his shoulder. "Are you sure this is the right remote?"

Sharon, I presume, doesn't even look up as she calls back. "Yes,

Mister Thomas, I'm sure. I'll send Louie over to help as soon as he gets done with bedpans."

Burt snarls. I wouldn't want Louie's nasty hands on my remote either.

"I could give it a try if you want," I offer.

He holds it out with another sigh as if I am the last person he really wants to put his trust in. Again, can't say that I blame him. But a man should at least have TV if he's going to sit around in this depressing place all day. I test it out, pressing the channel up button with the same result Burt had.

"It's on the wrong input," I tell him and hold it so he can see. I press TV and then the channel button again, this time with success.

He keeps frowning as he takes it back in a liver-spotted hand and tries it for himself. I don't get a thank you or even an acknowledgment before I leave him to CSI.

If the options are going out young and unaware or old and hating the world... I think I'm in favor of the first. Live hard and die happy.

DESERT ROSE TREATS US TO LUNCH AFTER WE'RE DONE. THE GUYS are all in good spirits. Everyone's talking and laughing as we go through the buffet line set up for us. We're starting to get a nice camaraderie among the group, and I hope it translates to the ice when we get out there.

We spread out under the pavilion, sweaty and dirty but so hungry. Mav and I sit across from one another. The place goes silent as we eat. Even Mav barely speaks as we devour everything on our plates and then grab seconds. I finish and then guzzle what remains of my water.

"You want to grab a beer after this?" Mav asks.

"Nah, not today."

"Xbox?" he asks as we stand to leave.

I shake my head and we walk to his car. I need a shower and to find Ginny. She still hasn't responded to my text from earlier.

"Movie?"

"No." I slide into the passenger seat and Mav opens the driver's side door and gets in.

"Running out of options, buddy." He starts the car and taps his thumb on the steering wheel as he thinks. "Girls?"

"Now you've got it, but just one girl."

"Sharesies?" He seems surprised, but dare I say a little excited about the idea.

I lean back against the headrest. Tired laughter slips out. "Really, man?"

I don't have an exact plan. Find Ginny, make sure she's good, then convince her to spend more time with me.

"You wouldn't share with me? What if I sing Mariah and promise to keep my hands to myself?"

I don't know if he's kidding or not, but I wouldn't put anything past Maverick.

"Absolutely fucking not." I don't want to share one second of my time with Ginny. Not with anyone.

Chapter Eleven

GINNY

And that's the story of why I'm never going back to my brother's apartment."

"I'm sure it wasn't that bad." Reagan gives me a hopeful smile across the table. I snuck out of Adam's early this morning and went straight to Dakota and Reagan's. They're consoling me over brunch at a cute little café they like.

"I was having a full-on panic attack in the bathtub. I have an issue with dark, enclosed spaces." I wave it off, hoping they don't ask more about that piece because I don't really feel like going into the specifics. "It was absolutely that bad."

Dakota snickers and takes a bite of her bagel.

"It's kind of romantic," Reagan insists. "Crawling into the tub with you and calming you down. I'm impressed, although not all that surprised that Heath was the one to come to your rescue. He's got that cocky but capable look about him. Still, I'm not sure I would have known what to do, so you were really lucky."

"It wasn't romantic. It was pity." I groan and bury my head in my arm on the table for a second. When I lift it back up, they're both smiling at me. "It's too bad. I liked Heath. Now I'm going to have to avoid him until I can look at him without wanting to disappear into the ground."

"Are you a drama major like this one?" Dakota asks and points her bagel toward Reagan.

"No, why?"

She smiles and I toss a crumpled napkin at her. "Ha. Ha. Very funny."

"We've all made fools of ourselves one time or another. It's college. It's fine." Dakota finishes her bagel and grabs her coffee. "Do you need to get back to the dorm or do you want to hang out today?"

"I need to shower and change, but I don't have anything after that."

"You'll want to shower after, but we can swing by the dorm on the way because you need sneakers."

"On the way where?" I ask, standing and following them out of the booth.

I GASP AS WE JOG AROUND THE VALLEY U CAMPUS TRACK. "WHEN you said hang out, I was picturing Netflix or mani-pedis."

"Two more laps and then we switch to speed walking," Dakota says, sounding far too comfortable talking while jogging.

The Scott pride and competitive nature keeps me pushing on, but when we finally begin walking, I'm a lot more sweaty and tired than these two.

"Do you guys do this often?"

"Three times a week," Reagan says, sounding only slightly out of breath.

"Why?"

"I like to run," Dakota says.

"She was on the track team," Reagan adds. "I let her drag me along because it justifies the really big slice of cheesecake I'm going to have later while I make Dakota watch Lifetime movies."

"What's Ava, your roommate, like?" Dakota asks, swiftly changing the subject.

Ava and Trent hadn't been at the dorm when we'd stopped by, but Trent's things were still there. I can't wait to sleep in my own bed tonight.

"She's really nice. Her boyfriend goes to school at Northern. That's why I was at Adam's this weekend. He was visiting, and I wanted to give them some privacy. Hopefully next weekend she goes to his campus because I'm going to need a few weeks while I'm in hiding."

"You can always crash with us. The bathtub is all yours," Reagan teases.

"Thanks a lot, jerks," I say with a smile.

Trent's gone and Ava's asleep in her bed when I get back. I shower and then get into my own bed to nap, but last night plays over and over in my mind. Adam and Heath have both texted, but I only responded to my brother and with a quick—I'm fine, it was nothing—that will hopefully keep him from asking more.

A knock at our door gets me out of bed and I'm half expecting it to be Adam. It would be just like him to skip texting back altogether and want to check on me in person, but it's Heath standing in the hallway.

"What are you doing here?"

He smirks and adjusts the baseball hat on his head. "It's nice to see you too."

"Sorry. Hello, how are you today? Great weather we're having. What the heck are you doing at my dorm? And how did you know where I lived?"

His rough chuckle pulls a smile from my lips. "Good. Agreed. I wanted to see you and…" He leans in closer. "I can't reveal all my secrets." He's full-on grinning at me with a mocking glint in his eyes. "Come on, take a walk with me."

"A walk?"

"Sure. You got something better to do?"

"I was planning on taking a nap."

"Sleep's boring. Come on, am I really having to talk you into this? It's gorgeous outside and we can stop at the dining hall to feed you."

"Me?"

"Now that you mention it, I could eat."

He doesn't move and I relent. "One minute."

I leave him in the hallway, shut the door, and change out of my comfy yoga pants and into a pair of shorts. I swipe on lip gloss and a dab of mascara. When I pull the door open, he's leaning against the wall, one ankle crossed over the other and hands in his pockets.

"Ready?"

He pushes off the wall and motions for me to go first. "If you are."

We cross the street to the dining hall in silence. Heath seems perfectly at ease with the quiet, while I have a million questions on the tip of my tongue. He holds the door out for me.

"I should have assumed spending time with you would mean eating."

"Always," he says. "Plus, it's where we met. We have history here."

I huff a laugh and grab a tray. Now that we're here, I am kind of hungry. Heath gets a much smaller portion of food than normal and I raise a brow.

"I already ate lunch once," he admits.

We take our food to our usual table.

"What time did you sneak out this morning?" he asks.

I hesitate with a chip up to my mouth. "I didn't sneak out."

His left brow rises as he takes a bite of food.

"Okay, fine. I very quietly left at a ridiculously early time. Happy?"

"Obviously not since I tracked you down."

"I'm fine, okay?"

He shrugs. As we eat, he tells me about his morning with the team doing community service and I tell him about running with the girls.

"Congrats on being drafted, by the way. Adam mentioned it this summer, but I didn't piece together it was you until Reagan mentioned it last night."

"Thanks." He sits back in his chair, drinking his water and studying me.

"What?" I ask self-consciously.

"Trying to figure you out. What are you into?"

"Everything and nothing. I didn't play sports in high school or anything like that."

"Had to have been into something."

"I was into socializing. Turns out you can't make a career out of that unless your parents are rich and famous."

"Damn those Kardashians."

"Right?"

"Genevieve, Genevieve, Genevieve."

I love the way my full name sounds when he says it. I was always sort of embarrassed by it. Teachers would comment on how beautiful it was, which to a middle schooler, is super humiliating. Kids would taunt me with it, at least until I got boobs, then it became some sort of bad pickup line. *Genevieve, huh? Cool name.*

Cue swooning. Not.

Except, I'm sort of swooning now and all he did was say my name. And I'm also staring at him when I'm supposed to be saying something. Anything.

"Heath, Heath, Heath."

His playful smile makes my stomach flip.

"I'm going to get ice cream." I stand before he can comment and take my time at the dessert bar creating a perfect sundae.

He's picking at the chips on my tray when I get back. "I assumed you were done."

"They're all yours."

"What is that?" he asks, face twisted in disgust as he eyes my bowl of ice cream.

"Neapolitan with sprinkles and gummy bears."

"All the flavors are touching."

I laugh and bring a big spoonful of all three flavors to my mouth. He continues to watch on horrified.

"I don't understand Neapolitan flavor. It's ice cream for people who can't make a decision."

"Not true. The decision is we want all three and don't want to settle for one boring flavor." I offer him my spoon. "Wanna try it?"

His mouth pulls into a tight line and he shakes his head.

"Come on." I sit forward and lean over the table to get the spoon closer to his mouth. He opens and I feed him, which turns out to be a surprisingly intimate thing. His throat works, eyes locked on mine, as I sit back and study his reaction to the food.

"Well?"

"I think I swallowed a gummy bear whole," he says, voice tight.

We finish the rest of my ice cream and if Heath eating more than half of it is any indication, I'd say he likes my Neapolitan sundae just fine.

After, we take a walk around campus. It isn't as busy as it is during the week, but lots of other people are out walking, hanging out in the shaded areas, playing frisbee, and some are even going in and out of buildings.

Eventually we take a seat on the ledge of the fountain in the center of campus. It's one of my favorite spots.

"So, you're all right?"

"What?" I try to play it off like I don't know what he's talking about, but his serious expression says it all. "Oh, yeah, I'm fine."

I dig through my pocket for a penny, close my eyes, and toss it into the fountain.

"What'd you wish for?"

"I can't tell you or it won't come true."

It's quiet and I hope we've successfully avoided talking any more about last night until he asks, "You've had them before, right? Panic attacks? Adam said you had a thing with the dark."

I consider lying, but it feels as if it couldn't get any more embarrassing with the truth.

"Really, I'm fine. I don't like being trapped in dark places. And, sure, I've had them before, but it isn't like a common occurrence." I quit talking and hope I've said enough to make me seem less crazy.

"My mom used to have them. The first time she thought she was dying or having a heart attack. Scared the shit out of both of us."

I finger the hem of my shorts and avoid meeting his gaze.

"It's okay. I didn't bring it up to make you embarrassed. I just wanted you to know it's nothing to be ashamed of."

"I'm not ashamed. I'd just prefer not to need to be rescued by my brother's insanely hot friend." I slap a hand over my mouth. "Forget I said that. Clearly there was something wrong with those gummy bears and it's making me say crazy things."

He quirks a brow. "You think I'm insanely hot?"

"Did I say insanely? That was the gummy bears talking. I mean, objectively yes, you're hot. But it isn't like *I* think you're hot."

His hand comes up and brushes my hair back from my face. His thumb traces my bottom lip. He leans in and the seconds while his lips descend on mine seem to happen in slow motion while my pulse quickens.

My eyes flutter closed and finally his mouth covers mine. His lips are soft, but his scruff is scratchy against my smooth skin. His hand at my face slides to the back of my neck, cupping it with his large palm as his mouth widens and his tongue asks for entrance.

His tongue feels divine. Kissing Heath feels divine. He's a great kisser, and even though it's only my neck and lips he's touching, I feel it everywhere.

When he pulls back, I'm breathless and turned on. Jesus.

"I'm sorry. I shouldn't have done that."

His words are like a bucket of cold water dumped over my lady parts. "Why not?"

"Because maybe you were right. You're off men, I'm not capable of being more than your friend without ruining everything else, your brother is my teammate, pick a reason I guess."

"Those gummy bears are making you do crazy things too."

He smirks. "Friends?"

Is he serious? He wants to be friends after that kiss? But I did just get out of a relationship and it's probably not the best idea to jump into something one week into college, so I nod. "Friends."

SEPTEMBER

Chapter Twelve

HEATH

Ginny takes the seat across from me with her bowl of ice cream. "I'm ready for fall. My boobs are sweaty just from walking across the street."

"I totally get it," Mav says. "My balls—"

"All right. Too much information, man," I tell him.

"I don't see how it's any different than Ginny's boobs." Mav shrugs and goes back to his homework laid out on the table in front of him.

"Boobs, Mav. It's different because boobs."

Ginny giggles, not the least bit offended by my buddy or me and slides the bowl along the top of the table to me without asking if I want any. The chemistry between Ginny and I is hard to ignore. I thought friend-zoning myself would take away the tension, but even when she says things like sweaty boobs, I find I'm wishing the clock would move a little slower so we could spend more time together.

There are too many complications. For one, I don't need the team captain having it out for me. And then there's the fact that

I don't want to stop hanging out with Ginny. If that means being friends instead of kissing her so I don't screw things up, then so be it. Better friends than nothing at all.

I smile as I stare down at her bowl of ice cream. She never gets gummy bears on top anymore. I don't know if she really believes it was their fault she admitted I was hot and let me kiss her or not, but the loss of them makes me a little sad. Hard, awful little things.

I take a small bite and push it back.

"That's all you're eating?"

"Gotta get the season diet back on track. We're taking the ice today."

I can barely keep from jumping out of my skin I want to be out there so badly.

Mav looks up and nods, but then groans. "It's going to be short-lived for me if I fail this British literature test." He hits his head on his book several times and then sits up and closes it. He barely scraped by with grades good enough to play last year and Coach is watching him closely. "You still have Tonya's number? I think she tutors."

"Uhh… yeah, maybe." I pull my phone up and find her and hand the phone to Maverick. "I wouldn't tell her you got her number from me though, she's not my biggest fan."

"Did she *tutor* you?" Ginny asks.

"No, she did not." What we had was much more honest—a quickie in a bathroom at a party last year. She wanted to continue the fun and I didn't.

"Maybe I can help," Ginny says. "I love literature."

"Really?" Mav looks hopeful.

"Sure. Tonight?"

While they make plans, I sit back and watch Ginny. She's nice, interesting, funny, and a little naïve. But naïve in that way that she still believes in the good of people and situations, and being around her makes me believe a little more too. There isn't anything I don't like about her. Every little detail. It's safe to say Ginny Scott's grown on me just like Neapolitan ice cream.

I look forward to our meals together. She's never mentioned the gummy bear induced illicit kiss, and neither have I, but we both show up at the same time for breakfast and lunch every day to eat together. Sometimes Maverick and the guys are with us, sometimes not, but the two of us never miss.

Lunch friends. I can think of worse things to be. I can think of better things, too.

After lunch, I head to the rink for practice. I'm early, but I can't wait another minute to get out on the ice. The weeks of preseason workouts on the football field are hot and grueling, but I'd do it three times a day if it meant stepping on the ice sooner.

Adam's in the locker room already dressed when I walk in.

"Hey," he says when he sees me. "Couldn't wait either?"

"I barely slept last night," I admit.

He chuckles and heads toward the door. "Guess it'll be easy to stop you from scoring today."

"You wish," I call after him.

As I walk to the ice, I feel a sense of peace and an unbridled excitement. One month without skating and I feel like I'm regaining a limb. I respect Coach's idea that a month of practice on the turf learning to work as a team makes us stronger before we step out onto the ice, but man, how I've missed it.

I breathe in the cool air as my skates glide over the fresh ice. I nod to Adam, who's skating with that same look of joy on his face. We skate in silence for a few minutes before he juts his chin for me to join him. We take turns passing and shooting. I'm sweaty and breathless but in the best way.

When the rest of the team arrives, Coach Meyers and Coach Kelley start us with speed drills and then some power play scenarios.

My heart races and adrenaline courses through me as I skate hard.

"Move your feet," Coach Meyers bellows from his spot in the opposing side fan section. "There you go. Nice."

"I'm gonna puke," Maverick says on a raspy breath as I fall back into line.

"How are you out of shape? We spent the last month running our asses off."

"Can't run this sweet ass off," he says straight-faced. "Beautiful genetics, but not great for speed."

I laugh. "You're blaming your ass for being slow? Really?"

He smirks and takes off as Coach blows the whistle for the next person to go.

Practice goes by entirely too fast. The girls' team practices in thirty minutes, so I can't even linger like I want to.

Not everyone is so sad to be done.

Jordan's face is red and splotchy and he mutters, "Oh thank god. I was burping ham and cheese. I swear it was coming up in the next five minutes."

I'm the last one off the ice. Adam notices and laughs at what I'm guessing is close to a pout on my face. I'm totally not beyond kicking and screaming and throwing a tantrum if I thought it'd work instead of Coach Meyers making me run laps around the football field.

"Come on, Payne, I'll buy you a beer."

At The Hideout, Adam pays for two pitchers and sets it down on the table before handing out glasses.

Mav's filled his glass and taken a long drink before the pitcher even makes its way to me. "Dude, maybe it's the beer gut and not your ass that's the problem."

He flips me off, continues drinking and then says, "Hey man, how much do you think Coach Meyer will pay you to babysit Liam and Jordan this year? Minimum wage?"

I grimace and he laughs, knowing he's hit a sore spot. Coach had me on a line with two freshmen forwards today, both need a lot of work.

"It's going to be a great season," Adam insists, always wearing his captain hat. "Frozen four this year. Last chance to secure my legacy as a frozen four champ before graduation."

I lift my glass.

Ginny is waiting at the apartment when we get back.

"What are you doing here?" Adam asks and takes a seat on the couch next to her.

"Maverick and I are studying Shakespeare."

Adam looks to Mav. "You know, you don't live here, man."

"I ordered pizzas," he says, standing in the doorway. "Gotta take Charli out. Back in five."

When he's gone, Ginny looks from Adam to me. "How was it

being back on the ice?"

"Amazing," we say in unison.

Ginny giggles.

"I'm going to shower," Adam says, standing and pulling off his shirt. "Save me some thin crust."

"Come keep me company while Mav is gone." I motion for Ginny to follow me back to my room and she does.

She walks in and scans the room before taking a seat on the bed, feet dangling off the side. I drop my bag and then pull out a pair of basketball shorts and T-shirt. I take off the shirt I'm wearing and toss it in the hamper without thinking about it. Ginny's eyes are fixed on my chest. I wait for her to catch herself, but she's full-on checking me out.

"Hey, friend?"

"Hmm?"

"Eyes are up here," I say with a wink.

She rolls her brown eyes, but then they land back on my bare upper body. "You're seriously cut. Maybe I should give up ice cream."

"Don't you dare. You're perfect."

Charli zips into my room, jumps onto the bed, and covers Ginny with slobbery kisses. She smiles and leans away but pets her behind the ears.

"Down, Charli."

Mav appears in the doorway and Charli goes to his side. "Ready, Ginny?"

"Yeah." She scoots off the bed. "See you out there?"

I nod and watch my friend and the object of my fascination walk out of my room. I might need a shower and some Mariah first.

Chapter Thirteen

GINNY

The following night Reagan's sitting at her vanity with the laptop open in front of her while I stand off to the side doing her makeup.

"I can't believe how much it looks like the girl on the video. I swear I've tried a few of these and it never looks anything like it's supposed to."

"Ava's been letting me practice on her." I glance at the girl on the screen and back to Reagan. "The winged eye looks really good on you."

Putting makeup on Reagan is fun. She's so naturally beautiful I probably couldn't make her look bad if I tried, but she's right, I managed to get it pretty close to the girl on camera.

"You're hired. Someday when I'm a big well-known actress, I'm going to force you to do my makeup every day. In fact, I wish you could do my makeup for the winter play."

Reagan is a theater major, and according to Dakota, she kicks ass in the school plays.

"Doesn't the department hire someone to do makeup for the

performances?"

"Yes. The previous stage director's mother, Ms. Morrison. She's lovely and nice and has been doing makeup for the university performances for something like twenty years, but last spring she had me looking like a clown. There's stage makeup, and then, there's straight-up too much blush."

I brush a little shimmer powder along her cheekbones. "Well, I'm happy to do it anytime. Seriously, doing your makeup every day is my dream job."

"Why aren't you going to school to be a makeup artist?" Dakota asks from the bed. She's lying on her side looking at her phone.

"Unless you work in a salon or store, it's a lot of freelance gigs like wedding days and special occasions. Plus, there's so much pressure to get it perfect so they feel beautiful and confident."

"Well, I feel both right now, so I think you'd be great at it." Reagan purses her lips and then smiles.

"Speaking of jobs, I need to find one if I'm going to be able to move out next year. Do you guys know of anything on campus or off? I was thinking about checking local restaurants and cafés." Rooming with Ava's been great. We get along well, and she doesn't have any crazy habits like leaving out old food or rummaging through my things without asking, but I don't want to do dorm life again next year.

"The Hall of Fame is always looking for guides," Dakota says.

"Guides?"

She sits up and abandons her phone. "Yeah, we do tours for local groups like schools and other organizations, but we also get to help with recruitment. I can ask my boss if you want."

"Just like that?"

"Well, I'm not going to lie, the fact that you're Adam Scott's little sister will probably help. My boss has a giant crush on him."

"What?" I ask at the same time Reagan mutters, "Who doesn't?"

Dakota and I look to her. "What? Come on, he's hot. No, not only hot, he's nice and..." She trails off. "I'm just saying, it isn't totally ridiculous that she has a crush on him."

Dakota shakes her head. "Well, whatever, but every time he's around, she gets all flustered and blushes."

Gross. "That's so weird, but whatever, the job sounds fun."

"Great. I'm working tomorrow, so I'll ask."

I get up and pull my phone out of my pocket so I can take pictures of my work. "Stand against the wall." I point to a blank section of white wall in her room and Reagan moves in front of it. "The guy you were crushing on earlier this year, it wasn't Adam, right?"

"What?" Reagan freezes. "No, of course not. I only meant I could understand it."

"Is it Heath?" Seems like a long shot since he's not dating anyone, but I need her to rule him out anyway. It would be too weird if she was into him.

"Definitely no."

"Why 'definitely no'? Heath is great."

"Rhett?" Dakota asks.

"Would you two stop trying to guess. I'm not telling you and it doesn't matter anyway. Every time I'm around him, I go stupid shy. I need a guy more on my level. Plus, I have a new crush and he is single and he asked for my number."

My phone pings as I take a few photos of Reagan's makeup. "That's Maverick. I'm going over to study with him again."

"Can you do this for my date?" Reagan makes a circle in front of her face.

"Absolutely, but you don't need my help to look gorgeous." I grab my stuff and wave as I head out.

Maverick is already at Adam's apartment when I get there. He's on the couch with Charli next to him. Rhett and Heath are playing video games.

"Did I miss Adam?" I sit in the chair next to Heath.

He bumps my shoulder. "Yeah, he left for Taryn's a few minutes ago."

"Does she ever come here?"

"Nah, not really."

I get up and haul my backpack to the table and pull out my laptop and a copy of Shakespeare's sonnets I borrowed from the library. Maverick follows and takes the chair across from me. Charli lies at his feet.

"Do you want me to take a look at your notes or should we jump into the study questions?"

He heaves a dramatic sigh. "My notes might be shit."

He hands over a notebook filled with three pages of his small penmanship.

"Did you write down everything the professor said?" I ask, baffled as I scan over them. The amount of detail he's captured is crazy.

"Uh, yeah. I wasn't sure what was important and what wasn't, so I wrote down damn near everything."

"I'm not sure either. Wow okay. The test is an essay?"

"Yeah. Payne, phone's going off in your room," Maverick calls to him.

Heath stands with the controller, backing out of the room. "Ah, ah, fuck. I'm cornered. Pause, one second." He rushes into his room and out of view, but I hear him answer the phone.

His voice lowers and softens, that tells me immediately he's talking to a girl. A surge of white-hot jealousy heats my face. He comes back out, phone to his ear, and tosses the controller on the couch.

"Sorry, man, gotta take this," he says to Rhett and then disappears back into his room, shutting the door behind him.

"So, what do you think?" Maverick asks, bringing me back to the present.

"These notes are great." We spend the next fifteen minutes picking out things we think he can use. Maverick is detailed and thorough in his studying. It surprises me he's failing actually. At least until I start asking him questions about it and his attention is about as focused as Charli's.

"What was the question again?" he asks.

I laugh and he gives me a sheepish grin. "I really fucking hate this class."

"Why are you taking it?"

"I thought it would be an easy A. I breezed through American Literature."

"Okay, well, how did you study for that class?"

"I don't know." He leans over and pets his dog and a smile pulls at his lips. "Heath and I read the books out loud to each other in funny accents."

"Heath helped you study? Did you have the class together?"

"Not together, but we were both taking it, different professors. Most of the reading was the same though."

"Were you roommates?"

"Yeah, we lived in the dorms together last year."

I'm suddenly less interested in studying than I am hearing about Heath helping Maverick study. What I would give for a peek into the past of those two reading Hemingway.

"Okay, well, we can try that." I grab the book off the table between us. "The first five sonnets?"

"I've already read them."

"But now that you know the form and themes, I think you'll be able to pick them out easier. Maybe they'll make more sense."

"Yeah, all right."

I clear my throat and open it to the first page and start reading.

As I'm finishing it and handing the book over to Maverick for a turn, Heath's door opens and he steps out.

"Payne! Sit your sexy ass down and read me some Shakespeare."

Heath takes a seat and to my surprise takes the book. "You're reading it out loud?"

"It helped last year. Worth a try, right?"

Heath crosses one ankle over the other. "What do we have here?"

"Sonnets," Maverick says.

A deep laugh rolls out of him as he brings the paperback up and starts reading. His voice is crisp, and the gravelly timber is easy to slip right under. His pitch varies and practically sings along the stanzas. I'm falling into it so deeply and I'm not even the one who needs to be paying attention.

Heath looks up as he's flipping the page and our eyes meet over the top of the book.

"Do it in your British accent," Maverick begs.

Heath looks like he might object, but then Maverick sticks his bottom lip out like he's pouting.

Heath looks to me again quickly before he starts again. I giggle at his accent, but my stomach flips. Shakespeare will never be the same.

As I'm packing up to leave, Maverick thanks me.

"I'm not sure how much I actually helped, but it was fun. Do you feel good about it?"

"Yeah, Shakespeare's the shit."

I laugh.

"Next week, then?"

"Sure. Also, I was thinking, if listening helps, you could try audiobooks."

"Maybe, but then I'd miss out on Heath reading to me." He winks at Heath and then whistles to get Charli's attention. "I'm out. See you tomorrow."

The man has a point. My body still tingles from Heath's voice reading such beautiful words.

Rhett went to his room earlier, so it's just me and Heath as I shoulder my backpack. "He's right — you have a really nice voice."

One side of his mouth pulls up into a boyish smile. "Thanks. I have no idea what I was reading."

"I won't tell Maverick."

"Do you have to run off or do you want to stay and hang out?"

"I can stay for a bit."

"Yeah?" He smiles wider like he'd been expecting me to say no, then takes my backpack off my shoulder and carries it to his room.

He puts my bag on the floor and then clears the clothes and books off his bed so we can sit. There's a box addressed to him at the end, still unopened. "What's that?"

"Oh, uh, my brother and his fiancée send me these care packages every month." He looks a little uncomfortable to admit it.

"My mom did that for Adam his first semester." Now that I think of it, she hasn't sent me one yet, although she has been distracted with all the fabulous trips they've been taking. The last time I talked to her, she and my dad had just returned from one trip and she was already planning another with her girlfriends. "Every month?"

"Yeah, pretty much without fail."

"What's inside?"

"Random shit, different every month." He pulls at the tape and dives in, looking more excited than he'd seemed a few seconds ago.

"Gift card." He sets it on the bed. "Granola bars, gum. Nathan must have put this one together."

"You guys are pretty close then?" I ask as I watch him pull out more stuff (all food-related, shocker) and lay it on the bed.

"Yeah, we're cool, but it makes me crazy how he's always trying to take care of me like I'm still a kid."

"I get that. Man, do I get that, but this is really nice." I motion to the gifts laid out on the bed.

"But I don't need him to send me stuff. I could buy all this on my own. Our dad passed when I was in middle school, so I think he feels like he needs to step into those shoes and make sure I'm okay."

"Or maybe he just wants to show you he cares with stuff he thinks you might need or want."

"Yeah, maybe." He laughs lightly and picks up a Ziploc bag filled with quarters. "What do you suppose he was trying to say with this?"

"I have no idea." I take the bag. It's heavy and must have at least ten dollars' worth of quarters in it. "Enjoy the vending machines?"

Chapter Fourteen

HEATH

A knock at the door breaks my concentration and I rub the back of my neck as I call, "Come in."

Adam steps into my room with a beer in each hand. He holds one out to me. "You know there's a party out there, yeah?"

I accept the drink and set it on the desk. "I'm just finishing up work."

He takes a seat on my bed. "You're still working for that sports website?"

"I am. Jon in Texas wants to know how many hours a day he needs to practice in order to make his high school team."

Adam pauses with the beer up to his lips. "Depends on how bad he is."

"Yeah, I'm gonna need a more polite way to say that."

He considers for a moment. "Tell him to focus on quality sessions, practicing until he masters small skills instead of focusing on time. Quality over quantity."

"Not bad."

"I won't even charge you for using it." He stands. "Hurry up, someone needs to beat Rauthruss at Halo and you're the only one that can. It's a matter of life or death, man. His ego is going to make his head explode."

I pop the top of the beer and take a long drink before answering Jon. Nathan got me a job working for Reeves Sports, an instructional sports website owned by pro-golfer Lincoln Reeves, the summer before I started college. Linc has become a good buddy, so even though things aren't so destitute anymore that I need to have a job, it's nice to have extra cash. And the job itself is fun. I answer questions from hockey players all over the world looking to up their game.

The party is loud, and Maverick is louder when I finally close my laptop and head out to the living room. I grab another beer and make a lap to see who came. It's mostly the usual suspects, the team, their girlfriends, puck bunnies, but the sight of Ginny on the deck playing flip cup makes me smile.

It's her turn, and she chugs her beer and then sets her cup on the edge of the table, flipping it over on the rim her first try. She squeals and the next person goes.

I step up behind her. "What happened to the girl who didn't like beer?"

"I guess she's getting used to it."

"I guess you are." Her hair is braided in pigtails and I tug one end.

"Excuse me." Dakota pokes her head between us. "I need my girl here for the next game. She's our secret weapon."

Ginny smiles as Dakota pulls her back toward the table.

"See you later, Genevieve."

I head inside where Rauthruss is still dominating anyone who

117

dares to take him on. He's got a puck bunny on either side, but I swear the guy doesn't even realize it. Or if he does, he's really good at acting disinterested.

Jordan groans as he takes his turn losing. "I give up."

I hold out my hand for the controller. "Don't take it so hard. Any kid with a name like Rhett Roger Rauthruss would be good at video games."

Rauthruss grunts a laugh. "He's not wrong. Kids are assholes. At least until I got big enough they were scared to mock me."

"That's awful," Jordan says. "Why would your parents name you that?"

Rauthruss stares blankly at him and doesn't answer.

"Move over, freshman, let me show you how it's done."

An hour or two must pass while I refuse to give up my seat, waving off anyone else who wants a turn. "This is personal," I tell them. "From one weird kid to another."

The girl sitting next to me drapes her hand on my thigh. I have no idea how long she's been there or how long she's been touching me. I guess now I understand why Rauthruss was oblivious to the two hanging next to him earlier.

"You were a nerd?" she asks. "I don't believe it."

"Not a nerd just weird." She looks at me unbelievingly, so I add, "Dead dad, non-functioning mom."

The words have barely left my mouth before I regret them. I don't talk about my family shit ever, but drunk Heath is a very sharing Heath. I don't usually drink so much, but I ran out of beer several games ago and instead of getting up to get another, I switched to sharing gulps of the Mad Dog bottle Maverick is passing around.

I glance around and notice the party is starting to die down. Inside it's me, Mav, Rauthruss, and the girls between us. Voices still carry from the deck outside.

"I'm gonna get some air." Standing, I'm much more aware of how drunk I am. My legs feel a little too light and kind of wobbly.

The group outside is almost as small as the one inside. Adam and the girl he's been seeing, Taryn, a few guys from the team, plus Reagan, Dakota, and Ginny.

Adam spots me first and his loud laughter barks into the night. "Gumby legs is back! Heath's druuuunk."

I lean against the railing beside Ginny. Her sweet smile hits me in the gut.

"Hi, Genevieve."

"Hi, Heath," she says, still smiling at me. "You look happy."

"I feel pretty happy."

"We should play sardines tonight," Dakota says. "Is Maverick still inside?"

I nod. "Yep."

"You guys in?" She looks around to everyone.

"What's sardines?" Taryn asks.

"I don't think that's a good idea," Adam says, arms wrapped around Taryn's waist, but his gaze is on Ginny.

"It's kind of like hide and seek," Dakota answers Taryn.

Ginny looks uncomfortable under her brother's scrutiny, but her words are enthusiastic. "Yeah, let's do it!"

The walk to campus in the dark with the fresh air sobers me up a little. Ginny's still smiling like something's funny as I walk beside her.

"What?"

"You're lifting your knees so high. It's adorable."

"You're adorable," I fire back.

She giggles, links her arm through mine, and leans in. Her boob presses into my forearm and all I can think about is reaching over and squeezing it like a stress ball. I completely understand that this is not acceptable behavior for friends—drunk or not, so I don't, but I think about it anyway.

At the edge of campus, Adam turns so he's walking backward. "Ginny, you good?"

"I'm fine." Her tone is playfully annoyed. "Seriously, Adam."

He waits a beat as if he expects her to change her mind. When she doesn't, he nods and says, "All right. We split into pairs. One couple hides and the rest of us try to find you. When you find them, you have to hide with them. The tighter the space, the better. No going inside buildings, no going on roofs." He looks at Maverick, who busts out laughing.

"Took you guys fucking forever to find us."

"So, wait," Taryn speaks up. "We're hiding on campus in the middle of the night? Campus is huge."

"There are some boundaries. You're with me. I'll show you." He winks and then looks to Ginny and me. "Heath, stay with Ginny. You can show her the boundaries."

"I'll be your guard, guardian, I mean guide, I think."

She smirks.

Adam points to Mav and Dakota. "It's your turn to hide and you get to make up a rule."

"We got this," Dakota says beside him. "Tonight's rule is that one partner has to carry the other by piggyback."

Everyone laughs.

Adam holds up his phone. "Five minutes and go."

While Dakota and Mav head off to hide, I lead Ginny over to the bottom of the economics building stairs and sit.

"You guys play this often, I take it?" she asks as she takes a seat next to me.

"It's fun. You'll see."

"I'm not really a fan of games where you have to hide in small, dark spaces."

It's then I notice she's staring down at her fingers and rubbing her thumb along the inside of the palm on her opposite hand.

I slide my hand in between hers and link our fingers. Shit, of course. Adam's words make sense now. "Do you want to go back? We can tell them we're going to go make out instead."

"Like they'd believe that." She huffs. "No, it'll be fine. Just don't leave me."

"I won't."

She pulls her hands away and glides them up and down her thighs. I don't really want to stop touching her, so I reach up and touch the end of her braid, rubbing the blonde ends between my fingers. "Adorable."

"You're a flirty drunk."

"I'm an honest drunk. Too honest. Don't ask me anything embarrassing."

"How'd you get so drunk?"

"Alcohol."

She giggles and then falls quiet. All around us, our friends are chatting and laughing, but we're in our own little bubble, which is nice. A Genevieve and Heath bubble that I kind of dig.

"Hmmm. What kind of dirt can I get on you while you're

drunk?" She narrows her gaze and smirks. "What's your favorite color?"

"Pink." I get the reaction I hoped for and then chuckle. "Kidding, it's green. What's yours?"

"Mine actually is pink, but not *pink* pink. Like a really dark pink. Cerise."

"That's cute."

"What is?"

"That you think I know what color cerise is."

She reaches over, catching me by surprise, and runs a thumb along my chin. "Did you get this scar from hockey?"

She's barely touching me, but I like it, so I lean in a bit and tilt my chin up so she can see it better. "No, I had a confrontation with a coffee table. It won."

Her hand falls away. "Ouch."

"Time," Adam calls, breaking the moment. He holds up his phone. "One-hour time limit."

"One hour?" Ginny squeaks.

"We're really good hiders," Rauthruss says before Reagan climbs on his back and he jogs off. Dude is super competitive.

Ginny and I move at a much slower pace. I manage to get her on my back, the feel of her pressing up against me is way too nice, but my legs aren't cooperating.

"Maybe I should carry you?"

"I got this," I say but then stumble a few feet.

"Which way, ya think?" she asks when we get to the first turning point.

Everyone else is going right, so I head left.

"I heard you got a job." I slow my pace. I'm not all that interested in searching for Maverick and Dakota, or generally being around anyone, but Ginny.

She smells like gummy bears which makes me think about kissing her again.

"I did. Dakota hooked me up with it actually. I start next week. I'll be leading tours of the Hall of Fame and athletic facilities, even doing recruitment tours once I get the hang of it."

"That's cool. I still remember mine."

"You do?" I pause when we come to another spot where we need to decide which way to go. "You decide."

She waves to the left, which really doesn't go anywhere and we're real close to being out of the borders of the game, but I keep that to myself. "Yeah, I had this guy named Clint. Wasn't nearly as cute as you."

Her light laughter tickles my ear. "You're incorrigible."

I'll be honest that I'm not really looking for Mav. I just want to keep talking, so I'm especially surprised when Ginny yells, "There they are!"

Dakota and Maverick are crouched down inside a fancy looking rectangular water fountain that's currently empty. It's a good spot and I don't see them myself until we're basically on top of them.

"How did you find us?" Dakota asks. "This spot is amazing. I've been waiting for weeks to use it."

"Maverick's shoes were reflecting in the light." Ginny points to his shoes.

Dakota throws her hands up.

Reluctantly, I set Ginny down.

"Now what?" Ginny asks, dropping off my back.

"We get in and wait for the others."

I hop down, not so gracefully, and then help Ginny down beside me. It's dark but not total blackout due to the lights around campus.

The space is really only big enough for us to sit side by side, but the more we spread out, the easier we are to see. Dakota and Maverick are sitting facing one another legs stretched out in front of them. I sit and pull Ginny down in front of me so her back is at my chest.

Maverick passes me the half-empty bottle of Mad Dog. Do I need another drink? Definitely not. However, we might be here for a while.

After taking a small drink, I tap Ginny on the shoulder with the bottle. Her fingers brush mine. They're cold and seem to tremble as she twists the cap off.

I wait until she passes it to Dakota before pulling her against me.

"Are you okay?" I whisper. Somehow the end of her braid gets stuck in my mouth in the process.

"Did you just eat my hair?" She runs her hand along her braid and flips it, so it lands in front of her.

"Unintentionally."

"Shh. I think I can hear someone coming," Dakota whispers.

Since I can't soothe her with words, I take her in a vise grip snug against me. Her shoulders are rigid, and I feel her take in a deep breath.

I hum the first song that comes to mind, 'Fantasy', and after a few minutes, she melts into me. She turns her head, so her lips are close to mine. "Thank you."

I'm frozen, staring at her mouth. The cupid's bow, the fullness of her bottom lip, how soft it feels under the trace of my thumb. I don't know when I touched it, but I keep doing it. Her eyes fall to my mouth and her tongue darts out, the warm tip wetting my thumb.

I lean in but hesitate to see how she reacts first. She nods her head a fraction, almost as if she's giving me permission to kiss her.

Adam's voice calls out, breaking the moment as the other four find us. "Twenty-five minutes. Mav, dude, your shoes are shining like a flashlight at anyone that walks by."

"Ow! Ow!" Mav yells and shields himself as Dakota pelts him and says, "Worst partner ever."

Chapter Fifteen

GINNY

T his is the coolest thing I've ever seen." I turn a circle. Flat screens cover every inch of the walls, floor to ceiling, all the way around.

Dakota grins and taps on the tablet in her hands. "Wait for it. It gets way cooler."

We stand in the middle of the room. It's cozy, not really meant for more than a few people comfortably. The recessed lighting above us dims and the screens all come alive at once.

Hype music pumps into the room and images and videos of the Valley U hockey team play like a highlight reel. My heart races as if I were sitting front row in a playoff game. My brother is shown a lot, which makes sense because he's been a big contributor to the team since his freshman year.

Sometimes the clips are of the players in action and sometimes it's media type posed images. One of the latter of Heath fills the screens. His face, jumbo-sized, stares back at me and my stomach does a somersault. He's so damn hot.

It goes on and on, a good five minutes of film, but when it ends,

I want to watch it all over again.

"Awesome, right?" Dakota asks as the screens go black and the overhead lighting returns.

"This is just for recruits?"

"Hockey, specifically. Each team has their own recruitment video and there's a generic one too that combines pieces from all the videos. We do tours for the community, local schools, and alumni too." She shows me the tablet where I can select and play the videos and then how to get in and out of the room because it's a very fancy coded system that seals you in and won't open while the video is playing.

I follow her out of the room, still a little awestruck.

"That's the last stop on the tour. Once you're finished in the hype room, you'll walk them to the front desk and the coach from whichever team they're here for will take over."

"I didn't realize how much effort they put into getting athletes to come to Valley."

"They recruit hard. Basketball and hockey especially. So, do you have any questions? Feel ready to lead one on your own?"

"No, I'm probably going to totally botch it. How long have you worked here?"

"Since my freshman year. I quit the track team, but I still wanted to be a part of something that was sports-related. They like to hire student-athletes since we're familiar with a lot of the facilities and can answer questions they might have."

She must read the panic on my face because she laughs and adds, "You'll be fine. It isn't that hard. You probably know more than you think from Adam."

"I'm not so sure about that."

Dakota smiles. "We're just here to get them excited about Valley. You're one of the few people they'll meet outside of the team. It's fun. You get to meet a lot of top athletes from all over the country, and if they come to Valley, you'll see them again and know you were part of getting them here. I'm doing two tours today, volleyball and hockey, so you'll shadow me and see how easy it is."

We take a break to grab lunch before our afternoon of leading recruits around campus.

I sit across from Dakota at an outdoor table outside of University Hall.

"So, you and Heath looked pretty cozy last night."

"He was drunk."

"Drunk Heath is hilariously honest. One time, he told me I was really pretty, but not his type because I was too bossy." She takes a sip from her straw and then adds, "Which is totally true. But you and him, I could see it."

"We're just friends."

"Except that time you kissed." She raises a brow pointedly and takes another bite of her sandwich.

"It was the gummy bears."

"Would it really be the worst thing to admit you like him?"

"Even if I did, Heath made it clear that he isn't interested in dating and that Adam's little sister was off-limits."

"Your brother shouldn't be giving anyone orders on being single. The man goes from one relationship to the next."

"He's always been like that. He got his first girlfriend in seventh grade and probably hasn't been without one for more than a week since."

"Taryn seems nice. I like her better than the last one, Heather."

"Heather wasn't the last one. He dated Maria over the summer." I shrug. "Taryn's okay. I try not to get attached anymore."

"Makes sense. Probably especially hard given Taryn's history with Heath."

My head pops up. "She dated Heath?"

"Dated might be a stretch. They were more like fuck buddies. Those two were going at it all the time loudly and everywhere."

My face heats and the food in my mouth turns to paste.

Dakota busts up laughing. "I'm totally kidding. I'm sorry; I couldn't resist." She points a fry at me. "I knew you liked him."

THE FIRST TOUR IS A LOCAL HIGH SCHOOL VOLLEYBALL PLAYER. She towers over me and I keep pushing up onto my tiptoes, so I don't feel so small. I barely say a word after introducing myself, and instead let Dakota take charge while I try to memorize every detail she says. I really don't want to screw this up when it's my turn to lead a tour on my own.

The hype room is just as cool the second time around and as we hand her off to the coach of the volleyball team, I'm feeling better about the job.

"The next one should be here in five." She reads from the tablet and then passes it to me. "Nick, a senior from Newburg High in Boston."

I look over Nick's information at the front desk while we wait. The scouting reports are detailed and makes me appreciate how much effort goes into recruiting athletes to Valley.

Maybe Adam and our parents downplayed it, but hockey was just sort of this thing he did. Adam never made a big deal out of touring colleges or getting a full-ride scholarship. Even when he had NHL teams inviting him to summer camps and agents asking about his plans after college, he waved it off like it was nothing. I'm not sure why he doesn't want to go pro, but he's wanted to be a doctor for as long as I can remember.

My thoughts briefly go to Bryan. He came to Valley and did a tour that probably looked a lot like this, too. He hadn't made a big deal out of it either. Maybe the jocks in my life are used to being fawned over like this. Freaking jocks.

I'm only checking Bryan's social media every other day now, a real step in the right direction from the hours I spent obsessing after we first broke up. Since I've started hanging out with Dakota and Reagan, I'm less jealous of his happy photos with new friends. He likes every single thing I post as if he truly believes we're cool and going to step right back into the way we were when we see each other again.

"There he is," Dakota says, breaking my thoughts. I look up to find Adam and Heath walking Nick through the front doors. Heath and my brother are wearing matching Valley Hockey T-shirts and jeans.

I smile and stand beside Dakota while we wait for them to approach the desk.

"Hey," Dakota says cheerily. "You must be Nick."

Dakota introduces me and then gives Nick a chance to use the restroom and grab a soda or water before we start. When he's gone, Adam leans against the desk. "Hey, Ginny. First day?"

"Yep."

"Anything we should know about him?" Dakota asks. It's good one of us is still thinking about the job because I'm ridiculously distracted by Heath. His hair looks like he tried to manage it into a style, but the long top curls and flips in every which direction.

Adam and Dakota talk and Heath smiles at me and takes a step to the side of the desk, motioning for me to follow.

"Look at you." His eyes scan my blue polo and khaki pants.

"Look at you," I toss back.

He runs a hand through his hair and his smile turns sheepish. "Missed you at lunch. Guess I'm going to have to find a new lunch buddy."

"It's only a couple of days a week."

He nods. "Tomorrow then?"

"Yeah, I'll be there tomorrow."

Nick rounds the corner and we all stop talking to give him our attention.

"Ready?" Dakota asks him with a big smile.

"Later, Genevieve." Heath winks and then he and Adam say their goodbyes to Nick.

I watch him leave and then blow out a long breath. Holy gummy bears.

OCTOBER

Chapter Sixteen

GINNY

We're decked out in Valley blue and yellow for the first home game of the season. Dakota, Reagan, and I sit in my parents' season ticket seats.

"I feel bad for not inviting Taryn," I admit as the team takes the ice.

Dakota waves me off. "She's fine. She said she was going to sit with her sorority sisters and meet up with us after."

"I think I'm going to have to get to know her."

"Why do you sound so defeated? She's nice," Reagan says, eyes forward watching the guys.

"Every time I get attached to one of Adam's girlfriends, they break up and it's like I lose them, too. I always wanted a sister."

Dakota and Reagan put their arms around my shoulders. "Well, now you have us and neither of us plans on banging your brother. Right, Reagan?"

Reagan's jaw drops. "Of course not. He's with Taryn."

When the game starts we cheer like crazy. It's nothing like being at a game with my parents and I feel so much more invested being a Valley student now.

And my brother is good. Really good. I spot Taryn jumping up and down in the front row of the student section as he scores a goal. Ugh. I really am going to have to make an effort with her. She seems to really like Adam and not be one of the crazy ones, but first I need to talk to my brother and make sure he isn't already thinking about breaking up with her.

There's a line switch and Heath and two other guys come off the ice. They sit not far from us. Jordan, a freshman I think, is drinking out of a water bottle. Heath shakes his head when someone tries to hand him his own water. Stick in hand, he's practically bouncing with untapped energy to get back out there.

He turns his head to follow the action on the ice, giving me a view of his strong profile. Dark hair peeks out around his helmet. His nose is straight, jaw sharp, nice lips that are soft despite all the ways the rest of him is hard.

I press two fingers against my lips remembering how it felt to be kissed by Heath. I've done my best to avoid going down this particular memory lane because I don't want to ruin the friendship we have, but I don't think I'll ever forget that kiss.

Valley wins and the girls and I head to The Hideout. The local restaurant and bar is a favorite among college students, and we have to push our way through a mass of people to find a table.

There's a collective cheer in the place when the guys arrive. Adam and Taryn lead the pack, Rhett, Maverick, and a few other guys from the team not far behind.

"Congratulations." I stand and hug my brother. "You were amazing."

"You've seen me play before."

"I know, but it was different this time. I can't explain it. I'm so proud of you."

One side of his mouth pulls up into a smile. "Thanks, Ginny."

We pull a couple of tables together so we can all sit. Pitchers of beer and shots arrive at the table, some the guys ordered and others that people buy for them.

My gaze falls to the front entrance every time someone new appears. I just assumed Heath would be coming, but now I'm not so sure and I'm disappointed. A friendly disappointment. We're friends — I'm allowed to be disappointed when a friend doesn't come out for the night.

I'm sitting at one end between my brother and Jordan. Adam's turned toward Taryn which kind of leaves me hidden behind his giant back from the rest of the table.

I'm leaning in and listening to a Celine Dion cover that Jordan promised would change my life when Heath's voice washes over me.

"Thanks for saving my seat, J."

Jordan looks from me to Heath and he nods slowly. "You two are...?"

"Friends," I say at the same time Heath says, "Yep."

"I'll send you the link," Jordan says as he stands to give Heath his seat.

"I wasn't sure you were coming."

"Came with the rest of the guys, but my brother called as we were walking in."

"You've been outside on the phone this whole time?"

He nods and reaches for one of the pitchers and a glass. "Yeah, what'd I miss? Other than Jordan hitting on you."

"He wasn't hitting on me."

Heath's brows rise and he takes a long drink from his glass then leans back and places his arm around the back of my chair.

"Five minutes talking with him and anyone would know he's totally hung up on his ex-girlfriend. He was playing me videos of her singing some Celine Dion song."

"That's why he picked that sappy-ass song."

"Picked it for what?"

"On game days, we do a light skate in the morning and we each get to pick one song that Mav compiles into a playlist for us."

"That's cool. What's your song?"

He smirks and instead of answering pulls out his phone. Like with Jordan, I have to lean in close to hear it. As the music plays I can see how it affects him, getting him pumped up. But unlike when I was this close to Jordan, I'm acutely aware of everything about Heath. The way he smells like soap and something masculine— sandalwood, I think. The fit of his shirt, tight around his chest and biceps but looser at his tapered waist. And the way my body reacts—heart racing and breathless.

Friends schmends. I want to kiss him again.

When the song ends, he pockets his phone and leans back, and I can think a little clearer without him so close. I push my chair back and stand. "I'm going to use the restroom."

I catch Dakota's gaze as I walk by the table and motion for her to come with me. She and Reagan tail me into the ladies' room.

"What's up? You were flashing panic eyes. Do you need a tampon?" Dakota asks as she checks herself in the mirror.

Reagan sets her giant purse on the counter and pulls out a tampon.

I wave her off. "No, I'm good."

Next, she pulls out lip gloss which I take.

"I like Heath," I admit after I swipe on the shiny pink gloss.

Dakota snorts. "Duh. What's the problem?"

"We're friends. He's one of my best friends here. He's already told me that he isn't interested in dating me. If I make a fool of myself, then I'll have to stop hanging out with you guys, and that would be a real bummer."

"First of all, we're not going anywhere. Second, don't be a pussy." Dakota meets my gaze in the mirror.

My mouth tingles and I rub my lips together. "What is this gloss?"

"Lip plumper," Reagan says, putting it back in her purse and pulling out mascara and adding a coat to her lashes.

"It stings. Holy crap." I grab a paper towel and wipe it off, but the burn only subsides a little. "That's awful. Do you have something else that will dull the pain?"

Reagan hands me another gloss, this one I inspect more closely before applying.

Dakota holds out her hand for the lip plumper. "I like the pain," she announces as she puts it on, turning so her back rests against the counter. "Listen, if you're sure that nothing is going to happen between you and Heath, then stop torturing yourself."

"She's right," Reagan says. "You guys spend a lot of time together which makes it hard to get over him."

"Or find someone else." Dakota's icy blue eyes bore into mine. "Come on. Let's go back out there. Sit with us and forget about Heath for tonight. There are a ton more guys at Valley, and we're going to introduce you to all of them."

"The ones out there anyway," Reagan says with a light laugh.

Not a terrible idea. I'm done being angry and sad about Bryan, and spending my time wondering what college would have been like if he were here. I'm ready to have fun, date, maybe even hook up with someone new. And if that's not Heath, then there are other people out there.

Heath is at the bar getting another pitcher when we make our way back to the table which makes my transition to sitting next to Reagan and Dakota less awkward. When he spots me down the table, he raises both hands in question, but I just smile at him like it's nothing.

Reagan and Dakota are true to their word and they casually introduce me to so many guys they start to blur together. I feel like I'm on a covert version of The Bachelorette.

"Okay, point taken. There are a lot of guys at Valley. You don't need to introduce me to any more." My gaze flits to Heath across the bar. He's talking to Maverick but looks up and smiles when he catches me staring.

"Hey, Ginny." Liam approaches with his hands in his pockets. "Are you going over to Adam's… I mean, your brother's after this?"

"Uhh." I look to Reagan and Dakota, who both nod eagerly. "I think so."

"Cool, I'll see you there."

I watch him walk off and then look to Reagan. "I think I'm going to need more lip gloss."

She digs into her purse and hands it to me. "Keep it. You may need to reapply many times."

Chapter Seventeen

HEATH

I get a ride back to the apartment with Maverick. I'm riding shotgun while Taryn and Adam sit in the backseat sucking face.

"Is that Liam's truck?" Adam asks as Mav parks and we get out.

"Yeah, I think so," I answer, looking over the silver F-150. There's like a million of these trucks and they all look the same, but this one has a Valley University Hockey license plate.

His brows draw together, and he has a weird look on his face as he passes it. Adam isn't one to care who comes over—it's one area he's actually chill about. He's got the whole, "everyone's welcome" mentality when it comes to the apartment.

"Something wrong with Liam being here?"

"He asked for permission to ask out my sister." He makes a little grunt of annoyance and Taryn smiles and pats his arm.

"Ginny?"

Now I'm the one getting the weird look from Adam. "I only have one sister, dude."

"Right."

I hang back, trailing the guys up to our apartment. I pull out my phone and text Ginny.

Me: Where'd you go? You coming by? Halo rematch?

I cringe a little at my borderline needy message, slide my phone back into my pocket, and force myself to chill the fuck out.

After grabbing a beer, I look for Ginny. I don't see her or Dakota and Reagan. The three of them are inseparable these days. I check my phone, but she hasn't texted back.

Liam is outside and I head toward him.

"What's up, Liam?" I tip my chin up in acknowledgment to the other guys on the team standing with him.

"Hey, Payne. Nice assist tonight."

"Thanks."

I spot Dakota walking out the back door to the deck first. Ginny and Reagan follow.

They go to the opposite side, stopping to talk to Taryn and Adam.

"Heard you asked Scott for permission to ask out Ginny?" I go for a teasing tone, but don't quite hit the mark.

Liam nods. "She seems like a cool chick. You two are friends, right? Any advice?"

Back the fuck off. Find someone else. Anyone else.

But that's not really fair. Ginny *is* a cool chick and Liam is a decent guy and hockey player.

I avoid his question altogether. "Scott gave his blessing?"

"He didn't seem all that happy about it, but he said Ginny could make up her own mind who she dated."

Jordan laughs and elbows Liam. "And threatened to beat your

ass if you hurt her."

"And that," Liam admits. "But I'd never screw over a teammate's sister."

God, I hate that he's such a nice guy.

"I think it's a terrible idea," Tiny says with a shake of his head. "It's messy. If things don't work out, then you're on the outs with the team captain. No chick is worth that much trouble."

I watch Liam's face to see if he agrees. Part of me hopes he does and backs off.

"Some girls are worth the risk," he says, and I grind down on my teeth.

Of-fucking-course Ginny is worth it, but Liam and Ginny? I can't see it.

"Well, good luck, man."

I go inside, do a shot, and grab another beer.

"Everything okay?" Mav says as he gets two beers from the fridge.

"Fine."

He lingers as he pops the top on the first can. "You sure? You look... off."

"Off?"

"Yeah, like at practice that time Coach tried to switch you to the left side. You do this weird thing with your face." He looks like a deer caught in headlights in some shit imitation of me.

"I don't look like that. Fuck off. I'm fine." I run a hand through my hair.

"Seriously, man, what's up?"

"It's nothing. Liam is interested in Ginny, and I can't see it."

"Because—"

"Adam asked me to look out for her, and I don't know, it doesn't feel right."

"Because you like her."

"I don't… it's not…"

He waits for me to string a complete sentence together, a smug expression on his face. "It isn't a big deal. Ginny's cool. Just tell Liam you're interested and ask her out yourself."

I tap my foot on the linoleum, consider it, and shake my head. "She probably isn't even interested in him like that."

Mav clears his throat and points with a finger wrapped around the beer can to Ginny and Liam standing in the doorway between the deck and dining area. They're both smiling. Liam leans a hand above her, and she doesn't look at all uncomfortable.

I take off in their direction without a plan and hear Mav mutter behind me, "Yeah, that's what I thought."

Four steps. Four, big, hurried steps is all it takes to get to her. I grab Ginny's hand, mumble an apology I don't really mean to Liam, and pull her through the party to my room.

She laughs, obviously not concerned that I'm dragging her to my bedroom like some sort of caveman. "What's going on?"

"We need to talk," I say once I close the door.

"About?" she asks, sounding concerned but still smiling.

"Do you like Liam?"

"Sure. He's nice."

"Nice like you'd let him feel you up or…"

She laughs. Loudly and I think at me. She walks forward and pokes me in the chest. "You're jealous."

"Am not." I don't know why I bother denying it. Gut reaction, I guess.

She laughs again and moves to sit on my bed, digging through her purse. "I'm sorry I didn't respond to your text earlier. I thought we needed a little space. We're friends, but we've kissed, and I know you've probably already forgotten, but I haven't and sometimes things with us feel messy. So, yes, I think Liam is nice like maybe someday I'll let him feel me up, but I'm not going anywhere. You and I will still be friends, no matter what. You don't need to worry about me dating Liam or anyone else and forgetting about my favorite cafeteria buddy."

I grunt at being called her fucking cafeteria buddy. She pulls out a long tube of pink gloss and coats her lips. I'm mesmerized by the action and the way her lips catch the light. She rubs her lips together and puckers them and all I can imagine is her walking out there and every guy in the place wanting to kiss her and smear that perfect, pink outline.

She stands. "I promise not to be one of those people who ignores her friends when she meets a guy, or, in our case, another guy."

"Don't date him."

"Why not?"

"He's not good enough."

"Good enough for what?" She rolls her eyes. "Thank you for wanting to look out for me, but I'm a big girl. I can take care of myself. I swear, if it were up to you and my brother, I'd spend the next four years alone while everyone else hooks up and pairs off. I want to do those things too, go on dates and make bad decisions, and I know it's possible that he'll hurt me or he'll be a total bore, but I won't know unless I go out with him."

"Don't date him."

She looks like she's going to start arguing again, but I keep going before she can get a word in. "Don't date him. We could…"

"We could what?"

"You know."

"Date?" She fights a grin. "You can't even say the word."

I close the space between us and drop my mouth to hers. Her lips part in a surprised squeak and I take full advantage, sweeping my tongue inside. She tastes so good and so right. I'm breathless when she takes a step back. Breathless and filled with so much energy, my steps feel light as I fill the gap again.

"Wait." She puts a hand at my chest. "I don't understand. You don't date. You told me that you weren't interested in dating anyone, especially me."

"I never said 'especially you'."

"It was implied."

"Fuck no, it wasn't. We already hang out more than I ever have with any other chick, so let's do that and make out. That's basically dating, right?"

She gives her head a little shake. "I'm confused. Is this some trick to keep me from dating Liam?"

"Hell no. I don't care who Liam dates as long as it isn't you."

My mouth tingles. Fucking tingles. This girl… fuuuck.

"I said we shouldn't date because you had just gotten out of a relationship and in the past, dating hadn't really been my thing. Enjoying college has been my top priority. I only have a few years before I'm going to be married to hockey. I didn't want us to hook up and then never talk again, and I wasn't sure I was capable of more. I like hanging with you and I don't want to mess that up."

"Oh."

"But I was overthinking it. If what you're looking for is the same thing I am—to have fun, hang out, hook up." I pull her against me so she can feel how hard I am. "Then of course I want to date you."

"Really?" Her eyes light up.

I swipe a hand over my mouth. It's on fire and sticky from her lipstick.

"Really, but I should talk to your brother first."

She groans. "You don't need his permission."

"I know." I give in and press my lips to hers again. It's almost painful with how much my mouth aches to be on hers. I kiss her harder and the burn intensifies. "Fuck, baby, your lips are on fire."

Her hand flies to her mouth. "Oh no."

"Oh yes. Don't move. I'm going to talk to your brother."

"Right now?"

"I promised him I'd look out for you. I don't want him to feel like I took advantage or... I don't know, maybe it's stupid, but I respect your brother and you, and I can't kiss you like I want to until I talk to him."

"Kiss me like you want to?" she asks with a laugh.

I walk to the door and pause with my hand on the doorknob. "Naked."

Adam's in the living room. I call his name and motion for him, going to the kitchen where I can pour a couple shots just in case one, or both of us, needs it.

"Dude, what's going on with your face?"

I rub absently at my face, which still stings. Since I can't very well tell him my body is having some sort of physical reaction to kissing his sister, I avoid his question altogether.

"I need to talk to you about Ginny."

I slide one of the shot glasses in front of him. He looks but doesn't touch it. "What about her? Is she okay?"

"Yeah, she's fine."

Reagan picks this inopportune time to join us. "Hey, have either of you seen Ginny?"

I glance at her. "She's—"

"Oh my god, Heath, what happened to your face." Dakota appears next to Reagan and steps forward and inspects my face. "I think your body is rejecting whichever random bunny you were making out with."

I swipe a hand over my mouth.

"Pink's not really your color." Adam laughs.

I grab a paper towel and wet it so I can wipe his sister's lipstick off my face. It can't be helping the situation. "I think I'm allergic to this shit. It stings."

Reagan starts giggling, and within a few seconds, it's full-blown hysterical laughter that has tears coming from her eyes.

"The lip plumper," she manages to get out and that sets Dakota off.

"What the hell is going on?" Adam asks.

"I was kissing—"

My body is yanked to the right by Ginny as she pulls me away. "Sorry, I need to borrow him for flip cup."

I hear Reagan say, "I must have given it to her again by accident." And then Adam's gruff voice asks, "What the fuck is lip plumper?"

Chapter Eighteen

GINNY

I don't stop until we're in the corner of the deck outside, far away from my brother. "We can't tell him."

Heath's rubbing at his lips. "Why not?"

"Because he'll freak out and make a big deal out of it. And any chance of low-key and fun will go right out the window with it."

"I don't know. He was pretty cool about Liam asking to date you."

"Liam asked to date me?" Ugh. I hate that they all feel like they need to ask permission. He's not the boss of me.

Heath puts his hands in his pockets and nods.

"Just trust me on this. He might have said he was cool with it, but he'll interfere somehow. We don't need his okay."

"I don't relish the idea of going behind his back. We may not see eye to eye on everything, but we're teammates."

"I know and it isn't forever, only until we decide if there's anything even worth telling him."

Heath raises a dark brow.

"You know what I mean."

"All right. If that's what you want."

I let out a sigh of relief. "Thank you."

"What the hell did you do to my lips?" He rubs at them again and I bite back a laugh and run a thumb over the tender skin. It's red and irritated, but his lips look nice and full, so I guess the stuff works.

I press my lips to his. A chaste kiss, but I linger, enjoying the feel of him being so close and his mouth against mine. Thirty seconds into this, and I'm already having a hard time keeping my hands off him around other people. He makes a little humming noise when I pull back.

"You expect me to keep this a secret?" He shakes his head. At least I'm not alone in wanting to jump him.

I take a step back as Maverick approaches.

"Hey, you two." He looks from Heath to me with a big smile and then sniffs the air. "Is that... romance I smell?"

Heath smirks at me. Busted.

"Well, so much for keeping it from everyone." I huff a laugh.

WE DO A SLIGHTLY BETTER JOB OF STAYING APART AFTER WE make Mav swear to secrecy. With a butt squeeze and a whispered promise to find me later, Heath goes with Maverick to play Xbox and I find Reagan.

She's sitting in a folding chair in a circle of people, but she's quiet, playing with the label on the beer bottle in her hand. I grab a chair and pull it up beside her.

"Hey, are you okay? You look a little bummed."

"Sam, the guy I went out with last week, was supposed to meet up with me tonight, but he flaked."

"Oh, babe, I'm sorry."

"It's fine. He was kind of boring, but it still hurts to be blown off." Her shoulders rise and fall with a big sigh. "And the worst part is I'm still not over…" She pauses and fidgets with her beer again.

"Are you ever going to tell me who it is?"

"No, probably not."

"Well, at least tell me what it is about him that has you so spun up?"

"He's smart and caring." She bites her lip. "And so hot. Have you ever been totally into a guy and no matter how hard you try to move on, you can't stop hoping he notices you?" She groans. "I just realized how pathetic I am. God, I hate being the girl who can't even enjoy the party because of a boy."

"No, I totally get it. Been there."

"I think you're there now." She smiles, dimples popping out. "At least with you and Heath, it's mutual. You kissed again, right? He had gloss all over his face."

"Listen, can we keep that between us for now? I don't want my brother all up in my business with this."

"I won't tell him, but good luck hiding it—you've got a ridiculous grin on your face just talking about him."

"I do?"

She nods.

"You know what? You helped me earlier by introducing me to guys, let's do the same for you now."

"I already know all of these guys."

"Humor me? Maybe you were too caught up in this other guy to notice how great some of these other boys are."

"You think?" She looks so hopeful.

I stand and hold my hand out. She takes it and gets out of her chair. "Okay, but you're sleeping over tonight. I need a safety net, so I don't do something crazy and end up having sad, forget-you sex."

"You never know," I say as we head inside. I make eye contact with Heath and my stomach flips.

LATER AFTER EVERYONE ELSE LEAVES AND IT'S JUST A HANDFUL of us left, Adam convinces us to play sardines.

Heath and I walk just ahead of the group toward campus. I'm holding his arm in a friendly way that we've done a hundred times before, but this time is completely about touching him any way I can.

"Which pair was the first to find Maverick and Dakota last time?" Adam asks when we arrive.

"Me and Heath," I speak up, briefly catching my brother's eye. I hold my breath to see if there's any indication from his expression that he knows. Maybe it really is written all over my face.

"All right, one of you gets to make the rule."

Heath looks to me. "You pick."

I think for a minute. "Partners have to swap shirts."

Heath eyes my white tank top and nods his approval.

"That's kind of easy, Ginny," Adam says, but then Rhett groans loudly and we all look to him and Reagan, who's wearing a dress.

Heath and I start our search for the perfect hiding spot, but only make it as far as the first corner away from the group before he backs me up against the building.

His lips take mine, and his body presses into me. I'm stuck in between a rock and a hard place quite literally. The brick building bites into my back and the rigid swell in Heath's jeans presses into my hipbone.

My body hums with excitement. I drop my hands to his waist and slip my fingers under the hem of his shirt. He keeps kissing me as I glide my palms over his abs and chest. His muscles tighten under my touch, and he grinds into me harder.

Who knew secret relationships were so hot?

Removing my hands from his body, which is exceedingly difficult, I take off my shirt, letting the breeze and his gaze pebble my skin.

"Fuck, Ginny," he rasps.

"We're supposed to swap shirts," I say, voice a little too breathy.

"Oh, right." Without taking his eyes off me, he pulls his shirt off and we trade. He tucks my shirt into the front pocket of his jeans and runs his fingers up the curve of my waist, stopping when his thumbs brush against the sides of my bra.

I don't make any move to put on his shirt because he's looking at me with so much admiration and hunger, I don't want it to end.

Wrapping my arms around his neck, I lift up on my toes to kiss him. The skin to skin contact feels better than anything I've ever experienced. Kissing down his jaw, which flexes under my lips, I move to his neck and chest.

He holds my hair back with one hand as I learn the contours of his body with my hands and mouth. I'm circling his nipple with my tongue, which he seems to like very much, when he curses and flattens me against the wall.

Footsteps approach and Adam and Taryn come into view holding hands. Adam's wearing Taryn's strapless top around his neck and she's in his oversized T-shirt.

Our only saving grace seems to be that we're so close they aren't looking for us yet. My chest rises and falls, and I fight to slow down my breathing as the others go off in search of us.

"Shit, that was close," Heath says when they're out of sight. He steps back and looks me over again, hunger flashing in his gaze and a smile on his lips. "We should hide." He takes his shirt from me and slowly pulls it down over me. His scent covers me, warmth still clinging to the material.

"Now? They're already looking for us."

He glances around and clicks his tongue. "I got it. Come with me."

"Is this in bounds?" I ask after he leads me back around the corner to the spot the seekers usually wait.

He shrugs and takes a seat on the top stair so we're as far out of sight as we can be while still pretty much being in plain view of anyone who walks by. He pulls me down into the space between his legs. "Technically it is, but no one has ever hidden here as far as I know."

"Probably because it isn't a very good hiding spot."

"I disagree. It'll take them at least ten minutes to double back, and in the meantime, I have you all alone." His mouth brushes against my neck. His shirt is baggy on me, giving him more access and his lips trail along my collarbone.

I start to turn around so I can touch him, but he stops me. "If you get any closer, they're going to find us naked."

Naked sounds great, but not in front of my brother, so I don't move.

There's something about holding still and just receiving his affection that is hotter than anything I could have imagined. Fingertips tease my waist and occasionally dip down to the top of my jeans, but he doesn't slide his hand lower to rub the ache between my legs like I desperately want.

This time, I'm the one who hears our friends approaching and I squeeze his calf hard enough it gets his attention. He hunkers down like he's hiding behind me, and we sit still until Rhett wearing Reagan's dress, a sight I'll never be able to unsee, spots us.

"What the hell, man?" he asks as he and Reagan take a seat on the stairs beside us. "You had to have switched hiding spots after we started. Is that legal?"

He's heated about it, talking loudly, and it isn't long before the others find us.

It turns out that it isn't legal, but I don't even feel a little bit bad about it when Heath and I get chastised for ruining the game. Totally worth it.

Taryn's chatting with Dakota on the walk back, so I take advantage of her not being attached to my brother's side and fall into step beside him.

"Sorry I ruined your game."

Hands in his pockets, his long stride is slow. "Eh, it's fine. Rauthruss takes games of any kind real serious. For me, it's just fun getting out and doing it."

"Taryn seems nice. Should I get to know this one?"

He shoots me an annoyed glare.

"What? Come on, your track record isn't stellar. It can't surprise you to know I'm hesitant to get attached to one of your girlfriends."

"Taryn's great." He shrugs. "Get to know her if you want or not, whatever."

"So it isn't serious?"

"I didn't say that."

"You're not saying anything." Good god, sometimes I want to shake him.

He huffs a quiet laugh. "Look, I like her. She's nice and a lot of fun, but I have no idea where it'll go. Dating in college isn't like it was in high school. People don't go into it thinking they've found their forever person or at least I don't."

I wonder if that's a universal thing or just my brother. Heath basically summed it up the same way. Seems a little depressing if I follow their logic too deep, but fun—fun I'm in for.

When the apartment building comes into view, I fall back beside Heath.

"I promised Reagan I'd stay over tonight to talk boys."

He smirks and his eyes darken. "You could come over later when you're done talking."

"I'd like to, really, but sneaking into your place with Adam there... I don't know."

He nods and I can't tell if he's disappointed or not. I'm glad he doesn't push any harder to get me to change my mind though. I'd probably cave, and some part of me knows I'm not ready to get naked with him yet.

I'm not a virgin, but my experience is pretty limited. And if what Adam says is true, that this isn't a big deal, I need to capture the butterflies in my stomach and give them a good pep talk about slowing their flutter every time Heath is near.

"Breakfast tomorrow?" I offer.

"Yeah. Text me and we can go over to campus together in the morning."

"Are you coming, Ginny?" Dakota asks when we reach the top of the stairs. She and Reagan are headed into their apartment, and the rest of the group has already gone into the boys' place.

"Yeah, I'll be there in just a minute."

As the doors close, Heath's mouth finds mine. He kisses me like he's begging me to reconsider going inside with him. His large hands frame my face, and he walks me backward until I'm trapped between him and the wall.

Heath likes to be in charge, and my body doesn't mind one bit. His lips find the sensitive flesh at the curve of my neck and I sigh. "How many hours until the dining hall opens?"

"Five or six." The words are spoken against my skin between nips.

"That's a long time to wait."

"Hungry, baby?" His deep baritone rumbles.

I don't answer, not even sure I'm capable of stringing words together as his face nuzzles in between my boobs. We didn't bother switching shirts back, so I'm still in his. Even through the cotton material, the scrape of his scruff provides a delectable friction. His hands fall to my ass, and he pulls me against him. He's hard again, or maybe still, and I rub myself on him desperate for more.

He growls and pushes his hips forward, slamming me back to the wall.

"Yo, Heath—woah, sorry, man." Maverick covers his eyes but doesn't leave as I duck my head, embarrassed.

"What the fuck?" Heath asks, not moving. Even in my embarrassment, I can't resist moving just slightly so I can recapture the delicious friction. At my movement, he moves his hand lower on my ass and his fingers dig into me through my jeans. Deep circles giving me just the right amount of pressure.

Maverick can't see what's going on, but I nearly cry out as the orgasm hits. I stop myself by biting down on Heath's bare shoulder.

I miss whatever exchanges between them and I'm coming down, body still shuddering, when the door closes. My head falls forward into his chest as I catch my breath.

Heath pulls me into a hug and kisses the top of my head.

"Did that really just happen?" I squeak, apparently out loud though not intentionally.

He chuckles, deep and throaty. "God, I hope so, but we can try again if you need to be certain."

I lift my face and wrap my arms around his neck. "I should go before Dakota comes looking for me."

He steps back and adjusts himself.

"Are you going to be okay?" I bite my lip. Maybe there's time. Hand jobs for him and her.

"Go. I'm fine. I'll see you in the morning. I'll still be hard then — don't worry. Seems to be a constant thing around you."

Chapter Nineteen

GINNY

y brother will be home any minute." I squirm as Heath's hands slide up my shirt and his hot mouth sucks on my collarbone.

"All the more reason to get naked quicker then."

The door opens and I sit up straight and elbow Heath inadvertently. He groans and leans back in his chair as Adam and Rhett walk into the house.

"Hey guys," I say cheerily and reach for a pencil on the table.

"Ginny?" Adam's brows pull together. "What are you doing here?"

"Studying with Maverick."

Adam quirks a brow.

"He's on his way over. He had to let Charli out."

"Oh, cool. You wanna stay for dinner?"

"Actually, I promised Reagan and Dakota we'd grab food when I was done."

"Invite them too. Mav can grill."

"You cook?" I ask the always shirtless Maverick as he walks in the front door with Charli.

"I grill."

"Is that different?"

"It's manly and awesome."

"Which is different than cooking?"

He grins. "Open flame."

Dakota and Reagan agree to come over to the guys' place for dinner and the seven of us sit around the outdoor table.

My brother might be oblivious to me and Heath, but my friends are not. Dakota corners me when I go inside to grab ketchup.

"What is going on with you and Heath? More kissing since last weekend?"

Reagan is right behind her, shutting the door and joining us.

"It's no big deal," I try, but I'm sure the smile on my face gives me away.

Reagan's dimples pop out and Dakota shakes her head. "You absolutely slept with him!"

"No, we haven't yet, but you cannot tell anyone that we're… whatever. Promise?"

Dakota looks to Reagan. "She's talking to you."

Reagan tries to look offended but then rolls her eyes. "I already knew. Besides, I'm good at keeping secrets of the heart. I won't say anything."

"Do you really think your brother would care?" Dakota asks. "I mean, he's one to talk."

"I'm not sure, but I don't want to cause a big thing. Heath and I are just… hanging out. If Adam finds out, he'll be all overbearing about it, and I don't want that. Judgment free fun."

"And hot, dirty sex?" Dakota smirks.

I feel my face warm.

"How are you planning on keeping it from him? They live together, G," Reagan reminds me.

"I don't know. I haven't thought that far ahead." I don't like the idea of outright lying to my brother and I hope it doesn't come to that.

Dakota snickers. "Well, you better figure it out because the two of you are beyond obvious. He's going to catch on."

There's no reason to worry tonight, though. As soon as dinner is over, Adam leaves to go to Taryn's and Rhett goes to his room to call his girlfriend. Maverick already knows so when Heath pins me against the counter in the kitchen, I let him kiss me like I've been dying to for the past two hours.

He hums into my mouth as his hands come up and wrap around the back of my neck. My fingers fly to the hem of his shirt, craving the feel of his skin against mine.

"I need to get you naked," he mumbles into my mouth.

"You two want to watch a movie?" Maverick asks.

Neither of us answers as we keep on kissing. Heath's hard and he presses into me with a groan. A pillow flies by our head and hits the cabinet door to my left.

"What the hell, Mav?"

"You two are a major bummer. Everyone's getting laid but me. Come hang out with me. Let me feel up your girl a little. Seems fair."

"Like hell," Heath growls, but he pulls me to the living room.

I can tell by Maverick's smile that he's just trying to get a rise out of Heath. Not that I doubt he'd like to feel me up because I think Mav is game to feel up just about anyone, but there are zero sexual vibes between us.

Heath's possessive side is hot though, so I follow him. He sits in the chair and pulls me on top of him. I hesitate to get comfortable, knowing Rhett could catch us at any moment. Heath doesn't seem to give it a second thought.

We watch the first half of some action movie. Heath teases me, fingers absently roaming over my skin. He doesn't seem all that affected, minus the huge erection poking me, until suddenly he stands and carries me to his room, calling out to Mav as we leave, "Sorry, buddy, you're on your own."

I giggle as he lays me down on the bed and stands tall to remove his shirt. "What if I wanted to watch the rest of the movie?"

He unbuttons my shorts and pulls them and my panties down before he answers. "Say the word and we can move this back out to the living room." His head dips and then his tongue flattens over my center, sending a jolt through my body. He glances up, eyes dark and taunting. "What do you say, baby? Wanna watch the movie while I lick you? Maybe you want Mav to watch as I eat your sweet pussy."

I arch into him wanting more. More of his mouth and more of the dirty, obscene things coming out of it. I don't know how much of it he's actually serious about, but the idea of him going down on me like this not giving one single fuck that people might watch is hot. Not that I actually want to give in to the fantasy.

He wraps his arms around my legs spreading me wider and lifting me to his mouth. His moans and grunts rival mine as the orgasm builds. I come once, crying out and trying to move away. It's so intense and my body can't decide if it wants more or to curl up in a ball and let the sensations slowly disappear. Heath doesn't give me an option. He keeps his grip tight on my legs, holding me in place.

He eases the pressure on my sensitive clit. His tongue laps slowly and tenderly until another orgasm begins to build and I start to writhe beneath him. He adds a finger, ever so slowly, matching the tempo of his mouth.

I reach for him, for any part of him to cling to like a lifeline as the second wave slams into me. I pull at his glorious hair and his ears, his shoulders. I'm not sure I've ever maimed a guy while he went down on me before.

I roll away from him as my body quivers and I try to catch my breath. Heath chuckles and lets me loose this time. He lies beside me and wraps his arm around my waist.

I shiver at the contact. "Even that feels like I might get off another time."

"Cuddle orgasms. I don't think that's a thing."

"There's nothing cuddly about you. Even your cuddles feel like foreplay."

"Oh, it's foreplay. It's all foreplay."

"I need like two minutes for my soul to float back inside of me and then it's your turn."

"Your soul floated away? Damn, girl, can I get that in a Yelp review?"

"Five orgasmic stars," I mumble as I wiggle back against him and his thick erection. I must doze off because when I wake up it's to Heath pulling on his T-shirt and answering the bedroom door. He talks so quietly I can't make out who he is talking to or what they're saying. He shuts the door and locks it and returns to bed.

"Who was that?"

"Rauthruss. They're playing Xbox, asked if I wanted to join."

"I haven't made good on my end of the bargain yet." I yawn again as I reach for him, which makes Heath chuckle.

He wraps me in his arms, and I tip my head up to look at him. "It's okay. I'm getting used to you leaving me with blue balls."

My jaw drops and he shakes his head. "I'm kidding, baby doll. Come on, I'll distract them while you make a getaway."

As I get to my feet, Mav's deep voice shouts from the living room. I can't make out his words, but it's his presence that makes me pause. "Oh, crap. I totally forgot about helping Maverick with his literature class."

"I'll help him."

"You're gonna read aloud to him in that sexy British accent?" Swoon. Maybe I can stay for that.

"Don't look at me like that Genevieve or I'll never let you out of here."

He goes first while I hide in his room, peeking out the crack of his mostly closed door. He calls for Rhett and then walks into the bathroom.

Rauthruss's tone sounds confused as he asks why he's going into the bathroom, but I don't stick around to figure out what Heath says to keep him in there while I hurry out of the apartment.

When Ava and I get to the dining hall the next morning, Heath is waiting outside, leaning against the wall, his phone in hand. He looks up as I approach and a smile spreads across his face.

"Took you two long enough. I'm starving."

I hadn't asked him to wait for me, so I find it particularly endearing that he did. Especially when I know how important food is to him.

"I'm going to grab something quick and sit outside to call Trent," Ava says before we split to grab breakfast.

"You don't need to do that. We can all sit together."

"Eh, it's fine. I get all tongue-tied around your brother and his hockey friends anyway and end up feeling like a bumbling idiot."

I fill a tray and find Heath at our usual table, already digging into his first plate of food.

He raises his brows and smiles around a big mouthful as I sit. His long legs find mine under the table and he spreads them to frame mine from either side.

We eat in silence. Heath somehow devours all his food before I do, and he leans back and eyes my tray as if he's hoping I might leave him some.

"Stop eye fucking my food, Payne."

"That strawberry jelly looks good."

"Should have gotten some then," I say and take a big bite of my jelly toast.

I'm teasing him, but now that he's watching my mouth while I chew, I'm a little turned on. Leave it to Heath to turn cafeteria breakfast into foreplay. In his words, it's all foreplay.

Chapter Twenty

HEATH

"Has anyone seen my hat?" Rauthruss walks around the living room moving cushions and checking under the couch.

"Bathroom," Mav and I say at the same time.

He narrows his gaze. "Why the hell is it in the bathroom?" He disappears and returns with the faded Bruins hat on his head.

"Hell if I know. You and Heath went in there and you came back with a frustrated scowl and without a hat. Did he violate you? You could tell me, you know?"

"I needed him to rub a little Icy Hot on my back," I say

"Mhmmm. And he took his hat off for that?" Mav grins big and looks to me. He knows damn well why I called Rauthruss in there yesterday. Getting Ginny in and out of our place without being seen is a great source of entertainment.

"I couldn't reach it!" I protest, playing along.

"The ol' reach-around." Mav hands me a controller as I take a seat next to him. "Where's Adam? I haven't seen him since practice this morning."

"Probably at Taryn's," I offer.

"He was having dinner with Ginny." Rhett sits in the chair messing with his phone, most likely texting his girl. Which is good because he misses the way my head pops up at the information.

"Dinner…" I look to Maverick. "I could eat."

"You could always eat." He sets down the controller. "I'm in. Any idea where they went?"

When we walk into The Hideout and crash the Scott's family dinner, Adam laughs. "Miss me, guys?"

"Nah, man, missed your sister," I say jokingly. Ginny turns red and Mav goes into a coughing fit. I slide in next to her and drape my arm over her shoulder.

Adam rolls his eyes, not taking me serious for a second, which is hilarious since I'm not kidding.

Rauthruss takes a seat next to Adam, and Maverick grabs a chair for the end.

"Smells good." I lean in close as she bites the end of a fry.

She elbows me. "Get your own."

We order food, but I continue to sneak fries off her plate while we wait. Ginny's so much nicer than I am. I'd never let anyone get away with taking food from me. *Heath doesn't share food.* I totally said that in my Joey from *Friends* voice. He had the right idea.

After dinner we linger. Maverick grabs a pitcher of beer and a few guys from the team show up. All the extra commotion means it's easier for me to flirt with Ginny without anyone noticing.

I place my hand on her leg under the table and she pins me with a playfully annoyed smirk. "Whatcha doing?"

She glances around.

"No one is paying us any attention," I tell her without looking. "Do you want to go into the bathroom and make out?" I waggle my eyebrows, and she laughs.

"No, thanks." She scrunches up her nose.

"I knew I should have gone with the dumpster out back."

"So much better." She leans in and my heart rate picks up. Sneaking around is hot. It isn't something I ever planned on doing. My sexcapades have never been secret but moving my hand up her thigh and brushing two fingers against her jean-clad pussy with no one being the wiser while Ginny tries hard not to react is awesome. I may never go public with a chick again.

"Seriously, though, I drove. Meet you at my car?" I motion with my head to the door.

She studies my face. "You're serious?"

"Hell yeah, I'm serious." I scoot out of the booth. "Are you coming?"

Her mouth opens and she looks around. This time I do too, but no one is staring at us. I mean, honestly, who'd picture us together? Ginny is sugar and spice and everything nice, while I'm the dude who propositioned her for a quickie in the public bathroom thirty seconds ago.

She nods. I put cash on the table to cover my food and a portion of the alcohol. I text Maverick that they are under no circumstance to come outside until I return, and I wait for her just outside the door. Maybe it'd be safer to wait inside the vehicle so that no one sees us walking together, but I'm not making her do the walk through the parking lot to my SUV for sex by herself. I'm a gentleman like that.

She pushes out of The Hideout and scans the parking lot, stopping when she finds my SUV and giving me a perfect opportunity to sneak up behind her and lift her at the waist.

"Oh my gosh," she squeals as I do an overhead press with her in my arms. When I bring her back down, she grabs hold of my neck. "What if you'd dropped me?"

"Such little faith." I unlock my car and open the back door.

"I can't believe I'm doing this."

She climbs in and I follow. I'm quick to shut the door and finally have her alone.

For whatever hesitation she had before, she attacks my face as soon as I turn my head. Her hands go to my hair and her mouth is on mine. I pull her onto my lap the best I can in this back seat, slouching down so our heads aren't bumping against the roof of the car.

God bless tinted windows. My fingers slip under her shirt and lift. I enjoy the way her skin pebbles at my touch. I push up the fabric so I can access her bra, pull the cups down and press my lips to one nipple. She arches into me and rubs herself against my crotch.

"Do you put something on your skin? Edible lotion?" I pop off just long enough to ask and then move to the next nipple.

"Edible lotion?" She giggles and then moans.

"You always taste so good." I lick and bite. Seriously, Ginny-flavored nipples are my favorite food and I am starving.

"It's just me." She pulls away, scrambling onto the seat beside me and unbuttoning my jeans. She smiles up timidly at me as she frees my dick.

I hiss as she licks the dot of precum. "Fuck, Ginny. Do that again."

She does, except this time, she takes me all the way in.

Dead. Gone. Rest in peace. Thought I was going to hell, but

this is heaven.

I hit the back of her throat, and she gags, but does she stop? Hell to the no.

I place my hands on her head, running my fingers through her hair. Gently, I guide the tempo, but I let her decide how much to take. I'm a big guy — no one has dared to deep throat me before, and she's the last person I expected to try.

I'm getting dangerously close with each swirl of her tongue and hollowing of her cheeks. I hold her hair back from her face like a ponytail. One blonde strand hangs in her eyes, the ends brushing my stomach as she bobs.

"I'm close," I warn her. "I think there are some napkins in the glove box." Unless her hearing is broken or she's in some sort of blow job focused trance, she hears me, but she doesn't stop until I've come in her pretty mouth.

I lean my head back against the leather. My whole body is trembling. "That was… holy shit."

She laughs. "And I thought the way to your heart was through your stomach."

"Only one thing I enjoy more than food, baby."

Fifteen minutes later, after returning the favor, we head back into The Hideout. She runs a hand over her hair and then her mouth.

"Relax, you look gorgeous."

"I should probably go in first." She takes out her phone. "I'll pretend like I was on my phone."

As she pushes through the door holding her phone up to her ear like she's on a call, mine buzzes in my pocket.

"Hey, I'm just walking into dinner," I say, taking a step away from the door.

"Hello, Mom. How are you?" she mocks and then chuckles, and that light sound makes me smile.

"Sorry. Hey, Mom. How are you?"

"Well, I'm good now that I finally hear your voice."

"Sorry," I say again. Not just for being a dick with how I answered, but for not calling her sooner.

"Can I assume no news is good news?"

"Yeah, everything's good. How are you? How's Kevin?"

"I'm good. Kevin's good too. He's actually why I'm calling."

My brows draw together. Oh shit, if she's calling to tell me she's getting remarried or some shit, it's going to be a real bummer to my night. I want her to be happy, but... "He is?"

"I was talking about coming down for your home games next weekend, and he offered to come with me."

I'm speechless, letting the information sink in. My mom hasn't been to a game since before Dad died. I stopped asking years ago. Now she's coming willingly and bringing the guy she's seeing?

"Heath? Are you there?"

"Yeah." I clear my throat. "Yeah, I'm here."

"Well, what do you think? I know I haven't—"

"Sounds great," I interrupt before she can finish that statement. "Can I text you later to hash out the details? I'm with some friends."

"Of course. Have fun and be safe."

"I will."

"Love you, honey."

I click end and blow out a breath as I head inside.

NOVEMBER

Chapter Twenty-One

GINNY

It's nice." My mom steps into my dorm and smiles. Dad hangs in the doorway and gives a tentative glance around.

"Dad, you can come in."

He moves only an inch farther inside. Since my parents were in Mexico when I left for college, this is the first time they're seeing my dorm outside of the pictures I've sent.

"Where's Ava?" my mom asks now inspecting her side. *The Vampire Diaries* poster and the collage of pictures that is basically a shrine to Trent.

"She's visiting her boyfriend."

Dad frowns. "You stay here by yourself on the weekends?"

"Not every weekend. Besides I'm not exactly alone." I motion behind him where people are moving up and down the hallway.

I set the bag of new towels Mom brought me on the floor by my desk. "Should we head over to the arena?"

Riding to the game with my parents feels a little strange like I'm back in high school and reminds me of the times Bryan and I rode down to Valley with them. It's a fleeting feeling of sadness at the thought of my ex, but as soon as Valley U takes the ice and I see Heath, Bryan is completely forgotten. I sit forward in my seat to get a better look.

He and Adam skate out next to one another. Adam scans until he finds us in the crowd. He smiles and lifts a hand to greet my parents. Heath notices and follows the movement to our family. I wave back as I stare at Heath.

He smiles, drops his gaze, and then does his own scan of the crowd. His mom and her boyfriend are in for the weekend too. And though he didn't tell me, I know it's the first time she's come to a game. I heard Adam and Rhett asking him about it earlier this week when I was hiding in his room.

Grand Canyon is the worst team in the division, and they didn't bring their A game tonight. Valley leads by two after the first period. On the plus side, Adam is playing great, so my parents don't care that the game is a snooze fest.

I head to the bathroom during intermission and run into Taryn as I'm going back to my seat.

"Hey." I pause and move out of the flow of traffic. "I wasn't sure if you were here tonight."

"Yeah, of course, I am. Wouldn't miss it." Her red hair is pulled back in a high ponytail with blue and yellow ribbons. Adam's number is painted on her face. I have a flash of jealousy at how proudly and openly she displays her loyalty and fandom for my brother.

"Are you going to meet up with us for dinner after?"

She twists her hands in front of her and nods. "Yeah, Adam asked me to come. I'm a little nervous about meeting your family."

"Don't be. They'll love you. Do you want to come meet them

now and get it over with?"

"I don't know."

"Come on. Let me introduce you, and by dinner, you'll be sharing embarrassing Adam stories with my mom."

A slow smile spreads across her face. "Yeah, okay."

As I predicted, my parents love Taryn. By the time the game ends and we get to The Hideout, they're completely enthralled with catching up on Adam and learning more about his girlfriend. I'm able to half-listen and stare across the restaurant to Heath and his table.

Maverick is with him, and they sit across from a woman with light brown hair and small features. I catch her smile as she turns her head to the man sitting beside her. He has a thick head of gray hair and a strong jawline and muscular arms that defy his age. They look happy. Heath looks... well not uncomfortable exactly, but like the outsider. To a bystander, you'd think Maverick was the one related. He looks far more relaxed and like he's enjoying himself. That's just Maverick though — he's always comfortable in his skin.

Rhett's girlfriend Carrie is here this weekend too. They're celebrating their five-year anniversary and the two of them sit up at the bar. She's nothing like I expected. Rhett is so nice and sweet, and Carrie is a little harsh and rough around the edges. When he introduced us, she didn't even fake a smile. Maybe she has resting bitch face?

I glance back at Heath. He's got RBF right now too.

"Right, Ginny?" Adam asks, breaking my surveillance of the Payne family.

"Sorry, what?"

My brother smiles like he's onto me and my cheeks warm. Shit, was that just totally obvious I was staring at Heath?

"I was telling Mom and Dad that you hang out at our apartment pretty often too. That it's nice and not the pigsty they are imagining."

"I wouldn't say often, no." I shake my head. "I've been over a couple of times."

"What? No way. You're over at Reagan and Dakota's all the time." He looks to my parents. "Our neighbors are cool, and we hang out a lot."

I'm slow to nod and my pulse is thrumming much too quickly as I realize he isn't talking about the times I've been over at his place and hidden in Heath's room.

"Right. Yes. We've become good friends. I'm actually considering moving in with them next year."

"Out of the dorms?" My mom frowns.

"Yeah. Just like Adam did his sophomore year."

"That's not exactly the same," my dad points out.

Adam smirks, knowing how it rankles me when our parents give him differential treatment for being a guy. Yes, I get that some things are safer for him because he's male, but I don't think this is one of those things. I could probably pull up statistics for crime in dorms versus apartments, but can't they just trust me?

I don't argue for now. It's a year away, and I don't want to spend this weekend annoyed with my parents.

Heath's table finishes with dinner first, and they get up and head toward the door. We're just out of their path to the exit, but Maverick moves to us with a big grin.

"Hello, Scott family."

"Mom, Dad, you remember Johnny Maverick?" Adam asks,

dropping an arm around the back of Taryn's chair. "And Heath Payne?"

My parents say their hellos. Heath doesn't introduce his mom, and there's an awkward beat before she steps forward. "Hello, I'm Lana Payne. Heath's mom."

"It's nice to meet you," my mother responds with a warm smile. She's always been good at making people feel at ease.

"Are you guys heading out already?" Adam asks.

"We can pull up more chairs," my dad offers.

Mav looks to Heath, who glances to his mom. "You guys probably want to get back to the hotel?"

I'm not sure if it's a question or statement and neither is she. Lana nods, though I detect maybe the slightest disappointment. "It has been a long day." She smiles stiffly. "If you two want to stay with your friends…"

"Nah, I'm tired too. Mav?"

Mav's brows pull together. "Sure, man, let's go back. I'm beat."

"Catch you guys later," Heath says, finally meeting my gaze and letting it slide around the table. "Good meeting you Mr. and Mrs. Scott."

They walk off from the table and out of The Hideout.

After they're gone, my attention and desire to be out wanes. Don't get me wrong, I'm enjoying seeing my parents, but I talk to them almost weekly, so there's not a lot to add. And… I might also be thinking of a certain boy. I don't know his family dynamics. I know his father died when he was young and I know his mother hasn't visited him at Valley, but I don't know the why or how and if the two are related.

Heath isn't very chatty about his family, and okay, we haven't done a lot of talking lately. When we decided to date, we caved to months of sexual tension and haven't come up for air yet.

Mom and Dad drop me off in front of the dorm and I head up to my room. I unlock the door, push it open, and flip on the light. Movement catches my eye and my heart goes to my throat. "Oh my gosh, you scared me."

Heath sits on my bed, his back against the wall, and his long legs hanging off the side.

I glance back to the door. "That was locked, right?"

"Your RA let me in."

My brows raise up toward my hairline. "She did?"

Rachel, my RA, isn't known for being all that lenient on rules, which hasn't ever really bothered me since I don't spend that much time here.

"I told her I was surprising you for our one-year anniversary." He looks a little embarrassed which makes me laugh.

"Have you ever had a one-year anniversary?"

"Nah." He chuckles. "It was the first thing that came to mind with Rauthruss and his girl's big anniversary this weekend."

I move to the bed and sit next to him. "Six-month anniversary?"

He shakes his head. "I've never even had a one-month anniversary." A small shrug of his shoulders and then he leans into me. "What about you?"

"Bryan and I were together for two years. We didn't really celebrate the milestones. For one, we could never agree on the date. He thought it was March third and I swore it was the seventh."

Heath's chest moves with a silent laugh and he takes my hand, running his thumb along the inside of my palm.

"How was dinner?" I ask.

"Weird."

I scoot back against the wall and lean my head against his shoulder. "How so?"

He lets out a breath and brings our joined hands to his thigh. It's a few moments of silence before he answers. "I knew meeting Kevin would be weird. He seems nice, but he's just like this stranger who is the center of my mom's world now, and I don't know her life like I used to. Even Maverick's random jokes and comedic commentary couldn't push past the awkwardness."

"I'm sorry."

He sits tall and I do the same so I can look at him.

"It's over. Besides, she seems good so that's worth something." He clears his throat. "So, back to this anniversary thing. Why do people get hung up on the number of years or the exact date?"

I want to ask him more about his mom but can sense his need to talk about something else. "I'm not sure. I think people like to have milestones to celebrate or maybe it makes them feel like their relationship is the gold standard if they can slap an award on it."

He grunts a response.

"But also, it's just sort of nice to look back on a year or twenty of your life and reflect on how it might have been different if you hadn't been together."

He studies me carefully, and I feel like I've gone too girly on him. It's a romanticized version, I admit.

"What would you do if you made it an entire year with the same girl?"

His eyes widen, playfully exaggerating as if he's horrified by the idea of a relationship that long—maybe he's not exaggerating, but he grins. "I'm not sure."

His mouth finally captures mine. Maybe it's because we aren't in danger of being caught or maybe he's just exhausted from the day, but our kisses are lazier. We take our time just kissing without rubbing up on one another, no hands roaming beyond the face and neck. It's unexpected but nice. Soft and sweet in the sexiest way.

When we finally lay down on my bed, he removes my clothes between kisses dropped on my lips and body. I tug at the hem of his shirt and he lifts it and tosses it to the floor. We've never been completely naked at the same time. My heart rate skitters when I finally get the full skin to skin contact I'd only imagined until now.

Whether it's because he hasn't wanted to or because he's read my hesitation, I'm not sure, but Heath and I haven't had sex. We've done practically everything but.

The largest part of me wants to, but something inside of me still screams for me to hold back. I hate to acknowledge that something because I think it has everything to do with the way I held out on having sex with Bryan for years and then as soon as I did, he broke up with me. I get that it wasn't the sex, and maybe I still would have slept with him even if I knew it was going to end. But the fact of the matter is, it scares me that the same thing might happen with Heath.

His dick twitches between us and heat pools at my center. There's a lump in my throat as I find my voice. "I don't think I'm ready. Is that okay? I mean, I want to do other stuff, just not that."

His hands frame my face, and his blue eyes stare deeply into mine. "Of course, it's okay."

He savors my body in a way I'll remember forever. Taking sex off the table only makes him more creative, and he gets a well-deserved A plus in that department.

We fall asleep still naked and I take note of a different type of anniversary—the first time you realize you're falling for someone.

Chapter Twenty-Two

HEATH

My mom wants to go to breakfast Saturday morning before I head to the arena. Mav is still sleeping when I get back from Ginny's, so I'm on my own when I push through the door of the café.

She waves from a booth, her other hand wrapped around a coffee mug.

"Hey," I say as I sit across from her. "Sorry I'm late."

"It's okay. You know I like to have my first cup of coffee in silence anyway."

I smile at the reminder that something is still the same.

The waiter stops by to pour me a cup of coffee and take our order. After which, I lean back in the booth. "Kevin isn't joining us?"

"No. Just the two of us." Her smile is warm and genuine as she studies me. "I've missed you."

There's an uneasy ache in my chest as the sincerity of her words hit me. Maybe our bond wasn't always the healthiest—me taking care of her more than the other way around, but in some ways, it's good to know I'm still missed, if not needed.

I spent the first year of college trying not to fuck up. If I'm honest, I didn't even want to come to college. I mean, I did. Of course, I did. College is fucking awesome. But I was so scared. My mom was barely hanging on by a thread after my dad died. I'd lost one parent and the panic was real that I'd leave and the other one would disappear without me watching over her like I'd done for the past four years.

I was the one who made her smile when no one else could. The person she relied on to remember things like paying the electricity bill and mowing the grass.

And I wasn't perfect. I found a release for my teenage angst with other things. Fast cars, easy chicks, occasionally getting high. But I did my best to never bring any more burdens inside the four walls that were already crashing in on us.

So imagine my surprise when I go away to college and nearly give myself a fucking ulcer with worry only to return home this past summer and see she's fine.

No, not just fine. Fine is the word she used when she was wearing last week's clothes lying on the couch and staring at the TV in a comatose state. She wasn't fine. She was good. She didn't need me to walk around the house singing Disney songs or brush her hair while we watched *Friends* on repeat.

I should be happy that she is doing well. I am happy. I'm just also bitter. Where was this woman when I needed her to hold me and tell me everything was going to be okay?

It isn't fair. I know that. There's no right way to mourn, and my dad's death rocked us all to the core.

You don't get to tell people how to feel. Fuck. You don't even get to tell yourself how to feel. It's a real bitch of the human condition to be in control of everything and also nothing.

"Is everything going okay? You look good."

"I am." She reaches across the table and squeezes my hand. I can't bring myself to return the gesture. Her fingers linger and each second that passes feels like an eternity. I don't know why I can't just accept and enjoy her company.

She gives me one last squeeze and then pulls back. "You looked good on the ice last night, too. I still can't believe how talented you and your brother both turned out. I can barely walk a straight line. You got your athleticism from your father. He would be so proud."

"Can we not?"

She flinches and I wince.

Dammit. Why can't I just sit here and let her talk about him? Partly it's because I'm afraid that conversation leads to me telling her how bitter I feel. And what good would that do? She's finally on her feet and I knock her down with memories of how she hurt me when she was drowning? No way.

"Can we talk about something else?" I try again.

She nods. "Sure."

We suffer through breakfast talking about stupid shit like the weather and repairs she's having done on the house back in Michigan. My mood sours with each bite, and I'm all too eager to head to the arena when it's time.

Adam walks in just after I do. "Hey, man. Where were you this morning?"

"I'm sorry. Did I need to check in before I left?"

His brows raise.

"Shit, I'm sorry. I'm in an awful mood. Had breakfast with my mom this morning."

He nods and takes a seat on the bench, setting his bag on the floor. "Are you two not close?"

"We are… we were. I don't know. When my dad passed away shit was fucked up for a while."

"Sorry, man. I can't imagine what it'd be like if something happened to my parents. Anything I can do to help?"

"Nah. I just need to get on the ice."

One side of his mouth pulls up into a smile. "All right."

AFTER THE BEST GAME OF MY LIFE (APPARENTLY BITTER frustration works well for me), I find my mom waiting for me outside of the locker room with some of the other families, including the Scotts. Ginny smiles and approaches me.

"That was incredible. Congratulations." She hugs me, taking me by surprise given all the onlookers, but it feels too nice to pull away.

"Thanks. Hopefully not the last time I get a hat trick." Then I lean down close to her ear. "Maybe we can celebrate with a hat trick of our own."

She blushes and pulls back. I accept a hug from my mom and a handshake from Kevin and from Mr. Scott.

"We should celebrate." Adam claps me on the shoulder. "What do you feel like doing?"

Your sister.

Mav steps up, his bag slung over his body. "Party at our place.

Invite the 'rents. Let's get weird."

"I think we'll pass. Let you guys celebrate on your own." Mr. Scott wraps an arm around his wife, who nods her agreement. "We have reservations for dinner." She looks to my mom and Kevin. "Would you like to join us?"

"I think that sounds great," Kevin says. "What do you say, Lana?"

More of the parents make plans and the guys start heading out.

Ginny's still standing by my side, and I have the strongest urge to grab her hand.

"I'm going to find Reagan and Dakota. See you later?"

"Ride over with me."

"But?" She glances around. "Are you sure?"

"Yeah, no one will notice or care. Just give me a couple minutes to say goodbye to my mom."

"Okay."

My mom walks over to us before I get the chance to go to her.

Ginny smiles at her and then me. "See ya."

Mom watches her leave, only speaking once we're alone. A sad expression on her face as she lowers her voice. "I should have come alone and not brought Kevin. I wanted you to meet him to see that I'm happy. I thought it would give you some peace, but I see now that was my own selfish reasoning and I'm sorry. This isn't how I wanted this weekend to go."

"It isn't Kevin. It's us. I don't know how to do this with you." I motion between us. "Everything is so different."

"I know. But I still love you just the same. I'm so proud of you."

Love. I hate that damn word. Why does it always feel like it's an excuse? When she says it, all I hear is, I love you, so it's okay that I screwed up.

"Thanks, Mom. I am glad you came."

Kevin steps up behind her. "Nice game, Heath."

"Thanks."

The hall has cleared, and we start toward the door. Mom hugs me tightly before we head our separate ways. "Be safe."

I hug her back. She's heavier now, no longer the small, fragile thing she once was. "I will. I'll call next week."

She nods and smiles, maybe a little disbelieving that I really will.

Ginny leans against my vehicle, her phone in hand. It's dark and she's all alone and I feel like an ass for making her wait for me out here like this.

I hit the unlock button and she looks up, those light brown eyes meeting mine under the fluorescent parking lot lights. Instead of going to the driver's side, I go to her, kissing her hard out in the open where anyone might see us.

She doesn't seem to care either, though, because she wraps her arms around my neck and presses her body to mine. And it's the best damn part of the day. Well... unless she lets me hat trick her later.

Chapter Twenty-Three

GINNY

The following weekend the guys are gone for two away games. I sit on the floor in Reagan and Dakota's apartment. Reagan brings two bags of chips and a platter of dips and sets it down between me and Dakota.

Dakota stands. "I'm going to grab the bottle of wine so I don't have to get up again. You're staying over, right?" she asks.

"Yeah, might as well. Ava's out of town visiting Trent," I say before digging into the queso.

She grabs the wine and we all settle in.

"Does Heath stay with you then on the weekends or are you two getting it on with your brother on the other side of the wall?" Dakota asks.

I make a face and toss a chip at her. "Gross, and Adam isn't on the other side of the wall, thankfully. Maverick is always hanging in the living room, though, and sometimes has girls with him. I have no idea why he doesn't go to his own place."

Reagan scrunches up her nose.

"Yeah. I've heard entirely too much of his sex talk for my

liking."

"Dirty talk? Maverick?" Dakota asks. "That surprises me for some reason."

"Not dirty exactly. And I think he might be talking to himself." I make a face. "He's a weird dude."

"Come on, give us something. Anything. We're dying for details. You've barely said anything about this new hot thing between you and Heath." Dakota pulls her red hair over one shoulder.

I look between my friend's eager faces. "There's not much to tell."

"I don't buy it," Reagan says. "You two looked like you were gonna rip each other's clothes off playing video games last night."

"Some clothes have been ripped off, but we haven't had sex yet."

"Interesting."

She says it like "interesting" means bad or weird. Is it? We're making out every chance we get. He's given me more orgasms fully clothed than I would have thought possible. Technically we haven't slept together yet, but it's been fun and hot. None of it seemed odd before, but now I'm nervous that maybe he thinks it's weird too.

"Is that bad? Should I be worried?"

"Sounds sweet," Reagan says.

Dakota takes a sip of her wine. "Sounds very unlike Heath."

"Dakota," Reagan says in a shrill voice.

"What?" She looks to me. "You know he's not some innocent guy, right? I mean, I wouldn't call Heath a slut because I'm not into label shaming, buuut… he's not been shy about hooking up with chicks. And by hooking up, I mean sex."

"No, I know."

Reagan places a hand on my knee and squeezes. "But he hasn't dated anyone else as far as I know."

"When did dating become more romantic than sex?" I ask and then, "If I tell you guys something, will you promise not to laugh?"

"Yes," Reagan says at the same time Dakota says, "No way."

"Kota," Reagan admonishes.

"What? If it's funny, I won't be able to hold back. I will try."

"Good enough, I guess." I take a drink of the wine. "My last boyfriend, Bryan, broke up with me after."

"After?"

"After we'd had sex. Like still inside of me."

"Oh shit." Dakota's eyes widen.

I hide behind my hands stretched out over my face. "Now I wished you'd just laughed."

"Wait, wait, wait. We need the full story," Reagan says.

So, I tell them. How Bryan and I had planned to go to Valley U together, but then he'd received an offer to play football in Boise and how he'd broken the news to me after we'd had sex for the first time.

"What an asshole."

"He really isn't though. It was my idea. I was ready, and I thought it would bring us closer before we headed off on this great adventure together. After, he told me he wasn't going to Valley and that he thought it would be better if we broke up instead of trying to make it work."

I've gone over that day a million times looking for cues I missed, but I was ready and excited, and I think he could have shown me a million red flags and I would have ignored them.

"Sorry, babe." Dakota rubs my arm. "For what it's worth, even

Heath's not that cold."

"No, I know. And I'd had sex before Bryan. Just one other time with a guy I met at summer camp. It was right before Bryan and I started dating. Neither were great. I made Bryan wait because I wanted it to mean more than the first time. And, I think I'm doing it again with Heath. Does that make me too idealistic?"

Reagan shakes her head. "No, of course not, but holding out doesn't mean that it will mean more… it just means you build it up to an impossible standard."

"I hadn't thought about it like that," I admit.

We go through two bottles of wine and watch a movie before calling it a night.

Reagan brings me a blanket and pillow from her room. "Thank you."

The TV is muted, but I lie down and watch *Golden Girls* reruns with subtitles. I'm just about asleep when my phone buzzes.

Hottest guy on campus: You awake?

Me: No

Hottest guy on campus: Me either.

Me: Don't you have a big game tomorrow or something?

Hottest guy on campus: Maverick snores.

Me: I don't snore, and I miss you.

Hottest guy on campus: Now I really wish you were in this hotel room with me instead.

Me: Oh yeah? Need a cuddle buddy?

Hottest guy on campus: Yeah, just don't tell Mav – he thinks I only cuddle with him.

Me: Your secret is safe with me.

Hottest guy on campus: What'd you do tonight?

Me: Hung out with Reagan and Dakota at their place. You'll be back tomorrow night?

Hottest guy on campus: Yeah, but it'll be pretty late.

Me: Can I come over and stay the night?

Hottest guy on campus: You never need to ask, baby.

I smile and close my eyes. My phone buzzes with another text.

Hottest guy on campus: Hat trick?

I type out a dozen different responses trying to decide if I should go along with his playful banter or take this opportunity to confide in him. He takes the decision out of my hands by sending another when I've been quiet too long.

Hottest guy on campus: Shit. I'm sorry. Did I freak you out?

Me: Honestly? A little maybe. I mean, I want to do all those things. A LOT. But I'm nervous too. My experiences are... limited and were just blah.

Hottest guy on campus: I find it very hard (pun intended) that any form of sex could be blah with you.

Me: That might have more to do with you than me. You're fun and hot.

Hottest guy on campus: Right back at ya, baby doll.

Chapter Twenty-Four

HEATH

I drop into the seat next to Rauthruss as my phone buzzes in my pocket.

"Payne, how are your ribs?" Coach Meyers stands in the aisle, hands on the seats in front of me. "That was a nasty hit."

"Fine. Nothing's broken." I laugh and then wince as my side screams. I adjust the ice pack strapped around my waist.

"Try to take it easy tonight. Check in with the trainer first thing tomorrow."

I nod and he walks off. I wait to make sure he's not watching before leaning back with a groan. I dig my phone out, breathless by the maneuvering that's required.

I read Ginny's text asking me to give her a heads up so she can sneak into my room before we get home. She added three hat emojis and fuck my life... I don't think I can even make good on that tonight.

I text her back the tongue, peach, and eggplant emojis because I'm not an idiot and I think it might be worth dying for.

Another win under our belt and it feels good, even if my body aches. I took a hard hit in the last minute of the game, and my ribs hurt like a bitch.

"You all right?" Rauthruss asks from the seat next to me.

I grunt a response as I close my eyes. Somehow that seems to make the pain lessen.

"I'm gonna video chat my girl. Cool?"

I wave my hand to let him know I don't mind.

Rauthruss is the kind of guy who doesn't care who hears his conversations with Carrie, so he doesn't even bother putting in headphones.

"Hi, baby." She answers. "Congrats on the win."

I've only met Carrie a couple times. Seems okay. I don't get why Rauthruss is so hung up on her, but he didn't ask my opinion, so I don't give it.

"Thanks. How's your editorial coming?"

She sighs and goes into a long explanation. Rauthruss listens intently with his *mhmm* and *oh yeah* at all the right times. He's good at listening. Has to be, apparently. She barely takes a breath between sentences.

I doze off and when I wake up again, we're pulling off the freeway to Valley and the dude is still on the phone and she's still doing most of the talking.

I sit up with a wince and check my phone, but only have a couple of texts from my mom and Nathan congratulating me on the game and checking in on my wellbeing. I tap out responses to both of them in the time it takes Carrie to get out a single run-on sentence.

How do two people have so much to talk about? It isn't like they haven't talked in weeks or something. She was at Valley visiting just last weekend.

As the bus pulls into the campus lot, they say their goodbyes with promises to talk later tonight before bed. When he hangs up, I ask, "Seriously? You're going to talk to her again later?"

His hard, steel-blue eyes study me and then he chuckles. "You don't get it, but someday you will."

When I don't respond, he clarifies. "Some girl is going to make you so crazy that you'll want to talk to her all day, every day."

"What in the world do you have to talk about after being together so long? Not even Scott talks on the phone as much as you." I look across the aisle to where Scott is staring out the window.

"It's different for him. He's going to get off the bus and go see Taryn. I gotta take what I can get for now."

"Sounds pretty awful," I say truthfully. What's the point of being in a relationship if you have to do it through an electronic device?

We file off the bus, me much slower than the rest of the guys. Mav's got an energy drink in hand as he steps up beside me. "Hey, buddy, how ya feeling?"

"Like I got hit really fucking hard in the ribs."

He grins. "Need me to drive?"

I toss him the keys and manage to get myself into the passenger seat with a lot of wincing.

"Text Ginny," I tell the Bluetooth once Mav is headed to the house.

When prompted for the message, I say, "Back. On our way" and send.

Her response pings over the speakers and the feminine British voice asks if I'd like her to read it aloud. I glance at Mav. "Earmuffs." And then, "Yes."

"Already here," the British voice reads the text, but I hear it in Ginny's bubbly voice.

I blow out a breath. Tired, but excited to see her.

"Ginny's at your place waiting?" Mav asks. "How'd she get in?"

"Her brother gave her a spare key." I grin. Wasn't that nice of him? And super convenient for me.

"I hate to be the one to rain on anyone's parade, bro, but don't you think you oughta tell him?"

"What? No. Why would I do that?"

"Look, at first, I understood you guys wanting to keep it from him while you figured out what it was, but it's been weeks and you're spending a shit ton of time together. He's going to figure it out."

"Ginny doesn't want to. Besides, he won't understand. You know what he's like in relationships. All in. Balls to the wall." I squeeze the phone in my hand. "He won't understand," I repeat.

"Maybe not. I still think it should come from you."

"Hey, Scott, guess what? I'm hooking up with your sister, but don't worry, it isn't that serious." I glance at Maverick with an annoyed glare. "That what you had in mind?"

He laughs. "Maybe work on the delivery."

A bead of sweat has formed on my forehead by the time I make it into the apartment, and that's with Mav carrying my bag.

"Just set it there." I point to the spot in the living room where our bags usually end up. "I'll get it tomorrow. Thanks, buddy."

He grins, knowing exactly why I don't want him to bring it to my room. Adam went straight to Taryn's, and Rauthruss heads to his room while I limp to mine. The light's off, and I wonder how she's handling the dark. I push open the door and find her sitting on my bed with her laptop; the screen is dimmed but providing a decent amount of soft light.

I flip on the overhead light and she closes the laptop and sits up. As I walk, her eyes narrow in concern. "What's wrong with you?"

"Bruised ribs."

She gets on her knees and lifts her hands to touch me.

"Easy."

"Why didn't you tell me you were injured?"

"I'm fine."

"Lay down." Bossy. I can dig.

Gingerly, I sit and then fold over. "I'm pretty sure I'm stuck this way."

I kick off my shoes, and she lies beside me.

"Shit, I forgot the ice pack."

"Where is it?" she asks, angling like she's about to grab it for me.

"I left it in my car."

"I can get it."

"Nah, I got it. There's another in the freezer." I inch up, but not before Ginny is to her feet and padding to the door.

"Be right back." She opens it and peers out into the hallway.

"It should be all clear," I tell her, knowing Rauthruss is almost certainly still on the phone.

She nods and smiles back at me. "Okay. Be right back."

I manage to get out of my jeans although I think the shirt's going to have to stay because raising my arms hurts too damn much. I'm adjusting the pillow behind my head when she returns.

She hovers over me, lifts my shirt up to reveal my stomach, and gasps at the angry red and purple skin.

"Don't think I'm gonna be able to follow through on the hat trick tonight." I try to laugh, but my ribs dislike that a lot.

"It's fine. I've got my laptop for porn. Can I borrow your hand though?" She holds a serious gaze long enough that my dick starts to get ideas. "Oh my god, I'm kidding."

"Not a terrible idea though," I say and then have to clear my throat a few times. Not a terrible idea at all.

However, when she settles the ice on my skin, those ideas disappear pretty quickly.

"Want to watch a movie?" she asks as she gets up and takes her pants off.

Dammit, now I'm getting hard again. My body is so confused. She settles next to me and opens her laptop between us.

"Which one?" She scrolls between two. I'm starting to feel the exhaustion for the day, so I let her pick.

Once the movie is going, she places her head on my chest. Her hair smells like apples and tickles my face. This is nice, I'll admit. Maybe I can kind of see Rauthruss's point about wanting to talk to Carrie all the time. Though I can't really picture having an entire relationship through a phone. For Ginny though? My mind starts to conjure all types of ideas for phone sex.

Hanging out with Ginny is always nice. I'm not even disappointed we didn't have sex. Okay, I'm not *too* disappointed. When I finally get inside of her, I want full range of motion. Especially knowing her past experiences were blah. Seriously, what the fuck? How is that even possible?

There's so much passion in Ginny. Kissing her is a trip. Just lying next to her, there's an energy that flows through my veins that doesn't exist when she's not with me. Sex with Ginny blah? If I weren't so tired, the thought would be laughable.

Chapter Twenty-Five

GINNY

Thursday night, Heath and I ride over to The White House with Maverick and Dakota. We're in the backseat and Heath's big palm is stretched out over my knee. He's texting with his other hand.

"Sorry, he's getting married next summer, and for some reason, I need to decide what kind of tux I want right this second." His fingers keep flying over the screen as he and his brother text back and forth.

"A tux. Hmmm." The image of Heath in a nice suit or tux does not suck.

He glances up and winks. "Tuxes do it for you, huh?"

"*You* do it for me."

Mav groans. "You two are a real buzzkill. Should have stayed home and boned, left the party to the single people."

"Don't be a dick to my girl," Heath tells him, still staring at his phone.

Maverick turns in his seat. "You are ruining it for the rest of us. Girls see you two together, and you give them hope and ideas about what the rest of us want. And all I want is a good blow job."

"I hope that's not your best pickup line," I tell him.

Heath and Dakota laugh. Maverick shakes his head but smiles.

"You're such a liar," Heath says, finally putting his phone in his pocket. "Some girl gets her mouth anywhere near your junk and you'll be proposing marriage."

"Probably true." Mav sighs. "I'm a romantic at heart."

From the front of The White House it looks like a nice, respectable family home, but one foot inside the door, and it's college madness. Though, thankfully, not quite so mad as the pool party. I can actually see two feet in front of me tonight.

As we walk through the entryway, I look around to take it all in. The last time I was here it was so packed, it was hard to appreciate.

"I know, right?" Heath takes my hand. The other two have already gone ahead of us. "My brother lived here."

Since my interactions with Heath have mostly been limited to the hockey team and the dining hall, I didn't realize just how many people he knows. Guys on the basketball team call out to him, "Baby Payne!"

They ask him questions about Nathan and a few girls ask about Chloe, his brother's fiancée. With each group of people we talk to, Heath introduces me, we chat, and we accept drink after drink. Heath more so than me.

The end result is a very Gumby-like drunk Heath by the time we've made it outside where the main party is happening.

He wraps an arm around my shoulders and leans into me. "I think I might be drunk."

I stutter step my way to where our friends are sitting. Dakota's found Reagan and they've pulled lounge chairs together. They're sharing one and facing Maverick.

When they spot us, more specifically me desperately trying to unload a very heavy Heath, Mav moves to sit with Reagan and Dakota, and I manage to get Heath and I seated.

"The Oversharer is here!" Maverick lifts his cup with a smile. "How ya feeling, buddy? Feeling good? Feeling like you want to tell all your deepest secrets?"

Heath makes a motion like he's zipping his lips and tossing the key, nearly loses his balance and falls off the back of the chair.

"How do you get so drunk when you're this heavy?" I groan as I pull him upright.

"I wanna take you to The Olive Garden." He sways a little, staring at me. "You deserve The Olive Garden."

Our friends are laughing, but even drunk and out of his mind, I can't take my eyes off Heath.

"I'm pretty sure they're closed right now, but food isn't a terrible idea." I look to Reagan. "What do you have in that purse of yours to soak up the alcohol?"

As she pulls out snacks, everyone suddenly gets very interested in eating. I manage to snag a granola bar and a mini bag of pretzels for Heath.

"I think you might be my dream woman," Maverick says to Reagan as he opens a peanut butter cookie and takes a bite. He finishes that off and then downs two granola bars. "Let's go eat. We can hit IHOP or get Jack in the Box and head back to the apartment. Ooooh Jack in the Box tacos." He closes his eyes and moans.

"Can't," Heath interrupts. "I'm showing my girl a good time." He throws his arm around me again.

"You can show her a good time back at the apartment. Naked." Maverick stands and everyone else follows his lead.

"It isn't about sex," he says and looks at me dreamily. My stomach does a thousand backflips.

We aren't having sex, so even though our friends are reacting with a series of "aww" and laughter, he's only stating facts. It isn't about sex, but I think that needs to change soon.

I get to my feet and pull him up. "Come on."

"Are we going to The Olive Garden?"

THE NEXT MORNING, HEATH WAKES AS I'M GETTING DRESSED TO sneak out of his room.

"Where do you think you're going?" He pulls me down and hugs me against his chest.

"I have to go to class."

"In three hours." His eyes are barely open, but apparently he knows the time.

"I want to get out of here before the guys wake up."

The apartment is still silent, but it's game day, and I know the guys will be getting up soon to go skate.

"It'll be fine. Go to sleep," he murmurs against the top of my head.

I turn so we're facing one another and trace tiny circles on his chest. "You have to get up in thirty minutes."

I decide to try another approach. Sliding a leg over him, I scoot on top of him. He makes a strangled sound between a groan and a sigh. I pepper him with kisses—his jaw, his neck, his chest. His hands move to my back, and one comes up and fists my hair. He pulls back just hard enough to lift my chin.

"Whatcha doing, Ginny?"

Instead of answering, I close the space between our mouths and kiss him hard. I can feel him smiling, that is until I roll my hips against the bulge in his sweatpants.

In one smooth motion, he has me on my back and he holds himself over me. He dips his lower body to brush against me.

"This what you want, Genevieve?"

My cheeks flame. It is, but suddenly, I feel really shy about it.

He tips my chin up with a finger. "No need to be embarrassed. You can feel how much I want you, but what do you want, Genevieve?"

I'm having a hard time finding my voice.

"There's no rush." His sweet words comfort me, but man, do I wish I were ready. It isn't that I don't want to have sex with Heath. I do. Very much. But it's a big deal to me, more so maybe because I know in the past it hasn't been to him. And because of my previous experiences.

I nod and his thumb glides across my lower lip before he kisses me again. My head may have reservations, but my body does not. Fifteen minutes later, we're basically dry humping when Heath's palm slides up my leg. His fingers brush against the lacy material between my thighs and a shiver wracks my entire body.

His thumb rubs the tiny bundle of nerves over my panties while one finger slips underneath. I cry out and then slap a hand over my mouth.

Heath pries my hand away. "I want to hear how good I make

you feel."

He pumps in and out of me a few more times before he decides my underwear are hindering him too much and he yanks them down to my ankles. I think he's moving to free them and toss them to the ground, which he does, but then his large shoulders nudge my legs farther apart and he wraps an arm around me to open me wide.

I arch into his mouth, wanting more as his tongue flattens against my throbbing core.

He gives it to me, sucking and licking. Slow at first, but as I get louder and the orgasm draws closer, he pushes my legs wider and increases the pressure. As I start to go over the edge, I fist his hair in my hands and ride his face.

When one ends, another builds. He rumbles something that vibrates against my pussy and clamps down, sucking on my clit as the second wave hits.

My body melts into the mattress. Heath's head is still between my legs and he places chaste kisses along the inside of my thighs and along my hips. I reach for him, pushing my hand under his sweats.

He's not wearing any underwear which means I have easy access to wrap my fingers around his hard shaft. He hisses a breath and moves his hips. A slow pace that quickly turns into him fucking my hand, hips pumping fast. He growls out as his release fills the inside of his pants.

We lay shoulder to shoulder as we catch our breath.

"Shower with me?" he asks, brushing my hair away from my neck and kissing me there.

We pad down the hall to the bathroom quietly. He starts the

shower while I stare at my wild hair in the vanity mirror.

He turns back and drops his pants. I'll never get over seeing him naked. My throat closes and I just stare. He steps forward and kisses me then pulls the T-shirt I'm wearing over my head.

"You're beautiful."

I reach out and touch his once-again-hard dick. "You're huge." I swallow.

He chuckles. "Come on."

He lets me get in the shower first and then follows and pulls the curtain.

I wash and condition my hair and then Heath covers the both of us in his body wash. It's somehow fun and silly showering with him. He looks adorable with his hair matted down. His very hard penis keeps poking me, but he doesn't make any move to do anything about it.

We dry off and get back to his room before I hear other people in the house starting to move around.

I sit on the bed and finger comb my wet hair while I watch Heath pull on a gray Coyotes hockey T-shirt. "What was it like when you got drafted?"

"It was cool."

"Cool? That's the best you've got?"

He flashes a sexy smirk. "Really cool?"

"I'm serious."

"It was incredible and surreal. Easily one of the best days ever."

"I'm jealous that you have it all figured out. I can't even decide what classes I want to take next semester."

"I think you're missing the best part of college."

"And that is?"

"Having fun and not thinking too hard about the future."

I snort. "Says the guy who knows his future."

"Maybe, but there're no guarantees that when the time comes, I'll play. A million things might happen between now and then to fuck it all up."

I never considered that Heath would worry about his future when he has it mapped out. I don't stress about life beyond college, only planning for it. I guess once you have it figured out, the only thing to worry about is how things might go wrong.

"You just got here. Give yourself time to just be and let life happen. You don't need to have the next three years or beyond all planned out. What fun would that be? Four months ago, I didn't know you and now I do." He steps into my space and places his hands on the mattress on either side of me. "Not knowing can be exciting."

A knock at the door is followed by Maverick's voice. "Yo, Payne, let's go."

Heath brings his mouth to mine and kisses me softly.

"I think I'll wait for you guys to leave," I whisper.

"How are you going to get to the dorm?"

"I'll walk."

"No."

"No?"

He finds his keys on top of his desk and tosses them to me and then kisses me one last time before he heads out.

Chapter Twenty-Six

HEATH

We're sitting around the apartment before we head to the arena for tonight's game. Rauthruss is FaceTiming Carrie, and it doesn't annoy me quite as much as usual. Mav's sharing his pre-game peanut butter sandwich with Charli, and Adam's staring at the TV with a look of hard concentration.

I know he wears the weight of the world on his shoulders before games, worrying about how we'll play. He takes a lot of that pressure on himself, most I think isn't really necessary, but I guess that's why he's the captain.

"Scott, what are you going to do after graduation?" I ask him, surprised I don't know.

Mav's already signed with the Cats and Rauthruss's family runs a hockey camp that he plans to take over.

"I'm premed, man. Going to medical school."

"Really?"

The other guys look to me with equally surprised faces.

"I didn't know." Or maybe I did and forgot it already. I don't spend a lot of time thinking past next week. Even my own future feels weird. Pro hockey is like this thing I've agreed to but doesn't really feel like it's going to happen. Two and a half years feels so far away.

"We're gonna be busting people up and he's going to be putting them back together," Mav says, mouth full of peanut butter.

"I can see you being a team doctor or something; that'd be cool."

He laughs and says sarcastically, "Thanks. I hadn't thought of that."

"I'm sorry. You probably mentioned it before, and I let it go in one ear and out the other. Making plans isn't really my thing."

"Speaking of plans, is it okay if I crash here tonight?" Maverick asks. "I'm meeting up with that girl Holly later and I don't want her to know where I live."

"Dude, gross, stop hooking up on our couch. You have your own apartment for that." Adam's laughing as he says it though, the mood light before we have to get serious and ready for the game.

He looks to me. "What about you? I haven't seen any girls running out in the mornings."

"You're never here," Rauthruss points out, somehow managing to follow two conversations—his with Carrie and ours.

"Okay, well, fine, but I don't see them zipping through to your room at night before I leave to go to Taryn's either."

Mav's smile is big and mocking. "Yeah, Heath, what's up with that?"

Well, now I know why I don't try to make small talk with Adam.

I stand and start toward my room. "Just focused on hockey." I come back with my bag. It's a little early, but I need out of this conversation. "You guys ready to head over?"

None of them mention the time. They're all just as ready to get out of here as I am.

"Hey, can I catch a ride over to The Hideout?" Maverick asks after the game.

I'm pulling on a shirt and jeans, but I glance over to make sure Adam is out of earshot before I answer. "I can drop you off, but I'm not going."

"Why not?"

"Taking Ginny out."

"A date?" he asks, louder than I'd like.

Adam's still not paying us any attention, so I nod. "Yeah, a date, hanging out, whatever."

"Where are you going?"

"I don't know. Maybe Prickly Pear since all the guys will be at The Hideout." The Prickly Pear is our second favorite local hangout, but on the weekends. It's often taken over by townies, so we aren't likely to run into anyone we know there.

"That's a lame date."

"Then I guess it isn't a date."

"Yo, Scott," Mav calls and I fight the urge to pummel him. "What's the best spot in Valley to take a girl on a date?"

"On a Friday night?" Adam asks, eyebrows drawn together in consideration. "The drive-in up on Mount Loken or pretty much anywhere downtown. Araceli's has a nice outdoor patio and good food."

"Didn't take you for the romantic type, Mav," Jordan says.

"People are surprising, aren't they?" He chuckles. "Thanks, Scott, knew you'd come through for me." Maverick closes his locker and turns to me with a smug look. "Ready?"

I PICK UP GINNY AT HER DORM. SHE SLIDES INTO THE PASSENGER seat in a short dress smelling like apples and cinnamon and I can't help but kiss her while sitting in the no-parking zone. Someone honks and I reluctantly pull back and then guide the car back on the road.

"Where are we going?" Ginny's beaming at me and I'm suddenly glad I have some better suggestions than Prickly Pear.

"You'll see." I rest a hand on her thigh and head out of town.

I drive to the outskirts where the houses get bigger, set up on the base of the mountain, and are placed farther apart.

The roads are mostly quiet with as many people biking and walking as cars driving along it. It's still nice and warm in Arizona. A few trees have leaves that are changing colors, but mostly it's the usual dull greens and browns—nothing like what I'm used to from growing up in Michigan.

Even in the coldest part of the year, the days are too warm in Arizona to consider it real fall weather.

It takes almost an hour to get up to the top of the mountain. The road curves through the trees, and we follow a long line of cars all with the same idea.

I park and we get out to get food before the movie starts.

"It's so much cooler up here," she says, wrapping her arms around her body as the wind whips through the lot.

Ah, shit. Something I hadn't thought of. I double back and grab a sweatshirt from my car. She pulls it on over her dress. It's nearly as long and she looks freaking sexy as hell. I smooth her hair away from her face and drop a kiss to her lips. "Hungry?"

She presses her mouth to mine and nods. I tug her behind me to the concession stand. We order hot dogs and popcorn, soda, and more candy than any two people should eat (Ginny's words obviously) before walking back to the vehicle. The movie is just starting, and I open the back and help her into the cargo area of my SUV.

"How do you of all people know about this place?"

"Me of all people?"

She grins. "I said what I said."

Chuckling, I admit, "Actually, from your brother."

Her nose wrinkles up. "My brother? Ewww. He brings dates up here, doesn't he?"

"It's a good spot, gotta admit." I lay out a blanket and we sit, her nestling into my side. "Come on, it's gonna be fun."

We dive into the food while watching the first half hour or so. It's some old Cary Grant movie that I'm not really into, but Ginny is smiling and practically in my lap, so I'm dealing just fine.

When the movie fails to keep our attention any longer, we lie down flat in the bed of the SUV with our heads at the end so we can stare up at the stars.

"It's really nice up here," she says.

"Yeah, I think I'll start bringing more of my dates up here."

She turns her head to face me. We're both smiling. "Jerk."

Her eyes are lit with humor and a contentedness fills my chest as I slowly bring my mouth to hers.

Kissing Ginny is better than just about anything. She's fun and sexy, and when we're together, everything just feels good. Her nose is cold, and I pull the blanket around us and hug her tight against my chest.

"What's your major?"

She chuckles a little, caught off guard by the question as my dick poking her tells her just how much I'd like to be inside her. "I haven't decided yet. Why?"

"Just curious. I realized today I'm not great at asking people about themselves. I didn't even know your brother was premed."

"Adam's weirdly quiet about that. He is about everything he does, really. He takes things on and just holds it in so no one else can feel responsibility for it. I know I gripe about him butting into my life, but he's always looked out for me, always ready to save me from trouble. He'd do anything for me, no questions asked."

Am I trouble he'd try to save her from? The pit in my gut tells me yes.

Her hair blows into my face and she tries to tame it.

"The way you talk about Adam reminds me a lot of Nathan. Always looking out for me even when I didn't want him to."

"Maybe we're just good at giving them reasons to worry about us."

"That's probably accurate." I think back to all the times I gave Nathan reason to worry.

"What about you? You're going to be a big hockey star when college is over. Is it weird to have your future all mapped out?"

"Feels so far away it doesn't seem real yet, I guess."

"Will you get me tickets so I can come cheer you on?"

I like the vision of her being there even if it's unlikely to happen. "We might be able to work out some sort of barter system."

"Oh yeah? What'd you have in mind?" That sexy glint is back in her eyes.

"Nothing appropriate for the kids sitting in that minivan next to us," I tell her and sit up. I take her hand and pull her up next to me, drop a kiss to her forehead, and say, "We can discuss it back at my place."

Chapter Twenty-Seven

GINNY

On Sunday, I drag Heath over to my dorm to hang out. Ava's still gone, so we sit on my bed and watch TV, make out, watch TV, nap, make out—it's the perfect ending to a great weekend.

"You could stay the night," I offer as he's getting dressed to go.

"I wish I could, but I promised Maverick we'd work on Shakespeare. His test is tomorrow."

I let out a sigh. "I should probably do some homework too. Someone distracted me all weekend."

He leans down to kiss me. "You didn't seem to mind so much when you were riding my face."

Fresh desire blooms, and he must read it all over my expression because the next thing I know, I'm flat on my back and he's on top of me kissing me like the world will end if he doesn't.

A squeak and the slamming of a door breaks us apart.

I give Ava an apologetic smile. No matter how many times she sees Adam or Heath, she still gets shy around them.

"Hey, Ava," he says to my roommate and then slowly rises off me, but not without another quick kiss. "Bye, baby. See you at the dining hall tomorrow?"

"Umm... yeah." I think through my schedule. "Only for breakfast, though, I'm working at the Hall of Fame in the afternoon."

"Too bad." He winks and then heads out.

Monday afternoon I have three tours in a row. It's only my second time working by myself. Usually we do them in pairs, but today, I'm the only one available.

I have a junior high class, a soccer recruit, and then finally a hockey recruit. Knowing I might see Heath before or after the last tour makes the time go by at a snail's pace. It's nice out today, though. Perfect Arizona weather with blue skies and a light fall breeze. I take Andi, the soccer chick, over to the practice field and we sit while I let her ask me questions and soak up the experience.

We return just in time for my last tour. I hand her off to a girl on the Valley team as Rauthruss and Maverick walk in the hockey recruit, Tom.

"Genevieve!" Maverick calls, his voice echoing in the big, open space.

I wave and step forward. "Hey, nice to meet you." I smile and extend my hand to Tom.

"You're in good hands," Mav assures him. "Ginny is Adam's sister and Heath's—" He catches himself in time, but my blood pressure still rises. Mav coughs. "Friend."

"Thanks, guys." I bypass the weirdness by stepping away and inviting Tom to follow me with a head tilt in the opposite direction.

Tom is a quiet guy who doesn't say a lot as I show him around. We go by all the usual places on the tour, but I still can't get a read on him until we get to the last stop.

"And this is the hype room." I do my best Vanna White as he stares into the darkened room with wide eyes and an excited smile. Upbeat music already pumps into the space, and with the press of a button, the TVs come to life with the standard Welcome to Valley message splashed across the entire room.

Tom walks in, slowly giving it the appropriate amount of awe. "This is so dope."

"Right?" I follow behind him and close us inside.

I cue up the hockey team video and scoot to the back to let him enjoy the five-minute segment in as much privacy as I can.

The hype room is still my favorite part of this job. I could sit in here all day. Even I feel like a badass after watching the videos and I did not inherit the athleticism my brother did.

I wait for the bits with Heath in them, having practically memorized when his face or an action clip appear.

Things have been great. While I don't love keeping it from my brother, it's been nice to spend time with Heath without the judgment or questions from anyone. I love my brother and I understand why he wants to protect me, but I don't need it in this scenario, and I'm not willing to gamble that he'll be cool with it. Heath and I are having fun. A lot of it. And yes, maybe my feelings have gone beyond that, but I refuse to get swept up in analyzing it. But as Heath's face displays on the screen, flashing a cocky and disarming smile, my body melts.

Fine, I like him a lot. Who knew dating could be so much fun? I've never laughed so much or felt so wanted. And I don't mean his obvious appreciation for my body. We spend a lot of time together and only half of that is naked. Seventy percent tops.

As it gets to the end sequencing, I step closer and get my tablet ready. It's the last tour of the day, and there's a whole different set of steps for shutting down for the night that I haven't done before. Dakota's shown me a few times and she texted me instructions earlier today as a backup.

This room is worth a very pretty penny to the university and I don't want to break anything.

When it finally freezes on the end frame, Tom turns to me.

"Awesome, right?" I ask at his captivated grin. I've seen this look before. He's totally sold. "Let me just shut everything down and some of the guys should be waiting at the desk outside to take you over to the arena."

I tap the screen and begin to shut things down. I'm sweating a little with Tom staring at me while I try to juggle my phone and the tablet. "Sorry, it's my first time closing it out for the night."

"No problem." He shoves his hands in his pockets, and I turn slightly and walk toward the door. It isn't pitch dark in here, but it isn't exactly a comfortable light level either. Dakota is much better at sequencing everything, so it happens seamlessly.

"Okay, I think I got it," I say as I tap the final button. Except instead of opening the door it shuts off all the TVs and now we really are in the pitch black.

Shit. I forgot to open the door before shutting down.

No problem. I've got this. With trembling hands, I try to turn on the TVs, but they won't come back on until the system's reset. I search for another button hoping to find one labeled lights.

Oh shit. Shit, shit, shit, shit, shit.

"One second. I'm so sorry." My breaths come in quick, short gulps as I text Dakota and then press buttons at random on the tablet hoping I get lucky. I'm sure there is a very simple solution, but I'm panicking. Oh my god.

"Are you okay?" Tom asks.

I think I nod, but it isn't exactly believable because I cower against the wall retreating into myself.

One, two, three…

Chapter Twenty-Eight

HEATH

When Adam and I get over to the Hall of Fame, it's chaos. There's a crowd hanging out in the back of the main area, and a couple of security guards stand outside of the hype room.

"What the hell?" Adam asks.

My pulse accelerates and adrenaline swells as we head toward the commotion.

"What's going on?" I ask one of the football guys hanging out watching the security guards talk into their walkie talkies.

"Two people got trapped in the hype room."

At that moment, the doors open and a frazzled Ginny pushes out. Her breathing is so labored I can see the rise and fall of her chest, eyes wild, clutching the tablet to her stomach. Adam and I move to her, and when she sees us, her pace quickens.

"Oh, fuck," I hear Adam mutter quietly under his breath.

He's a step ahead of me and I'm so thankful he's here because she looks like she needs him. She's on the brink of a complete meltdown. But when we finally get to her, it isn't him she throws her arms around. It's me.

Her body is limp as she sucks in air with ragged breaths. My throat is tight, and my chest cracks open, letting her slip inside. I feel her fear with the force of a Mack truck slamming into me and then dragging me a mile down the road. I can't find the oxygen to speak, so I wrap my arms around her and pull her head under my chin.

I glance at Adam, feeling his presence like a dark cloud hovering over us. His glare goes from confused to pissed, but this isn't the time or place to have this conversation.

Adam senses the same thing, and I shield her while he gets us some privacy, calling for everyone to get lost with only slightly more polite words.

"Ginny." When his attention is back on us, his voice is softer than I expected for the rage rolling off him. "G, are you okay?"

She pulls herself away from me, not meeting my gaze, and hugs him instead. He looks relieved as she glues herself to his side.

"What happened?" he asks gently, cupping the back of her head.

She tries to speak, but her voice is shaky, and he shushes her. "Later, G. Just relax." He's calm and loving with her, and I feel a sense of relief that he's here with all the right words, even if it means he's going to kick my ass later.

Adam's jaw flexes and he nods over my head. "Can you see Tom to the arena?"

Ginny's face is buried in his side, giving me her profile. She's not crying, but her eyes are closed, and her dark lashes fan out against her smooth skin.

"Heath," Adam says again, voice as sharp as razors.

I take a step back. "Yeah. Yeah, okay."

ADAM DOESN'T SHOW UP TO THE ARENA WHILE I'M SHOWING TOM the locker rooms and team training facilities. The guys who are free this afternoon are hanging around, including Maverick and Rauthruss. They both question me on Adam's whereabouts. I shrug it off and focus on getting through the quick tour.

When Coach shows up, I hand off Tom and decide to do a quick skate to clear my head. I assume Adam is going to show up and slam me into the boards at any moment, but he doesn't.

I trudge home with dread and guilt weighing down each step. No matter how many times I tell myself it's none of his business, I can't find any solace in it.

Adam's sitting on the couch with his phone to his ear when I walk into the apartment. I hesitate, but ultimately decide a shower is what I need before he goes nuclear on me. When I'm clean and dressed, he's still sitting in the same spot—sans the phone to his ear. He doesn't even look at me as I join him in the living room.

I'm already sweating again with uncertainty on how to navigate this. Quick and honest, rip off the Band-Aid.

"It's not what you think."

A growl escapes from his chest and his eyes turn to angry slits. Fuck. Okay, that wasn't the best opening, I admit.

"Okay, it's what you think," I backtrack.

"Of all the girls, man. You can have any other one, but not her. Not my baby sister."

"I'm sorry if it pisses you off. Maybe I should have told you. Not because I think I need your permission, but out of respect. I'm sorry for that, but I'm not sorry for digging your sister. She's awesome and I like her a lot. I don't need your permission," I repeat. "And Ginny doesn't need it either, for any guy she decides to date."

"Ginny said as much." He stands. He's a good three inches taller than me and he uses every single one. "You can honestly tell me you think you're good enough for her? Fuck man, I see how you are with women. I don't want that for her, is that so hard to understand?"

He doesn't wait for my answer before heading to his room and slamming the door.

"He and Taryn are sitting guard in the living room," I tell Ginny on the phone later.

The two of them never hang out at our apartment. That's part of the Adam Scott boyfriend experience—bending over backward for his girl and always staying at their place. Or that's what I hear. Since this is my first year living with him I don't really know, but Rauthruss made an offhanded comment once that Adam hardly ever has girlfriends sleep over.

"So, I'll just come over. What's he going to do? Kick me out?"

"No, but he might kick me out."

She groans. "This is stupid. I can date whoever I want."

"He's just looking out for you."

"I don't need him to look out for me." She sighs into the phone.

"I guess it's best to give him a couple of days to cool off."

My chest tightens, and I wonder if in a couple of days she'll decide it isn't worth making waves. Maybe that'd be for the best.

The next morning, though, she's waiting outside of the dining hall for me and a goofy grin pulls at my lips.

I hug her and she laughs. "Miss me?"

"Yep." I take her hand and follow her through the line for omelets.

"I need my hand back," she says, and I realize I'm still holding her palm in mine.

We take our usual table. Mav drops into a chair beside her a few minutes later. "Hey there, Romeo and Juliet."

Ginny laughs. "Their families were enemies—this isn't really that sort of thing."

"Well, it *is* a Shakespearean tragedy, anyway. What are you going to do?"

I shrug. Thought about it all night long and I still don't have an answer.

"I'm heading home tonight. I'm sure by the time I get back on Sunday, he'll be over it."

I'm not so sure.

After my morning classes, I head back to the apartment. Ginny's on her way home for the long weekend, and the prospect of spending that many days without her is a real bummer.

Rauthruss is on the phone with Carrie. Mav and Adam are still on campus. I've got my newest package from Chloe and Nathan, so I grab it and walk to my room.

I call him as I cut open the tape.

"Hey," he answers on the second ring.

"Hey. Got your latest box."

"And?"

As soon as I pull back the flaps, a deep chuckle escapes from my throat. "This one is all you, bro."

"What? How can you tell?"

"It looks like you went down the aisles at Target and just threw random things in." I pull out deodorant, body soap, condoms (major eye roll), toothpaste, pencils, a giant tub of my favorite protein, and an Xbox gift card. "Plus it's all just shoved in here. Chloe's boxes are packed a lot nicer than yours."

"I knew I should have had her wrap it all up."

I chuckle again. "Thank you. I appreciate it."

Sitting in my desk chair, I lean back as he catches me up on the latest wedding details. Getting married takes an awful lot of planning, apparently.

"So, spill," he says eventually when he's done with the rundown on dinner entrees and cake tasting. "What'd you think of Kevin?"

"He was fine." I shrug even though Nathan can't see it. "Mom's happy so that's good, right?"

"Yeah, I guess so. It's weird seeing her with someone else though. No matter how nice he is."

I hum my agreement.

"Are you still calling her and checking in to see how she's doing?"

"Nah. I mean, we chat every other week or so, but she doesn't need me to do that anymore. She's got Kevin, plus Uncle Doug is still checking on her."

"Yeah, I guess. Chloe and I are going to fly up to have Thanksgiving with her. Bummed you can't make it."

"I'm sure you guys will make the most of it." We've got a game on Saturday, so it'll just be another Thursday around here, although the extra days off school are nice.

"I could never make her smile like you could. Remember that time we went to the water park in Wisconsin?"

I smile, knowing exactly where he's going with the story.

"She got up on the top of that big slide and she wouldn't budge. The line was backed up and people were yelling for her to hurry up. There were six-year-old kids going down that thing."

"She hates heights," I say.

"Yeah. I'm not even sure why she attempted it in the first place."

"Because I was too scared to go on my own and you were whining about me tagging along with you and that guy you used to hang out with…"

"Lee," he fills in.

I nod. "She came up there for me. I knew she was scared too but I didn't care."

"Dude, you were like nine."

"I still knew it was a bad idea."

"You sang to her, at the top of your lungs, the whole way back down the line."

"I had to scream so she could hear me over all the people yelling at us."

He laughs.

I'm smiling now, but I was so embarrassed at the time and Nathan made fun of me for weeks.

"You were always good at calming her down, being her rock. You still are. She might be doing better, but there's no one that can make her as happy as you. Call her."

When I get off the phone with Nathan, I send her a text checking in and promise myself I'll call her tomorrow. With my gift card in hand, I walk out into the living room. Everyone's back from campus, and Adam has parked himself back in his guard dog position between the door and my room.

I toss the gift card on the coffee table. "I was going to order pizza and get the new Call of Duty. You guys in?"

"Oh, no way." Rauthruss picks up the card. "Rad, man. I'm in."

We both look to Adam and he shrugs his big shoulders. I guess that's a start.

Chapter Twenty-Nine

GINNY

Hottest guy on campus: Hey, gorgeous. Why aren't you in my bed?

Me: Better offer.

Hottest guy on campus: Damn, woman. That's cold.

Me: I figured you would understand better than anyone. My mom's been cooking for days. SO MUCH FOOD.

Hottest guy on campus: My stomach just growled, for real. Also, my dick's hard just from texting you.

Me: Proof or it didn't happen.

Hottest guy on campus: Dick pics... always a bad idea, Genevieve.

Me: Like vag pics *shudders*

Hottest guy on campus: Not the same at all. Speaking of... feel free to send some my way.

Me: Tit for tat.

Hottest guy on campus: Tits okay too, I guess. Make sure you get front and side view... I very much enjoy a little side booby.

Me: How's Valley?

I don't want to ask specifically about how things are with Adam, but he must read between the lines.

Hottest guy on campus: Okay. We stayed in tonight and played video games. Adam hasn't punched me yet.

Me: I heard my mom say you guys are having a team dinner to celebrate Thanksgiving. That's nice.

Hottest guy on campus: Beats the dorm food. Don't tell Brenda.

Me: Brenda?

Hottest guy on campus: My favorite lunch lady.

Me: Of course, you have a favorite lunch lady.

Hottest guy on campus: Eyes keep closing. Gonna sleep. Don't forget (o) (o)

The following night I'm lying on the couch watching TV when there's noise outside. A car door followed by deep voices. I get up and peer out the window. Adam's Jeep is in the driveway, and I see his big frame climbing out of the driver's side. Heath, Rauthruss, and Mav follow.

I run to the door and fling it open as they approach. "What are you doing here?"

I hug Adam first. As excited as I am about the man behind him, it's been three years since Adam and I have celebrated a Thanksgiving together. He always stayed at Valley because of his hockey schedule.

"Decided to come up for the night, enjoy Mom's sour cream apple pie. We have to go back tomorrow night to have dinner with the team."

"Figures you found a way to have two Thanksgiving dinners."

Adam heads inside, so do Mav and Rhett. Heath lingers with a sexy smirk. "Hey, Genevieve."

I throw myself at him.

"Couch, Payne." Adam's voice comes from behind me. "Mav and Rhett, you guys can take the guest room."

Adam gets Heath a pillow and blanket, and I stay downstairs as Heath spreads out on the couch bed.

"Why didn't you tell me you were coming?"

"I wanted to surprise you. Also, I didn't know until about three hours ago. Your brother said he was heading up and asked if we wanted to come with him." He shrugs. "I was half expecting him to stop on the freeway somewhere and kick me out of the car."

"So you're here because of my brother?" I sneak a hand inside his shirt and up his chest.

"Yep. He really does it for me." He winces. "Shit, I can't even joke about it while I'm hard."

"Come up to my room." I start to stand, but he doesn't budge.

"I don't think I should."

"Because of Adam? He's had more girls in his room than Sephora on sale day."

"I don't know what that means, but I'm guessing it's a lot."

"Yes." I pull again, but he shakes his head.

"It's not just Adam. I'm a guest and I don't want your parents to think I came up to get in their daughter's pants.

"Oh my god, when did you turn into this good guy?"

"Don't worry, baby. I'm still bad." He pulls me down on top of him and quickly has me pinned underneath him on the couch bed.

He doesn't kiss me, though, just stares down at me.

"I'm so excited you're here."

He grins. "Me too."

I WAKE UP TO THE SMELL OF PUMPKIN AND TURKEY AND AM instantly giddy. A real Thanksgiving with the whole family. And Heath.

Adam and the guys are already up, their doors open and rooms empty as I pass by on my way downstairs. I slow as I get to the last step. Heath's pulling a gray T-shirt over his head and holding his phone up to his ear.

When he spots me, he smiles, and my insides turn to mush.

"All right, I should go. The guys are waiting on me." He continues staring at me as he says goodbye to whoever he's talking to. I meet him halfway as he pockets his phone.

"Was that your mom?"

"Yeah."

"She must miss having you home for the holidays. My mom's ecstatic Adam's here. She's been in the kitchen all morning making extra pies."

"Hope she doesn't mind we came along."

"Are you kidding? She's thrilled. My mother's happiest when she has lots of people to dote on."

He wraps his arms around my lower back. "What are you up to this morning? Can you save me from some lame football game outside?"

I gasp. "Lame? It's an honored tradition." I take his hand and pull him to the door. "You can be on my team. I've never lost."

The neighborhood football game on Thanksgiving morning is a tradition as far back as I can remember. When I was little, I'd sit along the sidelines and cheer on my dad and Adam and whatever boy I had a crush on at the time. But sometime in middle school I decided to join the other brave girls out there. I love it.

"Morning, sunshine." Mav jogs up to us.

"Morning," Heath says, voice cracking. He clears it a few times. His gruff morning voice is my favorite.

"Glad you got your sexy ass up; we need a QB."

Heath shakes his head. "I never played football."

Mav punches him. "I know, but you've got those QB good looks like Tom Brady."

"Did they already pick teams?" I ask.

"Nah," Mav says. "They're fighting over Adam."

"You four are the most athletically inclined people we've had in a while." I scan the yard to see who made it to play this year, and my gaze snags on someone I didn't expect. "Bryan's here?"

The question is more to myself than the guys, but Heath asks, "Who's Bryan?"

"My ex." Bryan and I make eye contact and he starts toward me. Seeing him for the first time in three months has my emotions whipping around like I'm on a merry-go-round.

"Hey, Ginny." Bryan envelopes me in a hug, pressing his large body against mine and squeezing tightly. Apparently he feels none of the awkwardness I do. I can't decide if that's comforting or not. "It's so good to see you."

"I didn't expect you to be home for break."

"Just for the day. I fly back tonight."

"Oh." I shift uncomfortably and wring my hands to have something to do. "How's Idaho?"

"Eh… you know."

"Actually, I don't."

"Well, it's not Arizona. How's Valley?"

I sneak a glance at Heath out of my periphery. He's got his arms crossed and a hard expression on his face. "It's great. I really love it."

"Yeah?"

I nod.

"That's awesome." He does a blatant once over of my body. "You look amazing."

"Thanks." I smile politely. He looks good too, but not in that way where I want to rip off his clothes. And the guy who I do want to do that to is standing beside me. I turn to him. "Bryan, this is my friend Heath."

"Hey, man." Bryan juts his chin in acknowledgment. "You play hockey with Adam, right?"

"That's right."

"The guys were talking about you earlier. Sounds like you're going to be the opposing QB. I'll try not to make you look too bad." He takes a step back and winks. "Good to see you, babe. I'll call you. Maybe we can hang while we're both in town for winter break."

I wait until he's gone to face Heath, prepared to stroke his ego, but he's... smiling?

"Your friend, huh?"

"Did you want me to introduce you as my make-out buddy?"

He chuckles and winces at the same time. "Guess not. You dated that douche?"

"He's... not so bad." I play down any lingering resentment because the last thing I need is Heath or my brother to make a scene. And honestly, it's not so much resentment as just dislike for the guy. Sure, he had his own reasoning for how things ended, but let's be real, he did it in a super shitty way. I can see that so much clearer now.

"He's a douche."

"Is this jealous Heath?" I wave a hand in front of his broody frame. He glares toward Bryan's retreating back.

"What? No, of course not." But he continues to stand close while we set up the game.

We've got enough people to play with two full teams and a couple alternates. Rauthruss and Heath end up on my team and Adam and Mav on the other with Bryan.

"We're just waiting on my dad," Adam says and glances toward the house. "Ginny, did you see him when you came out?"

"No, I haven't seen him this morning."

Adam's brows scrunch together. "That's weird."

"He probably had to run to town for something Mom forgot. Let's just start, I'm sure he'll show up."

Adam doesn't budge.

"I will go check on him." I nudge Heath playfully. "Don't screw up my winning streak, Payne."

I hurry back up to the house and to the kitchen where I can hear Mom and her sister, Zoe, talking and cooking. Mom's wearing a half apron chopping onions while Zoe sits on a stool peeling potatoes.

"Hey."

They both look up as I enter.

"Morning. Game over already?" Mom asks.

"No, we haven't started yet. We're waiting on Dad. Do you know where he is?"

Mom and Zoe exchange a look.

"What?" I ask when neither of them immediately answers.

Mom shakes her head. "I don't know where he went, but it's not like him to miss the big game. Start without him, and I'll text and let him know the team's missing him."

I grin. "Okay. Thanks, Mom. Are you staying for dinner, Aunt Zoe?"

"No, your uncle Wyatt and I are heading to his mom's. I'll stop by Sunday before you head back to school."

As I go out, Dad's pulling into the driveway. I run to him, pleased to see he's dressed to play in an old T-shirt and shorts. "You're late."

"How's the team looking, kid?" He gives me a one-arm hug as

we walk toward the game.

"We've got a few ringers thanks to Adam and his friends."

At the next break in play, Adam finds us on the sidelines, and he and my dad hug. Adam's taller and broader than him now, which is just another way things have changed over the last three years.

"Good to see you, son."

"You ready to get your ass kicked, old man?"

Adam and my dad smack talk like they're both twelve, but it's so good to see them together. Our whole family home at the same time.

"You're on Ginny's team," Adam tells him.

Our team huddles up, and Dad and I substitute in.

As we play, I have this sublime feeling of total completeness. Like I've never been this happy. Maybe it's just nostalgia and the sense that this is a rare moment. Adam will graduate, become a doctor with insane hours, and get married or move far away and who knows when we'll all be here again. Maybe another three years. Maybe longer.

Heath isn't as good of a QB as Bryan, as painful as that is to admit, and Adam is way better than I remember. While we grab water, Heath gives me a rueful smile. "You might want to think about a trade if you want to keep that winning streak."

"I would never leave my team in the final quarter," I say, faking shock then wrapping my arms around his sweaty neck. He grins and I kiss him in front of everyone. I definitely got the better QB and I'm not shy about letting the other team know it.

Chapter Thirty

HEATH

Ginny's ex is a piece of shit. *Hello, jealousy, nice to meet you.* But come on, this guy? I don't miss the way he tries to flirt with her or the little inside jokes he tosses out. I want to throw the football in a perfect spiral directly into his face... or maybe his balls.

I remind myself that Ginny referred to sex with this guy as blah. My jealousy? Petty as hell.

Adam makes the game winning touchdown and his team celebrates as I approach Ginny with a rueful smile.

"Sorry, baby doll."

My girl has a competitive streak I find as amusing as I do sexy. Her mouth pulls down in a disappointed pout. "It's fine. I was due for a loss. Besides, I was distracted more than normal."

I worry for a second that she means because of Bryan, but then her lips twist up and she fists my shirt to pull me closer. "You threw me off my game, Payne. Usually you're covered in layers of padding and I can't really see *you* when you're on the ice, but out here I could see every drip of sweat."

"That padding keeps me alive."

She brings her lips to mine and hums against my mouth. "Necessary evil."

"QB looks but missing that QB arm." Maverick places both hands on his hips when he stops beside us.

"Yeah, well, I'd like to see you get a pass through Adam and Rauthruss," I grumble.

Ginny drops another quick kiss and then steps back. "I better go check on my mom in the kitchen."

After everyone else leaves, the guys and I sit in the yard drinking beer. Adam and his dad are tossing the ball back and forth. They have this easy way about them. Like I can tell Adam respects him, but his dad has stopped being the hard-ass parent now that his son is older, and they just seem to enjoy being around one another.

I never got that. Never even knew it was a thing until now. I had lots of good times with my dad, but I was still a kid—we didn't talk girls or life, none of that. Losing a parent is one of those things that as soon as you think you're over it, something stops you in your tracks and the wound is as fresh as if it just happened. I have a feeling it'll be like that the rest of my life. But as sad as it makes me for what I missed out on, I enjoy being around Ginny's family. It's the first holiday I've had in years where my worries are only the limitations of my stomach and how much food I can stuff in it.

"We're eating in thirty minutes," Ginny says as she rejoins us outside. She's freshly showered and dressed in jeans and a ruffly shirt with a deep V-neck that's going to make it impossible to keep my eyes off her boobs while I feign the role of respectable friend.

She hasn't held back with the PDA since I showed up last night, but I still want to respect that Adam's not exactly on board.

She takes a seat on my lap and I glance around to see if anyone shoots daggers at me, but Mr. Scott and Adam barely seem to notice.

"I should shower." I'm dirty and sweaty and probably not presentable for a Thanksgiving table.

"Yeah, we all should get cleaned up," Mr. Scott says as he tosses the ball to Adam one last time and heads for the house.

"Adam, do you have some clothes I could borrow?" Mav asks. "I was so excited when I packed all I managed to grab were socks and boxers."

Adam chuckles but nods. "I'll see what my dad has."

They all head in, but Ginny doesn't budge to let me up.

"I can think of a few things to do while you wait for the shower."

"Oh yeah." I put my finger in the V of her shirt and pull the fabric away from her chest so I can look down it.

"Mhmm."

She presses her lips to mine and then pulls back so we're nose to nose. "I, uh, decided something last night."

"What's that?" I ask and kiss her again.

"I don't want to wait anymore."

"Wait for what?"

"Sex, dummy. I'm ready."

A few months ago, I would have thought going without sex this long would have been a real sacrifice, but Ginny's sexual appetite is ravenous... just without the actual sex. When we first started hooking up, I couldn't wait to get inside her, but Ginny's creative and I can't pretend to have been anything but satisfied with our hookups. However, now that she's giving me the green light, I am ready to skip dinner and just have her instead.

All the blood is rushing to my cock with all the new things this opens up for us. I can't freaking wait. I kiss her hard, giving her a taste of how excited I am about her news.

"Payne," Adam bellows from the house. "Quit sucking face with my sister and get in here."

I smile into her mouth as our kiss stops.

We walk up to the house and Ginny goes to the kitchen to help her mom. I grab my overnight bag and Adam and I head upstairs.

"You can take a shower in my room. Should have everything you need in there." He stops outside his room and motions for me to go ahead.

"Thanks, man."

"No problem. Lock the door on both sides."

"What?" I ask, confused.

"You'll see."

I walk in and set my bag on the floor and then wander to the bathroom. There's another bedroom on the other side and I grin as I get my first peek at Ginny's childhood. I go all the way in and turn a circle. The walls are painted teal and the bed has a white comforter with a thousand throw pillows piled on top. Framed photos line the top of a desk. Even without walking closer, I can tell Bryan is featured in a lot of them.

Her ex-boyfriend might be better at football, but Ginny barely even looked at him the entire game. I know it sounds conceited to say she's totally into me, but I know she is. I'm totally into her too. Still, I turn the largest frame around so I don't have to stare at their happy faces.

As I'm coming back through the bathroom, Adam walks in his room with brows furrowed. "Do you have any extra clothes Mav could wear?"

"Nah, man, I just brought the one change of clothes."

He goes to his dresser and rummages through the few items inside. "My dad doesn't have a single item of clothing in their closet."

I shrug and so does he as he says, "Guess Mav will have to wear some vintage duds of mine."

By the time I shower and head back down, the Scott's dining room table is filled with food and the guys are already sitting around practically salivating. There's an empty chair between Ginny and Mav, and I take it.

Mrs. Scott sets a final dish on the table and smiles. "I think 'hat's everything. Dig in everyone."

For five minutes no one speaks except to compliment the food between bites. Even my sweet little Ginny, who barely fills a plate most days, eats her weight in mashed potatoes and turkey.

I feel like I can't eat another bite, but then Mrs. Scott brings pies to the table and I can't help myself.

"I think I'm gonna be sick," Mav says after his second piece, leaning back and rubbing his stomach.

"What are you wearing, Mav?" Ginny asks. "Is that Adam's high school homecoming shirt?"

He looks down and shrugs.

Adam speaks from across the table. "Yeah, Dad. I went in your and Mom's closet to loan Mav a shirt, but I couldn't find anything. Did she finally take over the entire closet and ban your clothes to the basement?"

Adam laughs at the idea, but then an uncomfortable silence follows as Mr. and Mrs. Scott share a nervous glance.

My skin prickles with awareness even before I've put it together. I'm good at reading bad news. Ginny's confused expression is heartbreaking, and I rest a hand on her leg under the table.

Mrs. Scott frowns and then says, "We wanted to wait until after the weekend to tell you."

"To tell us what?" Adam asks, his tone hardened in anticipation. Uncomfortable silence falls over the room.

"Your mother and I have separated," Mr. Scott answers finally.

Mav goes into a coughing fit, unable to hide his surprise and I elbow him hard in the ribs. He grunts loudly, but no one is paying him any attention anyway.

"Separated?" Adam questions. "You're getting divorced?"

Mrs. Scott looks around the table. "Maybe we should talk about it later."

"Mom?" Ginny's voice wavers and my chest... my chest fucking aches.

Mrs. Scott's mouth pulls up into a smile, but it's sad as hell. "We love you both very much. That hasn't changed and it won't. We're still a family."

Rauthruss clears his throat. "Maybe the guys and I should give you some time to talk." He glances to me and Mav, and we start to stand only to have Adam beat us to it.

"No, you guys stay. I need some air."

Ginny pushes back her chair so quickly it scrapes against the wood floor. "Me too." She disappears after him.

"Holy uncomfortable Batman," Mav whispers.

"I'm going to talk to them," Mr. Scott says and looks to his wife, maybe for approval. She nods and he follows them out.

It isn't until Mrs. Scott stands and excuses herself that the guys and I take a breath.

"Fuck, man, that was rough." Rauthruss grimaces. "What do we do?"

"No clue," I tell him honestly.

Chapter Thirty-One

GINNY

Adam and I sit in the garage after Dad leaves to go back to his place.

"He has his own apartment. How weird is that?" I ask, mostly to myself.

"You really had no idea?" Adam looks to me again like I should have known and warned him. Maybe I should have, but I didn't.

I shake my head. "I didn't know. Dad was in Scottsdale for work when I got here earlier this week." I think back, not only to the days since I got home for Thanksgiving break, but over the last few months. "They were going on trips and…" It hits me then that those trips were probably a last-ditch effort to save their marriage, and I feel like throwing up.

At some point, my brother grabbed a bottle of wine from the kitchen and we are well on our way to finishing it off. Adam's drunk the lion's share. He seems to be taking this harder than me. I feel numb, but he… well, I haven't seen my brother so devastated since the day I got locked inside the pantry. He'd been nine then and took on the big brother protector role with a dedication second to none. Since then I'd thought of him as unbreakable.

He can't protect me from this though, and I can't protect him. Everything is going to be different whether we like it or not.

Rauthruss walks outside with his hands in his pockets about the time Adam is tossing the empty wine bottle in the trash. "Are you guys okay?"

"Getting there." Adam holds up his wine glass and takes a healthy drink.

"We thought you might want to stay another night, head back in the morning?"

Adam nods and his expression softens. "Yeah, thanks, I appreciate it. Sorry for the family drama."

Mav and Heath walk out. Heath's blue eyes fixate on me.

"You guys wanna go out?" Adam asks. "I need to get away from here for a bit."

They all agree, and I stare down into my wine.

"You coming, Little Scott?" Mav asks.

"I think I'm going to stay."

Heath hangs back as the rest of the guys head for Adam's Jeep. Rauthruss climbs into the driver's side, thankfully. I know he'll make sure they're safe.

"Do you want me to stay?" Heath offers.

"No. I think Adam needs you more than me right now. I'm going to check on my mom."

He squeezes my hand and drops a kiss to my forehead. "Sorry, baby doll. Text me if you need me and I'll come back."

I offer the biggest smile of appreciation I can, which probably isn't that big. He jogs off, hops into the Jeep, and I watch them pull away.

I find Mom in the kitchen wiping down the counters. She stops when she sees me and offers a sad smile. "Are you okay?"

I slide onto the stool in front of her. "Funny, I was going to ask you the same thing."

She lets out a sigh and nods. "Yeah, it's the best thing for your dad and I, but I know that's not easy for you and Adam to understand."

"What happened? Is that weird to ask?"

Her smile is soft and warm, and she holds her arms out. I hop off the stool and go to her, stepping in and letting her wrap me into a reassuring embrace. "It wasn't one big thing, honey. We grew apart and started seeing our futures differently."

I tilt my head up to look her in the eye and she runs a hand along the back of my head like she did when I was a little girl. "I love you. Your father loves you. We're still a family, even if it looks a little different now."

"It'll be weird to go back to Valley and not think of you and Dad together here."

"I so get that. It's taken some getting used to being here by myself."

I glance around the kitchen wondering if she'll even stay here in this big house without him. I'm not brave enough to ask. I can't take another blow today.

"I promise that we'll both still be there for you and that we won't be those awful parents who can't be in the same room together."

My heart hurts imagining any scenario that looks different than what I'm used to. Everything's changing.

"Adam's wrecked."

"Your brother is a romantic."

I huff a small laugh. "Adam?"

"It's true. He is. From the time he was old enough to talk, he'd tell everyone he wanted to be a husband when he grew up, just like his daddy."

"I don't remember that."

"Middle school happened, and that's when he decided he wanted to be a doctor, but he hasn't changed."

"But he goes through girlfriends faster than anyone I know."

"He's a romantic, but he's still a young man." She smiles and I notice how tired she looks and wonder how I didn't see it before. "I should talk to him."

"They went to the bar."

"Even Heath?"

"Yeah, he offered to stay, but I figured Adam needed him more than me."

She touches my face. "You're a good sister. I'll talk to him before he leaves, but he'll be okay. We all will."

I hope so.

"I was going to have some pie in bed and watch *It's a Wonderful Life*. Want to join me?"

"Is there any pumpkin left?"

"You didn't really think I put all the pies out on the table earlier?" She smiles and shakes her head as she goes to the oven and pulls out a pumpkin pie.

I barely ate earlier and my stomach growls at the delicious smell of pumpkin and nutmeg. "In that case, I want two slices."

MOM AND I EAT PIE CURLED UP ON HER KING-SIZE BED. AS I LAY there, I can still smell my dad in their room and wonder if she can too. I'm sad, but I know my parents didn't come to this decision lightly, so I do my best to not let it show too much.

Mom falls asleep right after the movie, and I head to my own room. The guys aren't back, and the last text Heath sent said he thought they were in for a late night.

Adam's always been my protector. I never thought I'd need to repay the favor, but it seems like now might be the time. I can be the strong one this time.

I doze off sometime after one and wake up to the bed dipping with Heath's weight. His familiar scent mixed with alcohol wraps around me.

"You're back," I say, voice thick with sleep. "How's Adam?"

"Took all three of us to get him upstairs. Rauthruss is sleeping on the floor in there to keep an eye on him."

"I'm really glad you were here."

"Me too." He pulls me tight against him and rubs my back in long, soft strokes. "How are you doing? I hated not being here for you tonight."

"Well, I've had better Thanksgivings, but I ate my weight in pie, so I'm okay for the moment. It doesn't feel real yet. Twenty-three years… can you imagine?"

His head shakes almost imperceptibly. The TV is still on and his face illuminates with flashing colors. His warmth heats the space between us.

"You can turn off the TV if it bugs you," I tell him.

"It doesn't bother me, and I know you prefer it."

"Being scared of the dark is embarrassing. Maybe even more embarrassing than my parents announcing they're separating over Thanksgiving dinner, but I've gotten used to sleeping without the TV since going to Valley."

"I realize it probably doesn't help, but you don't need to feel embarrassed in front of me. Not for any of it."

"It does help, actually. Thank you. What also might help is knowing your deepest darkest secrets and fears."

He chuckles. "I'm scared of all kinds of things."

"Like?"

"Worms."

"What?" I laugh. "Why worms?"

He shudders. "We used them for bait when fishing. I never liked touching them and once Nathan noticed, he started chasing me around dangling the little slimy fuckers in front of my face." He shudders again.

"Worms are gross but not scary."

"Fears don't have to be rational."

"That's true."

"Why are you scared of the dark? Did something happen or have you always been?"

"When I was five or six, me and Adam were playing at my grandparent's house. It was this old house with creaky wooden floors and doors that somehow no longer fit the frame, so you had to put all your weight into them to close. They had this great back yard with a treehouse and a trampoline. Before my grandmother passed away, the whole family on my dad's side would get together.

The adults would sit outside in lawn chairs and the kids could run wild."

"Sounds like something out of a fifties TV show."

"Well, it wasn't quite that idyllic. Uncle Walter showed up stoned more often than not, and my cousin Tillie was always teaching us Urban Dictionary slang. My mom almost had a stroke with some of the words I learned. Anyway, one day, the whole family was over there, I think it was one of my cousin's birthdays. Everyone was outside and the cousins decided we would play hide and seek. I'm the baby of the family and I really wanted to prove that I was a good hider, so I'd been scoping out places for weeks and finally found the best hiding spot. In the pantry there was this extra closet where grandma kept brooms and mops. It was really small, and I knew I was the only one who could fit in it and that no one else would think to look there. So, when everyone took off to hide, I hung back so not to give away my spot and then went and shut myself in."

Heath strokes my arm as my voice wavers. Part of the memory is so real I can almost smell the dust and Pledge mixture of that tiny closet. Other things I only remember like I watched someone else go through it, like the way I wrapped my arms around myself, squeezing tight and sobbing through the screams.

"I don't know how long I was in there. For a while I was so careful to be quiet. I didn't want to give myself away. I could hear Adam calling my name and I just felt so proud, you know? He's always been a total know-it-all. Cocky and just better at everything, so I was really excited to have beaten him at something. Anyway, eventually my cousins grew bored of the game and when I was certain I'd waited long enough that they were never going to find me, I pushed the door open ready to show off my awesome hiding skills, only I couldn't get out. The outside of the door had one of those hook latches and it'd fallen in place when I shut the door. I screamed and screamed until I lost my voice. It was so dark and so small."

"Fuck, Ginny."

I nod. "By everyone's best guess, I was in there for two hours before my mom noticed she hadn't seen me in a while and went looking for me. They called an ambulance because I couldn't get my breathing under control. Adam freaked. He knew I was missing but didn't think it was a big deal, so it really hit him harder than anyone. He didn't leave my side for weeks." Heath's hold tightens around me and I snuggle into him. "I know I probably should have gotten over it by now."

"I don't think fears work like that. I think they hang on until you face them in one way or another, poking holes in the pain and letting good shine through." He pulls the sheet up over our heads and smiles at me in the near darkness. "Let's make some good memories in the dark."

The thin sheet doesn't really block out the light of the TV, but it's a step and I take it.

Chapter Thirty-Two

HEATH

disappear from under the covers long enough to grab a condom and then hurry back underneath where a very eager Ginny is wiggling out of her clothes. I had big plans for undressing her with my teeth, but I'm too busy appreciating the view to complain.

"You're so beautiful."

Her smile, even in the near dark, is bright and genuine. She eyes the condom in my hand. "I'm on birth control. We can…" She hesitates. "I mean, if you're comfortable going without, so am I."

My already throbbing cock is now harder than it's ever been. I pull my shirt over my head and Ginny works on unbuttoning my jeans. Together we push them and my boxers down and before I can kick them off, Ginny's mouth is covering the head of my dick.

"Oh Jesus. Slow down, babe. I'm never gonna last, like that," I tell her, guiding her head up and down my length. Her warm mouth is heaven. She comes off with a pop and I groan at the loss. I pull her up and swipe a hand over her lips. She looks a little uncertain and I tuck a strand of hair behind her ear.

"You sure you wanna do this?"

"I do, but I'm a little nervous. I might suck at it."

"Well, in that case, you can just keep sucking me with your hot as fuck mouth." I wink so she knows I'm joking and shift so I'm on top of her, holding most of my weight off her slender frame. "Babe, don't take this any other way than I mean it—a compliment—but there's no way you're bad at sex. You're the sexiest, most enthusiastic partner I've ever had."

That earns me a grin and I take her mouth in a bruising kiss. And just like that, the wild Ginny I've come to know is back. The blanket falls, but she doesn't seem to notice or care. She pulls at my hair and rakes her nails down my shoulders. I swear I could make this girl orgasm from kissing alone, if I could ever bring myself to only kiss her.

There's no single part of her that I like better than the rest. I like it all and I show her so with a dedication to touching and kissing every inch.

She squirms underneath me as I move down her body, tracing a single finger along the middle of her stomach, past her belly button, and down to her slick pussy. She raises her hips to give me better access and I dip my head.

Her hands find my hair and her fingers slide along my scalp and tug the strands as I taste her. She writhes and moans and it's so fucking hot my dick leaks with desperation. I wait until she's so close she's panting my name before I finally line up at her entrance. I inch in slowly, her tight pussy squeezing me.

I'm worried about hurting her and making it good for her for all of two seconds before pleasure wraps around my spine and zaps my brain.

"I'm okay," she says when I don't immediately move.

"That makes one of us."

She laughs and the slight movement of her body nearly sends me over the edge, and I have to close my eyes and grind down on my back molars for a second to regain my composure. I move at a pace meant to keep me from coming, but that somehow tips Ginny over the edge. She looks up at me wide-eyed and gorgeous as she rides out her first orgasm.

Damn, she's beautiful.

I pull out and place a kiss to her lips and then turn her onto her stomach and lift her hips.

I bite one ass cheek and then kiss it before nudging the head of my cock inside her pussy. She pushes back into me. "Hold on, baby. This won't be as gentle."

She flashes me a grin over her shoulder. With one hand on her hip and the other at the base of her neck, I bury myself inside of her sweet heat.

We both shudder. My balls are heavy, and I resist the urge to pound into her like a jackhammer. Slowly, I ease in and out, finding a nice rhythm.

"Harder," she whispers so quietly it takes me a second to realize what she's asking.

"You're sure?"

She nods. "Fuck me hard like I know you want to."

Stars dot my vision and my voice is gruff. "Grab the headboard."

Her fingers find it in an instant. Her eagerness and the new angle gives new meaning to torturous pleasure. *Ermahgerd.*

I fuck her as hard as I've dreamed of doing, but with every thrust and every slap of skin against skin, it somehow feels more meaningful too. It's never felt this all-consuming before. I know

Ginny in a way I've never known anyone else and that makes this better in so many ways. I can read her body and the emotions on her face.

She owns me as she falls apart beneath me for a second time. I fight to hold off my orgasm so that I can keep watching her, but with two more hard thrusts, my eyes slam shut and I follow.

I wrap an arm around her waist and fall onto the bed with her tucked into my front. We're gasping for air together. I feel like I've landed in another dimension. This girl... fuck, *this girl*.

I really don't want to move, but I need to clean up and I know she'll want to, also.

I start to pull back and she grabs onto my forearm. "Don't go. Not yet."

"Just going to clean up. I'll be right back."

I slide out of bed and pad to the bathroom to wash up, grab a wet cloth and bring it back to her. She sits up and reaches for it.

"I got it."

She leans back on both elbows while I take care of her; she watches me with a sleepy smile. After getting rid of the rag, I climb back into bed with her.

Neither of us speaks as we lie there drifting off. A peacefulness I wasn't expecting after the day's events settles in.

"Heath," she says as I'm just about asleep.

"Yeah?"

"I don't think I'm bad at sex anymore."

"No, baby doll." I snicker. "You definitely aren't."

She yawns, snuggles into my side, and falls asleep in my arms.

THE NEXT MORNING I WAKE UP BEFORE GINNY AND HEAD downstairs. Rauthruss is already in the kitchen with a cup of coffee. He looks tired, hair sticking up everywhere.

"Long night?"

"Yeah, man. Real long night."

"How's Adam?"

"Sleeping hard. We've gotta get out of here soon though."

I nod and grab some coffee too.

His phone pings and he lets out a sigh. "What a weekend."

"That Carrie?"

"Yeah, she's pissed because I forgot to call her last night."

"Had a few things going on."

"No shit." He sighs. "I should call her, let her yell at me, and get it over with so I can start groveling."

"Sounds awesome." I chuckle as he heads outside.

I try to conjure an image of Ginny and me like that but can't summon it.

I take my coffee upstairs ready to wake my girl and enjoy the last moments before we head back. As I walk into Ginny's room, her voice carries through the bathroom from Adam's room. I glance in and see her legs hanging off the end of his bed and the bottoms of Adam's feet.

"Are you going to be okay?" she asks him.

"Yeah, I just can't believe it. They always seemed so solid. My whole life feels like a lie."

"That's a little dramatic."

"But seriously, if they can't work things out, what hope is there for anyone?"

"Oh, come on. You and Taryn are great. Me and Heath… it can work out."

"You and Heath." A deep, sarcastic laugh follows.

"Look, I know you're all anti-love right now, but don't rain on my parade. Heath is great."

"Sure, of course he is, Ginny. My issue with you two was never about him being a bad guy—he's not. Heath's fun and always up for a good time, but I've seen him go through a lot of women. Some he hooked up with more than once, most he didn't, but ultimately he moved on from all of them as easy as changing his underwear. I just don't want to see you get hurt again."

He's not wrong, but he's missing the thing that makes it different now. Ginny.

"Relax, we're good. Heath and I are…"

I'm holding my breath waiting for her to finish that sentence, but Adam lets out a long groan interrupting her.

"Oh, Jesus, you're in love with him."

"Stop it," she says playfully. It sounds like she tosses a pillow at him as her light laughter trickles from the next room. "But since you're being nosey, yes, I am. I love him, and I truly think what we have is special."

My hand tips forward and coffee spills on my bare toes. *Fuck.* I place the mug on Ginny's dresser, clean up the mess, and get dressed quickly. I manage to grab my stuff and head downstairs, heart in my throat, before either Ginny or Adam notices me.

Chapter Thirty-Three

GINNY

I walk out with the guys as they load up in Adam's Jeep. My brother looks as hungover as he smells. He slides into the passenger seat, Rhett gets behind the wheel, and Maverick hops into the back.

I follow Heath to the other side.

"Let me know how he is?" I ask, motioning with my head to Adam.

"We'll keep an eye on him," he promises. "We've got practice this afternoon. Hopefully that'll help."

"If he doesn't throw up all over the ice."

He makes a disgusted face and shifts from one foot to the other. I lean into him and close my eyes, and his arms wrap around me. Despite all the awful things that happened this weekend, I enjoyed being with Heath.

The Jeep starts up, and I know the guys need to get going.

"Later." He kisses my forehead and I step away.

The rest of the weekend is uneventful, a welcome change. Mom and I watch movies, I see a few of my friends from high school, I text with Heath between his practices, and I even have lunch with Mom and Dad together on Sunday before I head back.

After dropping my things at my dorm, I go to Reagan and Dakota's apartment.

"And all I did was eat turkey and watch college football," Reagan says when I've finished giving them the rundown of my crazy weekend.

"I saw Adam earlier," Dakota says from the kitchen where she's putting away groceries while Reagan and I sit in the living room. "He and Taryn looked like they were having a serious and depressing talk outside of the apartment. Trouble in paradise?"

"Oh no. I should probably check on him. I hope he didn't do anything stupid."

"Well, it has been what… three or four months? He's about due for a new girlfriend." Dakota smirks.

Maybe I'm turning into the new romantic of the family, but I really thought he and Taryn were a cute couple.

Reagan nudges my foot. "I want more details on you and Heath. So, he met the whole family?"

"Technically, yes. But it wasn't really like that. He was there as Adam's guest, not mine. Plus, with everything else going on, I don't think my parents even realized he snuck into my room at night."

"Ooooh. A sleepover! Fun." Dakota's eyes lit up from across the room. "Did you two finally…" She waggles her eyebrows.

A slow blush creeps up my face and I glance from friend to friend.

"Awww," Reagan says and tilts her head with a dreamy look on her face. Okay, maybe she's the romantic.

Dakota joins us in the living room. "You're totally gone for him."

There's little point in denying it. "Totally." I bury my head in my hands. "He's just so… perfect."

Dakota's eyebrows jump.

"Okay fine, not perfect, but the way I feel when we're together—*that's* perfect. Don't worry. Adam's already given me the 'Heath doesn't do relationships' talk."

"That was before you," Reagan insists.

I look to Dakota. I know she won't bullshit me. She shrugs. "If you'd asked me before you, I would have laughed in your face. Now, I'm not sure. Only one way to find out."

"You think I should tell him?" I squeak.

"Why is that so crazy?" Reagan laughs.

"I don't want to ruin what we have. What if it's too soon?"

"You'd be okay continuing to hook up even if you knew that's all it was to him? That he didn't feel the same way?"

A heavy pit settles in my stomach. "No, probably not, but things are great. I don't want to ruin it."

Dakota snorts. "Isn't love supposed to make everything better?"

"Yeah, yeah." I lean back and wave a hand of indifference.

"Well, I think you should tell him and soon." Reagan stands. "Do I look okay?"

I nod. Even if I couldn't see her, I'd know she does. Reagan always looks beautiful. "Date?"

"Yeah, a guy from my speech class. We're going to dinner." Her dimples pop out.

"You look gorgeous, as usual, babe," Dakota tells her. "Condoms in the purse? Phone charged in case you need to make a getaway?"

Reagan rolls her eyes. "I'm all set." Her phone buzzes. "He's here. Bye!"

Dakota and I watch her go and then I let out a sigh and lay my head on her shoulder.

"Wanna watch a movie or are you heading over to Heath's?" she asks.

"Nope, he has team stuff this evening. They're working out or watching film or something. I'm all yours."

THE NEXT DAY I CORNER ADAM OUTSIDE OF HIS LAST MORNING class. He gives me a half-hearted smile that tells me everything I need to know about how he's doing.

"What are you doing here?" he asks as he wraps me into a one-armed hug.

"You didn't respond to my texts." I extend both arms around his middle and squeeze tightly.

"Sorry." He doesn't bother offering an excuse.

"It's okay." We walk down the sidewalk slowly. "Have you talked to Mom or Dad since you got back?"

"Not yet. Mom called while I was in class."

It's a weird switch of roles for us with me worrying about him, but I want to be there for him the same way he's always been for me. I nudge him. "It's going to be okay. I know it won't be the same, but they'll still be here for us. Plus, you've got me."

He grins.

"Anyway, the real reason I came to find you was to see what you were doing tonight. We need a night out. A fun night with all our friends to let loose and forget about parent drama."

"I don't know. Maybe. Let me see what's going on tonight. It is a Monday night after all."

"Monday is a perfectly good day to drink. Live a little, bro."

"Bro?" He hitches the backpack higher on his shoulder. "You sound like Heath."

We get to his car and he quirks a brow as I open the passenger side door.

"I mean, since you're going home anyway, can you give me a ride?"

He shakes his head. "Get in."

At the apartment, I walk back toward Heath's room. He's sitting at his desk in front of his laptop.

"Hey," I say cheerily as I enter.

One side of his mouth pulls up. "Hey. Did I forget we were hanging out?"

"Nope, thought I'd surprise you. I didn't hear back from you last night after your hockey stuff."

"Yeah, sorry, I crashed."

I go to him and he swivels to make room for me on his lap. "Let's go out tonight."

"It's Monday."

"Why does everyone keep using that as an excuse?"

He chuckles softly.

I take a deep breath. The girls are right. I need to make sure we're on the same page. "Also, I have something I want to talk to you about later."

He stiffens under me. Okay, that was probably not the smoothest. "Don't worry, it's nothing too crazy. A proposition if you will."

God, now he probably thinks I want to chain him to the bed and peg him.

His phone pings on his desk, Maverick's name flashes on the screen with a text. "All right, sure. I'll text you later. I've gotta check on Maverick. He didn't make conditioning this morning. He's got the flu or something. He hasn't been by all day."

I stand to let him up. "Well, then he really must be sick."

He takes a step toward the door and then backtracks and brushes his lips against mine before hurrying out to go check on Maverick.

Chapter Thirty-Four

HEATH

Mav? Buddy, where are you?" I call as I enter his apartment. He's got a one-bedroom ground level unit. On a normal day it's already darker than ours upstairs, but today all the lights are off, the TV too, so it's like a cave.

The place is awesome. Nice leather furniture, a huge TV that takes up the better part of one wall, he's even got throw pillows. Why he always wants to hang at our place is beyond me.

Charli barks and I follow the sound to the bedroom where my buddy is on his back with the comforter and blanket thrown off the bed and an arm over his eyes. Charli lies at the end of the mattress near his feet.

"You don't look so good." I step closer and then back. "Or smell so good."

"I think I threw up a kidney." His voice is raspy and pained.

"What can I do? Do you need water? Soup? I can make a call about getting you a new kidney."

A knock at the door has me looking back through the living room to the front door. "Are you expecting someone else?"

"It's food. Can you grab it?"

I cross through the apartment and open the door, taking a deep breath of clean, uncontaminated air. After thanking the delivery guy, I take the bag of food back to the sick room.

"Here ya go."

"Not for me." He heaves. "Oh, just the smell makes me want to hurl again. It's for you, so you'll stay with me."

"You didn't need to bribe me."

"Look, I know I'm your favorite person, but eventually your stomach would have convinced you to leave me."

I chuckle and take the bag back out to the kitchen. "There is a lot of food in here."

"You're a hungry bitch."

He's in the same position, but Charli has moved up to his hip and Maverick strokes her with the hand closest.

"What do you need?"

"I just want to lie here until the room stops moving. Tell me a story."

I take a seat on the floor near the door and lean my back up against the wall. I like the dude, but he smells, and I don't want whatever he has. "A story?"

"Anything to distract me." He peeks out from under his arm and then reaches over to his nightstand and tosses me his Shakespeare textbook. "Read to me. Do the funny voices."

"I thought you were done with Shakespeare."

"I am. We're on Shelley now, but that book is all the way in my backpack."

I hesitate.

"Come on. Pleeeease? I dig the rhyming shit; it's beautiful."

"All right, all right." I open the book and start.

Maverick falls asleep about five minutes in, which is good because reading sappy words about love is the last thing I want to be doing. I go out to the living room and eat, feed Charli, and then take her out for a quick walk.

Back inside, I take my spot in his room sitting on the floor and I must pass out because the next thing I know, Charli is licking my face, and Maverick is standing in front of me with a grin.

"Feeling better?" I ask, nudging Charli away and wiping a hand across my slobbery cheek.

"I think so. I'm gonna try to eat."

I follow him out to the kitchen, and he heats up some of the Chinese he ordered. We sit on stools at the counter. The smell of food has me heating up a plate too a few minutes later. Ginny texted while I was asleep to let me know the plans for tonight, meeting up at The Hideout with our friends. I'm real nervous about whatever she wants to talk to me about, but I do my best to push it out of my mind for now.

Mav finishes about half the food on his plate and then pats his stomach. "Thanks for hanging."

"Yeah, of course."

"You're not as hot as Nanny Laura, but it did the trick."

"Nanny Laura?"

"She was my favorite. Had these gigantic boobs that were like pillows." He nuzzles his head to the side like he's remembering it. "She'd sing to me when I was sick or when I was upset—which was a lot because Dad was always flaking on shit. I think I got more hugs from her in the year or so that she was my nanny than I have from him my entire life. Parents are bullshit."

I'm quiet. Don't really know what to say. For all the shitty things that happened growing up, physical contact was never in short supply. Sometimes my mom clung to me all day as if I was the only thing keeping her connected to the planet.

My stomach twists and I push away my plate.

"Sorry, man, didn't mean to go dark."

"Nah, it's fine. I don't feel so well." I stand and I break out in a cool sweat, my mouth waters.

"Ah shit," Mav says right before I take off in a dead run toward the bathroom.

AFTER PUKING FOR THE BETTER PART OF THREE HOURS, I JOIN Maverick in the living room. I stripped down to my boxers—everything else is wet from sweat.

"God, you weren't kidding. All my organs feel like they've shifted. Is that a thing?"

"No clue." He nods with his head toward the kitchen. "Ginny brought soup and Jell-O."

"Ginny was here?"

"Your phone was going off, so I texted her."

I find my phone on the counter and see that she did text several times about tonight and then to tell me to feel better and let her know if I need anything.

"She wanted me to tell you that she'd be by later to check in." He shakes his head. "That Ginny, she's a peach."

"She's the best," I say because even though I'm a little freaked out, I know it's true.

I text her back to thank her for the food and tell her not to bother coming again until we're on the mend. The last thing she needs is to catch whatever this is. I feel like I've been run over by a bus. I take a seat in the recliner. The cool leather feels nice against my skin. I'm pretty sure I have a fever.

"I need a Ginny." Maverick sighs and Charli whines.

"I think Charli would take issue with getting kicked out of your bed for a chick."

We spend the late afternoon and evening watching TV. Just when I think things are taking a turn for the better, one of us gets sick again. We reek. The whole apartment probably does, but I've lost the ability to smell it.

Ginny continues to text, but I don't respond. Nobody needs to be around this. I miss her though. Weird to admit to myself how much I've gotten used to having her around. That even though I'm freaked about her loving me, I still want her.

I've had girls that I hung out with, not exactly friends but ones that were part of my circle of friends, and girls I've hooked up with for a month or two, but I've never had one that ticks both those boxes. I'm delirious enough I think about calling her and telling her that, but something tells me I'd fumble up the message. *Thanks for letting me do you, and also for being cool enough I want to be with you even when we're not naked. Let's keep things like they are. Cool?*

Shakespeare, I am not.

As I lie there, alternating sweating and then shivering, I think about her and what I'm going to say when she tells me she loves me. That's what she wants to talk to me about, right? Is she expecting me to say it back? And if I don't, what does it really change? Nothing? Everything?

My mom was quick to tell me she loved me, still is. And, yeah, I believe she means it, and even meant it then when she barely knew what day of the week it was, but it always felt like the words *I love you* came as a substitute for *I'm going to do right by you.*

Things with Ginny are amazing, and I don't want this pure and good thing we have to become an excuse to hurt one another when we could do better.

Fuck, I don't even know if I'm making sense. My head is fuzzy and my stomach aches.

I wake up sometime later that night, stuck to the recliner. Mav must have thrown a blanket over me and gone to bed because he's not here and I'm tucked in like a child.

The next forty-eight hours is much the same. I wake up Thursday morning finally feeling like I might be able to get up, but my entire body hurts. I'm laying here staring up at the ceiling when I notice Ginny on the couch.

"You're alive."

"Barely."

She sits up. "I tried to text a few times to check on you."

"My phone died. I wasn't in much shape to talk anyway."

"Do you want me to stay with you? I brought some more soup and Jell-O. It's in the kitchen." She jabs a thumb in that direction. "Do you want some?"

"You didn't need to do that. I'm fine. I just want to lie here for a minute before I go to practice."

"You're going to practice? Can't you take another day off?"

"Could, but I've played in worse shape. I'll be fine." We've got Vermont this weekend and I don't want to miss it.

She smiles and it hits me in the gut. Either that or I'm gonna be sick again.

"Okay, well, I'm going back to my dorm before class. Call me later?"

She looks uncertain and I hate that. Hate it but can't seem to bring myself to reassure her. I also don't want to get much closer in case I'm still contagious.

"Yeah, of course, I'll call you later tonight. I have a feeling after practice I'm going to need a nap."

"Okay." She steps back and gives me one of those sweet, Ginny smiles. "Feel better."

DECEMBER

Chapter Thirty-Five

GINNY

I'm sitting at the bar at The Hideout waiting for my friends and brother. Reagan's the first to show.

"Hey." I stand to hug her. "Where's Dakota?"

"She wasn't done studying for her biology test. She said to tell you she was sorry and that she'd make it up to you."

"Well, boo. I was hoping she'd come. Adam's running late and the rest of the guys didn't feel like going out. It feels like everyone is bailing." Monday night was a bust after Maverick and Heath got sick, but I was hoping tonight we could all finally hang out.

"Actually, I'm glad I have you alone. I need to talk to you."

"Okay." We sit and when the bartender comes over, she orders two shots of RumChata.

"You're making me nervous, Rea."

The shots come and she downs one without waiting for me.

I start to chuckle. "Woah, there, it can't be that—"

"I like your brother."

Her words hit me slowly, but she doesn't give me time to respond anyway.

"I'm sorry I lied, but we'd just met, and I didn't want you to think I was some weirdo or that I was pretending to be your friend because of Adam."

His name makes it all finally click.

"Your crush, the hockey player, is my brother?"

"Yes, and I'm going to tell him tonight, but I wanted to tell you first." She eyes the second shot. "Do you need that or do I?"

"I'm not upset. Adam would be lucky to have someone like you, but you can't tell him tonight."

"Why not?" Her brown eyes crinkle at the corners as she draws her eyebrows together.

"Because I invited Taryn and she just walked in. I'm sorry. I didn't know." As I stand to greet my brother's girlfriend, I see Reagan down the last shot.

"Hey," Taryn says tentatively.

"Hi, Taryn," I say and we hug. "Thanks for coming."

She laughs lightly. "You didn't leave me much choice. You said it was life or death."

"Maybe that was a little dramatic, but it is important." I glance to either side of me, but there's nowhere for her to sit.

Reagan hops out of her seat. "Here, you can have mine. I'm going to… go. I just realized I need to be somewhere."

"Are you sure?" I ask. I feel awful, not that I could have predicted this.

"I'll call you later."

Taryn takes a seat and I blow out a long breath. Best to just dive right in. "Whatever my brother did or said… he's an idiot. He's going through some things right now, so he's not to be trusted."

Her face twists into a surprised expression. "You mean your

278

parents separating?"

"He told you?"

"Yeah, of course. He's really torn up about it."

"Exactly. Don't let him push you away because of it. I think he just needs some time."

She smiles sweetly. "I agree, but that's not why we broke up."

"It's not?"

"No." She shakes her head. "It probably was the catalyst, but it wasn't the reason."

Well, shit. I guess this is what I get for meddling. "Oh." I slump in my chair. "You're sure? You two seemed great together."

"We are. Your brother is fantastic, and I really like him, but I'm transferring at semester and neither of us really wanted to try to manage a long-distance thing."

"Oh." Well, shit. "I didn't know."

"I just decided before Thanksgiving break. I got into a really competitive design program at my dream college." Her face lights up.

"Wow, well, congratulations."

"Thank you."

For the next half hour, I listen as she tells me about her plans and the program at her new school. The more we talk, the more I like her and the sadder I am that she's leaving. We part with a hug and a promise to keep in touch. I don't know if we actually will, but it's more than I can say for my relationships with most of Adam's ex-girlfriends.

I've got a bunch of texts from Adam apologizing for not being able to make it. This night is a giant failure.

I call Heath on my way to his apartment, but he doesn't answer.

Since he got sick, he's been keeping me away for fear I'd catch it, but right now, I'm willing to risk it to lay in his arms.

Noise filters out, laughter and loud voices, as I head up the stairs to their door. I knock twice before walking in. Rhett, Maverick, and Heath are in the living room. All eyes are on the TV and whatever video game they're playing. Beer cans line the coffee table. It's far from the scene I was expecting.

When they finally notice me, Maverick and Rhett's glassy stares and big smiles give me some idea of just how drunk they are. Heath doesn't look drunk, but I'm still a little irritated that they're all hanging out together when I tried to plan a night out with all of us.

"Genevieve!" Maverick calls. He's got a bottle in one hand and a controller in the other. "Come be on my team. They're kicking my ass."

Rhett puts his controller down and runs a hand through his dirty blond hair. "You can take my place. I'm out, boys. I need to call Carrie." He stands and heads to his room, leaving me with Heath and Maverick.

"Need another?" Mav stands, sways, and then walks to the kitchen. He grabs a beer and holds it up.

"No, thanks," Heath says. He motions me over to him and holds his arms out.

I go to him and climb into his lap. As he wraps his arms around me, I snuggle in close and breathe him in.

"Hey," I whisper into his jaw. He's unshaven and I love the way his scruff feels against my smooth skin. "Feeling better?"

"Mhmm." He places a thumb under my chin and lifts my mouth to his and places a quick kiss on my lips. I melt into him.

"I only had two beers and look at me, I'm a lightweight now. Sorry that we didn't make it out. How was it?"

"A total bust. You didn't miss anything."

"You two wanna cuddle?" Maverick asks. "Make a little Mav sandwich?"

"No chance," Heath says and stands, holding me in his arms. He's unsteady on his feet, but somehow he carries me without falling or dropping me.

"Night, Mav," I call over Heath's shoulder.

He kicks the door closed and deposits me on his bed and lies on top of me, burying his head in my neck. He kisses the spot. "You smell nice."

"You feel nice," I say, lifting my hips into the hard bulge in his pants.

I slip my hands under his T-shirt and up over his pecs. He leans up enough for me to pull the material all the way over his head. I love Heath's body. Every muscle and every ridge. The light smattering of hair covering his chest and the defined abs and V that disappears into his jeans.

A shiver of pleasure shoots through me as he kisses my neck and collarbone, first on one side and then the other.

I unbutton his jeans and slide the zipper down. As my palm meets skin, I chuckle.

"Had to freeball it," he says and leans up to give me a sheepish grin. "Haven't done laundry since I got back."

I free his cock from his pants. "Convenient."

He hisses and then moans as I slide my hand down his length. "I may never wear boxers again. Fuck. I missed you."

My insides are total mush when he voices his feelings. Even if

I am touching his dick while he's saying it.

"It's only been a few days."

"And your point is?" he asks, eyes closed and hips bucking into my palm.

I pause and his eyes open and lock onto mine. It's an opening to tell him how I feel, but instead of taking it, I slide down the bed and wrap my lips around the head of his cock.

AFTERWARD, WE'RE LYING ON THE BED CURLED UP TOGETHER. Heath's eyelids keep shutting even as he tells me he's not tired.

"Let me get you some water and Tylenol." I start to stand, but he captures my hand and tugs me back down.

"No. I don't need you to do that. People are always trying to take care of me. I just want you to lay here with me."

"You are very stubborn."

His mouth pulls up into a smile, eyes still closed.

"You know, it's okay to let people do nice things for you. It doesn't mean you're incapable. That's how relationships work." I bite at the corner of my lip. "Speaking of, I've been trying to talk to you since we got back from break, but with everything that's happened, we haven't had a chance. Maybe tomorrow we can hang out, just the two of us?"

His lids flutter open and those dark blue eyes focus on me. "It's okay, Ginny, I already know. I overheard you talking to Adam."

"You know what?"

"At your parents' house. I was in your room that morning

before we left, and I overheard you tell Adam that you… how you feel about me."

"Oh." *Crap*. Embarrassed, stilted laughter slips out and I sit up. "Why didn't you say anything before?"

"I didn't know what to say." His lips turn down at the corners and then his tongue darts out to wet them. "Ginny… I like you a lot."

All the blood drains from my face. The way he says it and his expression—it's excruciating. *Like*. He didn't tell me because he doesn't feel the same.

I'm absolutely horrified, and fleeing is the first thing that comes to mind. Get out of here before I start crying.

"I forgot how honest you are when you've been drinking." I try to laugh it off, but tears sting my eyes. I stand and look for my clothes. "I'm going. Let's talk tomorrow when you're sober."

"Please don't go. This is why I didn't bring it up before. I didn't want you to say it and be hurt if I didn't say it back. What we have is great and it's just a bullshit word." He runs a hand through his hair, making the dark strands stand up, then the other hand joins it. I love his hair. It's always such a beautiful mess. Even now when he's breaking my heart.

"Love is a bullshit word?" I shake my head in disbelief. "This is why I told Adam and not you. I thought it might be too soon and I didn't want to pressure you or make things weird. I had no intention of telling you that I love you." I swallow. I can't describe how much I hate that the first time I utter those three words to him, it's like this. I feel completely shattered that I've been his unknowing pity case while he's been secretly trying to figure out how to let me down easy.

"No, that's not what I'm saying. It isn't that you…" He pauses. "Wait, you weren't? But you said that you wanted to talk. I just assumed that's what it was about. I've been worrying about it all week."

"Oh my god." I glance to the ceiling and try to calm the anger rising. When I look back to him, I can no longer keep my eyes from welling. Hot, angry tears.

"Fuck, that came out wrong," he says.

"I was going to ask you to be my boyfriend, you big jerk."

His brows draw together. "Oh."

"But it's really nice to know you've been stressing about me using the L-word, heaven forbid. What an awful thing for you to cope with."

Anger. Yes, I need more anger to keep from feeling the sadness.

He gets to his feet. His jeans are on but unbuttoned and they slide down on his hips as he starts toward me. "Fuck, Ginny. I thought I already was your boyfriend."

"Yeah, well, we've never talked about it. Hence, *the talk*."

"I'm sorry."

"For what? Not loving me or thinking the whole concept of it is ludicrous?" My voice cracks.

He groans and he runs those big hands through his hair again while he struggles to find the right words. But it's too late. What could he possibly say now? Any illusion I had that he might feel the same way, today or someday in the future, is now gone. Dating a guy who isn't ready for a serious commitment is one thing, but once you tell them you love them (even by accident), there's no going back and pretending it's just a casual fling.

"This isn't going to work."

"Don't say that. Forget everything I said in the past five minutes. Start over. Ask me to be your boyfriend." He closes the distance between us and frames my face with his hands. "Ask me, Genevieve," he pleads.

He makes a strangled sound deep in his throat as I pull away and finish getting dressed, tossing the T-shirt of his I was wearing on the bed, yanking on my own clothes, and slipping into my shoes. I think he might say something else to try to stop me, but he doesn't. He just watches me prepare to leave, looking helpless. Before I go, I have to say it at least once—out loud and to him, if only for myself.

"I love you, Heath." He flinches. "I'm sorry if that's too much for you to deal with, but I do, and I don't want to just forget it."

Chapter Thirty-Six

HEATH

I haven't been this hungover in years." Mav drops on the couch and chugs half the Gatorade bottle in his hand with one long drink. "Getting drunk after being sick and hardly eating all week, I've basically got the tolerance of a high school chick."

I'm silent and he nudges my foot on the coffee table. "What's up with you? You've been quiet all morning."

"I'm fine."

"Girl fine or really fine?"

"I said I was fine."

His brows lift and he smiles, but he drops it. He finishes off his drink and stands. "Ready to go to campus? I'm starving."

"Let's go out for breakfast today instead of the dining hall."

"Yeah, that sounds rad. I want pancakes. Text Ginny and we can swing by and pick her up."

"She doesn't want to come."

"What? Of course she does. I'll text her."

"No, don't. We're not... she's..." Jesus, I can't even finish a sentence that puts an end to whatever we were.

Maverick stops and the hand holding his phone falls to his side. "What the fuck did you do, Payne?"

I'd like to resent his automatic assumption that I'm at fault, but of course I am. I let out a giant sigh. "I'll tell you over pancakes."

HE DOESN'T PRESS ME TO TALK UNTIL WE'VE BOTH GOT A HEAPING stack of pancakes on our plates. Only then does he ask what happened. I fill him in on last night, unable to eat more than a bite or two.

"That's cold."

"What was I supposed to say?"

"I'm not sure." He shrugs and takes a large bite of his food. He looks thoughtful as he chews and then swallows. "You really think love is bullshit?"

"Don't you?" If anyone would understand, I figured it'd be Maverick. His childhood was as fucked up as mine, just in a totally different way.

"No, man. Love is beautiful."

"How the fuck would you know?" Damn, I need a muzzle lately. "Sorry, that came out wrong, but you know what I mean. Who's ever said it to you and not screwed you over?"

"Well, you've never said it, but you love me and you've never screwed me over."

"That's not the same."

"Isn't it?"

"Not unless you're over there thinking about me naked."

His lips part and pull into a smile. "Relax, you're not nearly kinky enough for me."

"But seriously, man. You think there's someone out there that's capable of speaking the words to you and really meaning it? No strings, no ulterior motives, two people who care deeply and want to support one another?"

"Isn't that basically what you and Ginny had before you blew it up?" He sets an elbow on the table and waves his fork around. "I'm not much for trying to live up to other people's expectations. I know what it means to me and yeah." He shrugs. "At least I hope so. Otherwise, it's going to be me and you heading to the Early Bird special together. The only question you need to ask yourself is, do you believe Ginny means it?"

"Yeah, I think she does. She's never given me any reason to doubt her." I toss my napkin on the table. "I'm not hungry."

He takes my plate and I watch as he inhales my food and then sits back with a contented sigh.

"I don't know what to do. I want to be with her, but I can't tell her I… you know, when the words make me want to throw myself off a cliff."

"But you do?"

"If I didn't hate the word and everything in my past associated with it? Yeah, that's probably how I'd define it."

"Big gesture. Huge. I'm talking Kanye-antics."

"I think I'll just try to talk to her first."

"Talking got you into this mess," he points out.

WHEN WE GET TO CAMPUS, MAVERICK STARTS TOWARD CLASS. I'M going by the dorm first to see if I can find Ginny. Something tells me she didn't show up at the dining hall this morning either.

"Good luck, buddy. Try not to use the word like."

I flip him off. He turns and I call after him. "Hey, Mav."

My buddy glances over his shoulder.

"You can always count me in for the Early Bird special. No matter what."

I move at a clip across campus and jog up the stairs to the second floor.

I knock on the door and wait. No answer. Knock again.

"Ginny? Are you there? It's Heath. Open up if you're there. Please." It's quiet on the other side and I rest my head against the door. "I'm so sorry."

A few people pass by in the hall and give me weird looks, and the door continues to mock me by staying shut. I blow out a breath, the magnitude of how badly I screwed this up makes my whole body ache something fierce.

I'm caught off guard when the door finally opens, and I stumble forward. My heart soars and then plummets when it's Ava's face that appears and not Ginny's.

"She's not here," Ginny's shy roommate says, her cheeks turning pink.

"Right, okay, could you give her a message?"

She nods, prompting me. Shit, what's the message? I'm sorry that I'm a giant prick doesn't really tell her anything she didn't already know, even if it's accurate.

"Just ask her to call me." I step back and then add, "Please?"

Chapter Thirty-Seven

GINNY

T hank you for doing this one with me," I say to Dakota as the group of local elementary students line up for a tour of the Hall of Fame. It's my first day back working after being locked in the hype room. I'm already a mess from last night and the idea of being in there by myself again is scary.

"Of course. These guys might look little but trust me, it's going to take two of us plus their teacher to keep them in line." She gives me a reassuring smile and steps forward and introduces herself.

I fall back and let her do the majority of the talking. I'm not feeling particularly chatty, but I answer questions and help keep the kids from wandering off. It's a totally different experience than the recruits get, less focused and more about letting the kids walk around awestruck by catching glimpses of college athletes working out or walking around campus. They look up to them like celebrities and it's pretty heartwarming. But since it's less intense than our recruit tours, I'm able to fade into the background, and today I'm extremely thankful for that.

When we walk into the hype room, Dakota goes first, the kids follow, and I bring up the end of the line. She glances to me as I enter. I nod to let her know I'm okay. Maybe the anxiousness I thought I'd feel coming in here again is dulled by the deep aching pain I've had since I walked out of Heath's apartment last night, but I'm able to stand and watch the video without panicking. It's a generic video, encompassing all sports, but since hockey is such a big deal at Valley, there are still lots of times that Heath's face splashes on the screen. Each and every time it feels like someone's pouring alcohol into an open wound.

I'm sad and mad, flipping between the two so frequently even I don't know which one is the prominent emotion. Does he really think we can keep dating like nothing happened? Even if I could get over the idea that he doesn't feel the same, and likely never will, I'd be a wreck waiting for the day he freaked out again or decided to move on. There's really only two ways a relationship can go, and he took one of those options away. When you know how something is going to end, it's harder to enjoy the moment.

As the video stops on the final frame, a drone shot overhead of campus, the kids' faces are lit up with joy and wonder. I step to the door so I can be the first out.

Dakota and I take them to the football field and let them loose to run around in the big, open space.

"How was it?" she asks as we stand on the fifty-yard line.

"I don't know if I'll ever feel the same about that room, but it was okay."

"Listen, I've got it from here. Take off, go see Heath, or go lay in bed and cry… whatever you need to do."

"You're sure?"

"Definitely. Five more minutes of them sprinting up and down the field and I can hand them back to their teacher."

I hug her. "Thank you."

I take off for my dorm with the intent of trying to nap. Needless to say, I spent last night tossing and turning, so I'm not only emotionally exhausted, but physically too. However, as soon as I fall into my bed and pull up the covers, I get a 911 text from Reagan.

I get back up and trudge across campus. I find her in the back of the theater in their dressing room. Her hair is in curlers and she's wearing her green silky robe.

"Hey, what's going on?"

"Ms. Morris fell and broke her wrist. She's out and now I don't have anyone to do my makeup. Can you help? We have our dress rehearsal in thirty minutes."

I'd gotten the first part from her text message and had come prepared to do her makeup, but dress rehearsal? The look on her face is pleading, though, so I suck it up. "I've never done stage makeup like that, but I can try."

"Thank you!"

The dressing room in the theater is a large open room with a long counter that extends on two walls with lighted mirrors. Stools are around the room in disarray. Some tucked under the counter, others have clothes and makeup bags on them, and the rest are occupied by girls as they get ready.

Reagan sits; her cosmetics litter the space in front of her. "So, what happened with Heath? Dakota heard from Rhett that Heath was not looking great at their morning skate."

I set down my backpack and add my makeup to the counter. "It was a very long night after you left."

I fill her in while I add primer to her face.

"All of this happened last night? And you haven't heard from him since?"

"Ava said he came by the dorm looking for me."

She smiles and tries to shoo me off. "Go. I can do my own face."

"No way. I've got you. Let's just talk about something else."

"Okay. Like what?"

"Like how nervous I am right now."

"What? Why? You've done my makeup lots of times. It always looks great."

"But the lights and the people..." My hands tremble. "I'm nervous and I'm not even the one who has to go out there."

Her sweet laughter relaxes me. "It's only a dress rehearsal."

As I work, she studies the script in front of her. I've heard her running lines with Dakota enough that I know she's already got it memorized, but I decide it's best not to mess with whatever process she has.

When she finally looks up, I'm ready to add another coat of mascara.

"Oh, wow, Ginny."

"Is it too much?"

"It's amazing." She turns her face to look at each side more closely. "You're a miracle worker."

"I don't know about that but thank you." Mascara wand in hand, I tell her, "Look down."

Instead of heading back to my dorm or going to class, I stay for the rehearsal. The play is a modern take on *A Christmas Story*, and Reagan plays the Ghost of Christmas Present. The green gown she wears could have been made specifically with her in mind. She looks exquisite. That's my first thought, but the longer she's on the stage, the more I fall into her character.

I smile as the clock strikes midnight, she bows her head and slowly walks backward until she disappears behind the curtain.

After the rehearsal, she comes down off the front of the stage and finds me in the third row.

"What did you think?"

I pull her into a tight hug. "You are so talented, Reagan." I let her go to look her in the eye, so she knows how much I mean it, and then I hug her again.

A woman who'd been sitting in the row ahead of me turns and walks toward us. Her blonde hair is pulled up into a tight bun and she wears red-framed glasses that she takes off when she reaches us. She has an air of sophistication and also looks like she might cut a bitch if necessary. "Really well done, Reagan. You found the lighting up there really well." She steps closer and inspects my friend's face. "Your makeup…" She makes a little humming noise in her throat. "Who did you use?"

"Oh, uh, I did it. I'm sorry if it isn't—"

"It looks amazing," she assures me. She tips her head to Reagan. "It needs to be a little darker to read at the back of the house, but it suits you. Great job today. See you tomorrow."

"Thank you, Dr. Rossen."

When she's gone, Reagan grabs my hand and squeals. "You did it."

"That woman is scary. Who is she?"

"She's the director."

"Well, she is not someone I want to cross."

"She's made more than one person cry since she took over last year. Come on, let me buy you coffee as a thank you."

We stay on campus and go to University Hall. It's busy with a late afternoon rush, but we order from the café and find a small table near the door.

"I'm so relieved that's over."

"Don't you have two real shows this weekend?"

"Yes, but the rehearsal is the only time I really get nervous. It's harder to be on when you're staring out into an empty theater."

"I so don't get that."

She smiles. "Thank you again. You might have been fleeing the Heath situation, but it benefited me greatly."

"Anytime." I take a sip of my coffee. "So, are we going to talk about that thing you said last night?"

She looks down to the table. "I was hoping we could pretend I never said a peep."

"Like you've been trying to pretend you don't have a thing for my brother all semester?"

"Longer than that," she mumbles.

I'm grinning ear to ear when she finally looks up at me. "I think you should go for it. He and Taryn are done for good. She's transferring at the end of the semester. Now's your shot."

"I don't know. Now that you and I are so close, wouldn't it be weird?"

I consider it for a few moments. "No, I don't think so. Not unless we make it weird."

"It's probably not even worth worrying about. Honestly, he hasn't noticed me in the three years we've known each other. I don't think he sees me like that."

"Only one way to find out."

"Listen to you, dishing out advice while you're hiding from your boyfriend."

"I'm not hiding... I'm giving us some time to breathe."

"And?"

"I prefer breathing his air."

I TURN MY PHONE ON SILENT, STUFF IT IN A DESK DRAWER, AND bury myself in schoolwork all afternoon. I don't allow myself to think about anything else. That is until a pounding on my door breaks my concentration. My heart is in my throat waiting for Heath's voice on the other side, but it's Adam that calls, "Ginny, open up."

I scramble off my bed and fling the door open. "Hey, what are you doing here?"

"I've been calling you all day."

"Oh, uh, I turned my phone on silent while I caught up on schoolwork. What's up?"

"I heard about last night."

"Oh, that."

"Yeah, oh that." He moves my books out of the way and sits on my bed. "I'm sure it's payback for meddling in your relationship with Heath, but I still can't believe you went to so much trouble to get Taryn and me back together."

Ooooh, right. *That*.

I sit and pull my pillow into my lap. "I know I overstepped. I thought you were having a reaction to Mom and Dad and I wanted to help. You've always looked out for me and I wanted to do the same for once."

"Taryn said as much."

"Are you mad?"

"No, I get it."

"I'm sorry about you and Taryn."

"Yeah, me too."

"On the plus side, I know lots of girls who will be thrilled you're single again." One in particular, but that's not my secret to tell.

His chest lifts and falls with a quiet chuckle. "I think I'm going to try being single for a change. With everything going on, I think the universe might be sending me a sign."

"Single, huh? I can't picture it."

"Me neither." He leans so his back rests against the concrete wall.

"I don't think I'm doing as well with Mom and Dad as I thought either. I came back and threw myself into making plans with our friends because I wanted so badly to pretend everything was normal. But it's not. I think it's going to be weird for a while no matter what. Plus, uh, Heath and I are... I don't even know."

"Yeah, that's actually why I'm here, but I figured that wouldn't get me in the door."

"You know?"

"One look at Heath this morning and I think we all knew something was up. Wanna tell me what happened?"

"The short version? He overheard me telling you that I loved him, freaked out, told me love was bullshit, and I ran."

"Why did you run? That's not like you."

"Because I was embarrassed. Do you know what it's like to tell someone you love them and have them not return the sentiment?"

"No." He shakes his head. "But I'm sure I've had a lot of people say it and not mean it. It's a risk either way."

"You know, I never thought about it before, but you're like the bravest person I know. You jump from girlfriend to girlfriend—"

He groans.

"Let me finish." I punch his leg. "You keep putting yourself out there no matter how many times it doesn't work. Maybe it's a *little* excessive, but definitely brave."

He rubs at the back of his neck. "Well, I guess that's one way to look at it."

We fall silent and I lean my head on his shoulder. The alarm on his phone sounds and I sit straight.

"I gotta go," he says. "Are you coming to the game?"

"I'm not sure. Probably."

"It's funny how even when you're pissed, you can't help but show up to support him."

"It's *you* I'm supporting."

"Mhmmm."

I roll my eyes.

"Are you gonna be okay?" He stops at the door and regards me seriously.

"Yeah, I will." I blow out a breath. "I was perfectly happy with our fun, college fling until he found out I love him. Freaking love."

He scrunches up his face. "And on that note, I'm out." He opens the door and winks back at me. "Later, G."

Chapter Thirty-Eight

HEATH

When we take the ice, I automatically look for Ginny in her usual seat. She's not there and the knife in my gut twists.

Vermont is tough. They've got a freshman, Lex Vonne, who's almost as fast as I am, and their defense is big and mean.

"I played against Vonne in high school," Adam says. "He was just a skinny kid who could barely stay upright back then."

We watched tape last weekend on Vermont and Jordan and Adam filled us in as best they could. All three of them are from Arizona, and Jordan went to high school with Vonne, playing together all four years. No one can believe the progress he's made. It seems the New England air agrees with him because every game he just gets better.

"Yeah, well, looks like he's improved. A lot."

"No shit." Adam laughs as we watch him warm up, looking steady and sharp.

The game matches our pace, a brutal intensity that's exactly what I need tonight. Neither team scores in the first period. I've skated nearly half of those twenty minutes and I'm sucking air, but the burn of my lungs is nothing compared to the feeling I get when I glance at Ginny's empty seat.

Coach gives us his usual quick and straightforward pep talk between periods. He's not big on grand speeches, but his words are always effective.

Vermont's goalie is one of the best in the country, not that we're making it hard on him. We're losing the puck before we can even do anything with it. I get a pass from Maverick and use some of my aggression on a mean slapshot. It's wide and I swear I feel him grin underneath that fucking mask.

The second line comes in and I get a breather and a moment to collect myself.

"You good?" Mav asks.

"Good enough to finish this," I grunt out. And then go find Ginny.

"Let's go then."

When we jump the boards it's another minute of skating my ass off before Vermont scores and the Valley crowd groans their disapproval.

We go into the third period down by one. Like some sort of masochist, I continue to glance to the spot Ginny's occupied at every home game. Every time I look is like another punch to the gut, but I can't stop myself.

"Payne!" Coach calls from the bench. "Are you standing still out there?"

I skate like the pain doesn't matter. I deke out a defenseman, pass to Jordan on the left side, and fly by two more players, just as he sends it back. I get a decent look at the net that's denied. At least this one requires the goalie to use a little of that all-star athleticism, but the end result is the same—with Valley losing. A shutout in front of our home crowd.

AFTER OUR LOSS, NO ONE FEELS LIKE GOING OUT AND THE GUYS and I head back to the apartment.

I take a seat on the couch with my phone in hand. I haven't heard from Ginny and I don't think it's because her roommate didn't give her the message. I tap out a bunch of texts but don't send any of them.

Rauthruss is playing video games. "Wanna play?"

"Yeah." I lift my hand and he tosses me a controller.

We play in silence for a few minutes.

"Can, uh, I ask you a question?"

"Sure," he says, not looking away from the screen.

"You and Carrie. How'd that come about?"

"We went to high school together."

"Right, but I mean, how did you make it official?"

"She told me we were no longer seeing other people."

"And that was it?"

He pauses the game and looks to me. "I probably said something real eloquent like 'uhh okay.' She was popular and I wasn't. I'd have done anything she asked."

Adam's bedroom door opens, and he walks out and drops into the armchair and blows out a long, exaggerated breath.

Rauthruss looks to him. "Not going to Taryn's?"

Adam waves a hand. "Nah, that's over."

"Another one bites the dust?" Rauthruss jokes then looks to me. "You want advice on getting a girlfriend." He nods his head to Adam. "Scott's the one to ask."

"You want to ask Ginny to be your girlfriend?" Adam asks.

Yeah, this would be a lot less awkward if I weren't having this conversation with her brother. He hated the idea before I made her cry, so I doubt he's pumped now.

I tread carefully. "To be honest, I thought she already was, but I guess that's a thing people talk about first?"

Adam's face slowly transforms from a stony wall of indifference to amusement and he laughs. "Have you ever had a girlfriend, Payne?"

I clear my throat and wipe a hand over my brow. Jesus, it's hot in here. "Clearly not."

He studies me and lets out another one of his new broody sighs. "Ginny doesn't need a big gesture, just tell her how you feel. Well, no, actually first, you need to convince her to speak to you again."

"Yeah, thanks a lot. Good talk."

Mav walks through the door. "Honey, I'm home." He plops down and reads the room. "What's going on?"

"Heath is gonna ask Ginny to go steady." Rauthruss smirks.

"Fuck off," I tell him but smile. Dammit, I should have known better than to ask him. Nothing is ever taken seriously around here.

"I take it *talking* didn't go over so well?" Mav asks with a knowing smirk.

I flip him off. "Are you guys going to help me or what?"

Maverick claps his hands together. "Let's brainstorm on the whiteboard."

"We don't have a whiteboard," Adam points out.

Maverick shakes his head, smiling. "Real oversight, minion. Task one, find something to write down ideas."

Surprisingly, Adam does get up and appears to search for something to write on. Maverick goes to the fridge and grabs four beers and then hands them out.

Adam comes back with a scrap of paper and a pen. "All right, ideas to ask a girl out. I feel like I'm back in middle school."

"I would have guessed you started more pre-K age," Rauthruss says and twists the cap on his beer.

Adam flips him off and then looks to me, poised to write down our ideas.

"You're on board with this?" I ask him.

He shrugs. "If it's what she wants. Besides, it's going to be fun as hell to watch you try to pull this off."

Maverick takes the lead and I let him. For as much shit as he talks about his dad, I can see the family resemblance. When he sets his mind to it, he's a good leader.

An hour later, we've got a handful of ideas and they're all pretty awful. Rauthruss is the straightforward one—take her to dinner, buy her roses. Maverick is elaborate and has so many suggestions only about half are being written down. They range from renting out a movie theater to hiring a Mariachi band and everything else you can imagine in between. Adam has some good insight since he knows Ginny the best, but none of his suggestions feel right either.

I'm probably overthinking it. I don't know anything about love or being a good boyfriend, but I know Ginny and I know that I'm better when I'm with her.

"Well?" Rauthruss asks once we're out of new suggestions and beer.

"Maybe dinner?" It isn't the most creative, but a lot easier than renting out a movie theater. I have no idea how to pull off the latter and I feel like that kind of thing might take days or weeks, and I don't want to wait that long.

"Dinner?" Maverick's face twists up in clear disappointment. "Dinner is so... *dinner*. Unless..." He sits forward, elbows on knees. "You buy out the restaurant so it's just the two of you and then—"

I cut him off. "Let me stop you right there, buddy. `Preciate your dedication, but I don't want it to feel like I'm being someone else for the night."

Some of my favorite memories with Ginny over the past semester have been hanging out with our friends or chilling just the two of us. None of that was elaborate or over the top, but maybe this is different? Maybe big and bold is what I need.

I scrub a hand down my face and then look to Adam. "Does anyone know her favorite song?"

"You're going with *that* one?" Rauthruss's eyebrows shoot up. "This I gotta see."

Maverick fist pumps. "Yeah, I love that one."

"Of course, you do. It was your idea."

Chapter Thirty-Nine

GINNY

Dakota and Reagan sit on one end of my bed, their concerned faces staring back at me. Ava's gone for the weekend visiting Trent, and when I'd told my friends I was going back to my dorm alone after the game, they insisted on coming with me.

My phone pings on my desk and Dakota reaches to get it for me.

"Read it for me."

"It's Adam. He says he didn't see you at the game and wants to know if you're in your dorm watching *Notting Hill?*"

She looks up to me for an explanation.

"When I was in like seventh grade, my first boyfriend broke up with me and I was so devastated I watched *Notting Hill* on repeat for an entire weekend. Something like twenty times. It became my go-to breakup movie." I could so go for watching that movie on repeat about now.

"I love that movie," Reagan says. "Julia Roberts is a goddess."

Dakota sets my phone on the bed. "Guess they didn't see us. That's good."

"Yeah," I agree. I mean, I think it's good. I'm not sure what difference it would have made, but there was no way I could sit in my usual seat so close to the bench where he could read the sadness on my face. The game was brutal enough as it was.

Instead, the girls and I sat at the top of the student section blending in with the sea of blue and yellow. It was hard to watch them lose, but it fit my depressing mood nicely.

My phone pings again, and this time I reach for it.

Adam: Are you okay? Just let me know you're at the dorm and that all is well and I'll leave you alone.

Me: Yes, I'm safe and sound in my dorm.

He doesn't respond right away, and I toss my phone back onto the bed. Holding it reminds me I haven't talked to Heath. "Well, should we watch *Notting Hill*?"

We're just cueing up the movie when there's noise outside of my window. My window faces a parking lot, so it isn't unusual that it's noisy, but this noise is... well, it's different.

"Do you hear that?" I ask.

"Sounds like a bunch of drunk guys heading out to party. It's too early to be so obnoxious, must be freshmen. No offense." She stands and goes to look. "Uh, Ginny, I think you need to see this."

I scramble from the bed to look. There's shrubbery along the edge of the building, so the aforementioned obnoxious guys aren't directly under my window, but they're as close as they can get.

Adam and Rhett are on all fours on the ground and Maverick is on top of them on his hands and knees and then Heath stands on his back. They've built a freaking pyramid. Reagan and Dakota laugh. We open my window as far as it goes, which is only a couple of inches.

Heath holds his cell phone over his head and sings along with the music.

"What in the world is he doing?" Dakota asks.

"Shh! He's serenading her," Reagan says.

"Why Mariah Carey?" Dakota asks in a whisper.

A few other residents have opened their windows and call out or sing along. People walking by in the parking lot are stopping. Some have their phones out videoing it, no doubt.

Heath wears a shy expression, one I wasn't sure he possessed, but he belts out the song confidently. When he's through the chorus for a second time, he stops.

Rhett calls, "Did she hear us? What's going on? I can't see shit down here."

"The whole dorm heard you, asshole," someone calls.

"What are you doing?" I ask through the crack. My heart hammers in my chest. Hope and excitement claw at the hurt and anger.

"I didn't think this all the way through. I don't know what to do now," he admits with a sheepish grin.

"Tell her how you feel," Mav urges. He looks up to me and lifts a hand to wave, which makes Heath wobble on his back.

"Maybe you should get down first," Adam prompts.

Heath jumps down and the rest of the guys get up. Heath walks closer and stares up at me. "I miss you."

"You could have said that over the phone."

"I was afraid you wouldn't answer."

"Trying to watch a movie in here!" someone else calls out a window not far from mine.

Heath looks toward the voice. "Sorry, man. Almost done."

Mav pushes forward. "Go fucking watch it then. Guy's trying to pour his heart out." He nods to Heath as if to say, *I've got you covered.*

Heath tilts his head to the side and speaks a little quieter. "Can we talk somewhere else, not through the window?"

I hesitate and he adds, "Doesn't have to be tonight. Tomorrow? Next week? Next month? You name it and I'll be there."

Reagan whispers beside me, "Go down there."

My heart is beating so fast, but the rest of me is frozen in place. "I'll call you, okay?"

He nods, a look of resignation taking over his features and he takes a step back.

"Come on, boys," Adam says.

Every one of them looks disappointed, but I can't bring myself to run down there and throw myself into his arms. Of course, that's what I want to do, but then what?

They head toward the parking lot. Adam's Jeep is parked in one of the fifteen-minute spots closest to my dorm.

"Heath," I yell out my window. They all turn with matching hopeful expressions. "I miss you too."

Last night, Reagan and Dakota stayed through the movie. They didn't ask if I was going to call Heath or say anything really, and I'm glad because I didn't know the answer. I still don't.

After they were gone, I laid in bed with my phone scrolling

through our text history and then my pictures. He's become such a big part of my life and I know that I can't cut him out completely. At least for another semester, he'll be living with my brother, but even if that weren't the case, I'd see him on campus. A glimpse across the crowd or maybe we'd run into one another at a party.

I've started a dozen different text messages, but I haven't been brave enough to send any of them.

I go to the game Saturday afternoon with Dakota and this time we sit in our usual seats. We're in our blue and yellow, and I do my best to plaster on a happy face as the team takes the ice.

Heath looks straight to my seat, and when he sees me, a hint of a smile pulls at his lips. Tonight's game is as fast-paced as last night's and we're on our feet, hands clenched in nervous excitement for most of it.

Vermont's defense is big and mean and they seem to have it out for Heath in particular. He takes hit after brutal hit.

I cringe when Maverick's slammed into the boards. In front of me, Adam and a guy from Vermont collide and both go down, but not before Adam passes the puck to Heath. It's like a wrestling match on skates, but Heath races to the net, past defenders, and finds the net. The horn blares and we go crazy with the rest of the crowd.

The goal seems to shift things and Vermont is sloppier, not quite recovering their composure. Valley holds on to win by one.

I decide to wait for Heath by the locker rooms. I have no idea what I'm going to say, but avoiding him forever isn't an option.

The guys are slow to come out and I'm pacing and wringing my hands when his dark head finally comes through the door. He pauses when he sees me and Maverick runs into the back of him. I start toward him and meet him halfway.

"Hey," he says tentatively.

"Congratulations."

"Thanks."

We both shift awkwardly, and I step forward and hug him. He hugs me back but hisses through his teeth.

"Oh, shit, sorry." I step back as he winces. "You got tossed around like a rag doll out there tonight."

"Yeah, it got a little rough."

"Are you headed to The Hideout?"

"That was the plan, unless…"

"Yeah, you should go. It was a big victory."

"You're not coming?" There's obvious disappointment on his face.

"Not tonight. Dakota and I are going to watch Reagan's play. It's opening night. But maybe we can talk tomorrow?"

"Really?" He looks so excited about it, I can't help but smile.

"Yeah, really. We should talk. It isn't like we can avoid each other forever."

"Wouldn't want to even if I could." I'm at a loss for words and he takes my hand. "Just give me a chance to explain."

I nod and take a step away, breaking our contact. "Tomorrow."

SEEING REAGAN PERFORM A SECOND TIME IS JUST AS AMAZING AS the first, and bonus that I get to watch as Dakota and the rest of the crowd react.

"She's so damn talented," Dakota says when it's over. She wipes an honest to goodness tear from her eye. "I don't even like theater."

"Let's go find her. She said she'd meet us out in the lobby."

I'm surprised to see my brother and Rhett as we crowd into the lobby with everyone else. Their tall and muscular frames make them easy to find, but getting to them takes a few minutes. When we do, I ask the obvious question, "What are you two doing here?"

A quick scan of them, and I can tell they're in their travel suits for away games.

Adam hugs me. "She always comes to support us, so we thought we'd return the favor."

"That's really nice of you. What'd you think?" I ask Rhett.

"I don't really like theater, but Reagan's part was cool."

"Maybe you could leave out the first part when you see her," I tell him as I spot her. "She's over there. Come on."

Chapter Forty

HEATH

After having a beer with some of the guys on the team at The Hideout, I head back to the apartment. My latest care package from Nathan and Chloe is waiting for me and I open it (definitely Chloe put this one together—it's covered in gold tissue paper) and call my brother.

"Thank Chloe for the package." I lie down on my bed and stare up at the ceiling.

"You can thank her yourself in three weeks. We're flying up to watch you play the weekend before Christmas."

"For real?" I ask and sit up.

"Yeah, Mom too. She didn't tell you?"

"Uh…"

"You haven't talked to her, have you?"

"She's my next call." I pull the phone away from my ear and look at the time. "Or tomorrow, maybe, it's kind of late there."

"She'll be up. You know what a night owl she is. Call her."

"I will, I will," I say begrudgingly.

"I get it," he says. "Trust me, I do. I did the same thing. I got to Valley and tried to live like the past hadn't happened. I barely talked to you or Mom my first two years of college."

"I know, I remember." I'd been sad at first and then pissed. Dad died, then Nathan left, Mom got worse, and before I knew it, everything had changed except me.

"She's trying. I know it doesn't magically make up for everything, but you can't be pissed at her forever if you really want to move on."

"I'm not pissed," I say and then backtrack. "Okay, maybe a little pissed."

"If it helps, the more I talk to her now, the easier it gets and the less I find myself thinking about the past."

"Yeah, all right."

"Well, I've gotta get to bed. We're flying to New York early tomorrow, but I'm really excited to see you in a few weeks. Also, Chloe started Christmas shopping two months ago, so be prepared—her level of excitement is intense."

"Can't wait," I say honestly. It's been a long time since we've had a holiday together or really any time together.

After we hang up, I call Mom, but she doesn't answer, so I shoot her a text and then change into sweats.

She returns my call as I fall back on my bed. "Hey, sorry I missed your call, my hands were covered in cookie dough. I'm doing some late-night baking."

"No problem. I'm about to head to bed."

"Have you talked to Nathan? Did he tell you we're coming to Valley?" Her voice is upbeat, and I realize she's excited, which makes me more excited.

"Yeah, I just got off the phone with him. I can't believe you guys are all coming."

"Visiting you at college and then your brother and Chloe coming home for Thanksgiving reminded me how much I miss my boys. I was so focused on myself and getting healthy that I've let us all go too long without getting together."

"You're doing great, Mom." She really is and it only takes her voicing her own regrets to make me feel like a giant douche for holding the past against her. I haven't magically forgiven her, and I don't know how long it'll be until I do, but I know Nathan is right—I've gotta meet her where she is now if I want any type of relationship with her.

The thing is I don't avoid calling her because I don't want her in my life. I'm just having a hard time figuring out what that looks like now while I try to let go of years of hurt I didn't even realize I was harboring until she was well enough for me to take a breath.

"I am," she says confidently. "And so are you. I'm so proud of you."

I clear my throat. "Thanks, Mom."

"Three weeks! I can't wait. I'm making a test batch of oatmeal raisin cookies now."

My stomach growls. "Those are my favorite."

"I know. I haven't made them in years."

The more we make plans, the more excited I am, but also cautious. "I'm excited too, but if it doesn't work out, then we'll still all be together next summer. Assuming they go through with the wedding."

"Of course, they'll go through with it. Your brother is head over heels for Chloe."

"Yeah, it's not her I'm worried about screwing it up," I joke.

Honestly, I know my brother would gnaw off a limb before doing anything to sabotage his relationship with Chloe. And she's awesome, so I get it. I'm happy for them.

"Oh, hush. Your brother is doing great. I'm proud of both my boys. I'm really glad you called. The house is still lonely without you. Especially at night."

I yawn and she laughs in my ear. "Get some sleep, honey. I'll call you this week."

"Okay, sounds great, Mom."

"I love you."

I try not to react to the word, but my muscles tighten, waiting for the thing that comes next… which used to be disappointment. It doesn't come, but it's too many years of hurt built up. I don't know if there'll ever be a day it doesn't fill me with a sense of dread coming from her lips. Or a day I'll be able to say it to her or Ginny or anyone else. "Thanks, Mom."

Sunday I'm practically glued to my phone waiting to hear from Ginny. I texted her as soon as I woke up, but by mid-afternoon, I'm starting to worry she's blowing me off.

"Give me your phone," Maverick prompts and holds out his hand.

"No way."

"Payne, give me the fucking phone before you do something stupid."

"Why can't I text her again?"

"Because it's pathetic," Rauthruss says.

"That's really something coming from you. You're on your phone constantly with Carrie."

"Yeah, but she wants to talk to me."

Ouch, but okay, point made. I place my phone in Mav's palm and not two seconds later, her name flashes on the screen. I swipe it back with a giant smile on my face.

"And?" Mav asks.

"She's been at the theater all day. Apparently they asked her to do the makeup for Reagan and a few other girls at the show today."

"Oh, right." Adam's in the kitchen making food. "Yeah, I think I heard them talking about that last night. Reagan looked as hot as she always does, but I guess it was too subtle for the stage or the lights or, fuck, I don't know."

"You're just telling me this now?"

"I didn't think of it until now."

I take my phone into my bedroom and dial Ginny.

"Hey," she answers, sounding out of breath. "I'm just now heading back to my dorm. Sorry about that. I didn't realize that I'd need to stay through the whole performance."

"Stage makeup, huh?"

"Yeah, they even offered me a job for future performances."

"That's great, Ginny. Congratulations."

"Thank you. So, today was kind of a bust. I need to shower and then head to the library. I have a group meeting for one of my classes. I'm not sure when it'll be done. Can we talk tomorrow?"

Tomorrow. Shit, that sounds so far away. "Breakfast?"

"Yeah, I'll meet you at our usual time."

"So," Mav starts as we're walking into the dining hall. "Which one did you decide to go with?"

"What are you talking about?" I scan the room for Ginny.

"Which big gesture is next? Rent out a theater? Dinner?"

"I decided to go with something that's more… me."

"You?"

I slap Mav on the back. "Yeah, but it's not because I didn't enjoy your suggestions. You save those for when you find the perfect girl and screw it up."

"Good luck, buddy." He gets in line for food.

I don't see Ginny yet, so I head to the back where I find Brenda. She smiles when she spots me.

"How's my favorite lunch lady?"

She snorts. Brenda is the no-nonsense lady who manages the dining hall. I won her over last year. It started with a lot of flattery. Much deserved flattery. She works hard to keep us fed and I appreciate that more than most people. Then I got to know her a little and found out she's a huge hockey fan.

"Sam and the kids good?"

She softens at the mention of her husband and children. "Matty is graduating high school this year, and Sophia is all about boys, God help us all."

She hands me a tray and quirks a brow. "Coach Meyers approve of this?"

"What he doesn't know won't hurt him." I wink. "Thanks, Brenda. I owe you."

"Mhmm. How about paying me back with another win next weekend?" she calls as I walk off.

My steps are light as I head to my usual table. Ginny waits, looking around for me. When she spots me, a shy smile tips up the corners of her lips. Aaand, I'm suddenly really nervous.

"Hey," she says tentatively. She looks as anxious as I feel.

I'd planned to say a lot of things, but fuck words. I drop the tray on the table, frame her face with both hands, and bring my lips to hers. She lets out a yelp of surprise, but then her body melts and she kisses me back. I've missed her so much. Not just this. *Her.*

I don't want to stop kissing her, but the sound of people bustling around us going about their usual morning routines makes me pull back. That and I know there are things she needs to hear.

"I missed you so damn much, baby doll."

"Same."

"And I'm really sorry."

"I know you are."

I sit and guide her to take the seat beside me. "I want to explain, but I'm sure I'm going to say it all wrong." I blow out a breath. The way she watches me, willing to hear me out even when I know I've hurt her, pushes me forward.

"The other night was six years of frustration coming out at once, but it shouldn't have been you I was saying all that to. For a big part of my childhood, my mom used the words like a Band-Aid. Every time I took care of something for her—paid the bills or made dinner—the repayment I got was with a string of 'I love yous.' It changed how I felt about it. Her love felt like an excuse to not show up any other way." I squeeze my eyes shut. "Trust me, I know that's fucked up. I know she was grieving; I know she was depressed, but it didn't change the fact that all I wanted was for my mom to act like everyone else's. I didn't want *I love you*. I wanted her to take care of me."

"Oh, Heath, I'm sorry." She squeezes my hand. "I won't pretend to understand what that must have been like. I'm certain that she loved you the best she could. That's all anyone does. It isn't perfect."

"I know. Knowing it and accepting it aren't the same." My heart's beating like a drum in my chest. "The thought of my feelings for you being tainted by the past... I hate it. I don't want anything bad to ever touch you. You are my favorite person. You're the only person I'd skip food for or that could convince me to eat Neapolitan ice cream or... a thousand other things. You. It's only you. And when I walked in here, I fully intended to stand firm on my stance of never speaking the words, of keeping the best thing in my life away from my worst memories, but then I saw you and I realized that it doesn't matter what it's meant before. If loving you is wanting to spend every day with you, laughing and having fun, supporting you, and having your back, then I do. I love you, Ginny. Of course, I do."

"Really?"

"Really, really. I love you. I love you. I freaking love you."

She smiles and closes her eyes like she's trying to savor the moment. When her brown eyes meet mine again, it's such a punch to the gut I wonder how it took me so long to realize it.

"We don't need to use the word. Not if it bothers you. I just want to know that you're as crazy about me as I am you. That we're in this together."

"Did I mention I'd skip food for you?" Her lips part into a happy grin and my chest tightens. "One last thing."

I hop up onto the table and clear my throat. "Genevieve Scott, will you be my girlfriend?"

People are staring and snickering. Ginny's cheeks go red with embarrassment, but she nods. "Of course I will. I'd skip food for you too."

I jump down and kiss her again, then pull back so my forehead rests against hers. "I had no idea it was ever unclear that you were my girlfriend. I've always thought of you as my girl. I'm sorry that I left any room for doubt, but I won't make that mistake again. I'll stand on this table and ask every day if you want me to."

"I'll consider that. Could be entertaining." She laces her fingers with mine. "Speaking of food though, is that for me?" She tips her head to the bowl of ice cream.

I push the tray toward her, a huge bowl of Neapolitan ice cream topped with gummy bears.

"That is a lot of gummy bears. How did you get ice cream at this hour?"

"I know people."

Her gorgeous smile will be the death of me. She picks up the spoon and brings a big bite to my lips. I take it and then kiss her again.

Maverick appears at the table. "Awww, look at you two, all smiles." He drops his tray and then drapes an arm around each of our shoulders. "Bring it in, you two crazy kids. I'm so dang happy I could cry. Way to go big, buddy." He nudges me with an elbow and then squeezes Ginny into his massive frame. "I love you two."

And I know he does. Whatever it means to him, he means it with his whole heart. It's freeing to know I get to make it mean whatever I want to, too.

"Love you too, Mav," I tell him.

He gives me a toothy grin. "Damn straight."

Chapter Forty-One

GINNY

One week later

I have to go to class, I'm going to be late," I protest, but make no move to actually go anywhere. Heath's arms are wrapped around me and I nuzzle into his chest, stealing some of his warmth. "It's so cold."

"This isn't cold."

"It's like forty degrees outside."

"Like I said, this isn't cold. Wait until you come to Michigan sometime in the winter. You'll need real winter clothes, not these cute accessories you have." He pulls my beanie down farther, so it completely covers my ears.

"It would be fun to see snow. It almost never snows here and when it does, it's gone too quickly to appreciate it."

Another chilly breeze whips through campus and I shiver.

"Come on, baby doll," he says. "Let's get you to class where it's warm."

As we're crossing to the humanities building, a guy headed

toward us slows and a big smile tips up his lips. Heath stops, as does the guy.

"Heath, hey."

"Wes!" Heath steps forward and they hug.

Wes is a few inches taller than Heath with lighter hair and a leaner build. He looks familiar, but I can't place him until Heath turns to me and introduces him as one of the coaches of the basketball team and an old teammate of his brother's.

Heath comes to stand beside me again. "And this is Ginny, my girlfriend."

My insides light up every time he calls me that.

Wes nods his head to me in greeting. "Nice to meet you, Ginny."

"You too."

"What are you doing on campus, old man?" Heath asks. "Shouldn't you be at the gym making guys run sprints or something?"

"Not for another hour." His smile is big, and his eyes crinkle up at the corners. "I'm meeting Blair for lunch." He takes a step past us and turns. "Hey, nice season, by the way. I'm hoping to make another game soon."

"Nathan's coming up in two weeks for the game against Western Michigan."

"Yeah? I'll have to call him and give him shit for not telling me himself. I'll see ya later."

He heads off in the opposite direction and Heath and I continue across campus. I slide my glove-covered hand around his and squeeze.

"Coming over tonight?" he asks, swinging our arms lightly between us.

"Yeah, but I need to do some laundry first. I've barely been at my dorm all week."

"I don't see a problem. Should just pack your stuff and bring it to my place."

I slow. "You'd give me a drawer?"

"I'll give you as many as you want."

I laugh lightly at how easy it is for him to share himself and his space. Although that's not really new. Heath may not have experience in being a boyfriend, but he's always gone out of his way to give me anything he thought I might want. But all I really want is him. No one has ever made me happier and I've never had more fun than when I'm with him.

It wasn't exactly my plan to fall for someone first semester, but I can't wait to see what new adventures the next one will bring.

"MAV, THESE BURGERS ARE AMAZING," REAGAN SAYS WITH A groan of pleasure.

"They really are," Rhett adds. "I bow down to the grill master."

Mav waves his hand and dips his head in a mock bow.

The guys bought a patio heater and we're outside having dinner. Me, Heath, Adam, Rhett, Maverick, Dakota, and Reagan—we're like our own little dysfunctional family.

My brother is leaned back, beer in hand, smiling as everyone eats and talks. He seems happier. I know our parents' separation hit him hard, but I think he's coming to terms with it. So am I. Things will look different now, but at least we've got each other.

It's so weird to think that if I'd come to college with Bryan, so many things would have been different, but the thing I'm the most thankful for is how close Adam and I are again.

Heath and I huddle under a blanket, eating and bumping shoulders occasionally since our hands are full.

"We should play sardines tonight," Rhett says as he crumples his napkin and sets it in the middle of his plate.

"We've got an odd number without Taryn," Adam says. "You guys play, I'll hang back."

"What, no way," I protest. "We can have three on a team."

"Mav needs two people to keep him in line anyway." Rhett nudges him. "Who's going with Adam?"

"Reagan," I say too quickly, and my friend's eyes get large as if she's afraid I'm going to out her. "Mav helps cancel out some of Rhett's hiding skills."

It's perfectly good logic and Adam nods. "Yeah, that makes sense. What do you say, Reagan?"

"Sure, I guess that's okay," she says, barely looking at him.

We head to campus. Heath and I are slower than the others,

stopping to kiss every few steps and generally being the obnoxious happy couple.

"Who's hiding tonight?" Dakota asks.

"Should be Rhett and Reagan, so let's go with Adam and Reagan," I say.

Everyone nods their agreement. Playing matchmaker is way too much fun.

"What's the rule?" I ask Reagan and Adam.

They share a look as they try to decide.

"You pick," Adam says to her.

"One person has to close their eyes and be led by their partner or partners," she says the last part looking at our group of three.

"All right. Let's do this." Adam's breath shows in the cold air, and he claps his hands together before he and Reagan head off to hide.

"I've got the time," I call as we all settle in to wait. The ground is cold, so we stay standing and form a small circle sharing our body heat. Heath's arms wrap around me from behind and I lean back into his chest.

"You two are annoyingly adorable," Dakota says as Heath leans down to kiss my cheek.

While our friends make fun of us, good-naturedly of course, Heath keeps right on hugging me and I soak it up. Him, our friends, all of it.

"Don't be jealous, Dakota," Heath says, speaking near my ear. "You've got two. Ginny only gets one."

Rhett and Maverick attack her from each side, hugging her tightly between them. She squeals and bats at their chests, but she's laughing as they bounce up and down, jostling her around.

"Okay, okay." She finally gets free. "Let's go find Adam and Rea."

"Close your eyes, Dakota. We'll lead you," Mav says.

"Not a chance." She shakes her head, making her light red hair toss around her shoulders.

Rhett takes a step. "Mav, close your eyes. Dakota and I will make sure you don't run into anything."

Dakota gets on the opposite side of Mav from Rhett. "No promises from me," she says before they start to guide him away.

Heath sweeps my feet out from under me. "Close your eyes, baby doll, I got you."

I wrap my arms around his neck and let him carry me. I close my eyes, playing along, though I hardly see the point.

"Are you really leading me to find the others or taking me somewhere to make out?"

"That last one sounds real tempting, but the sooner we find the others, the sooner I can take you home and make out with you in my warm bed."

His lips graze against mine and I lean forward to kiss him harder. He stops, wherever we are, and his tongue sweeps into my mouth, warm and demanding.

He pulls back way sooner than I want, but he doesn't move.

"Ginny, open your eyes." His voice is filled with wonder and excitement.

His head's thrown back and he stares up into the sky. A tiny snowflake falls onto his nose.

"It's snowing!"

The small white flurries fall around us, slowly at first. Heath sets me down and I hold my arms out to the side. "I love the snow.

It always feels so magical."

I can just make out Dakota's laughter and the guys shouting and know they're excited about it too. Heath and I walk toward them in the snow, joining them at the same time Reagan and Adam have abandoned their hiding spot.

"This is amazing," I say as I reach Adam.

"Right? I can't remember the last time it snowed like this in December."

"It won't last," I say sadly. Even by morning, it'll probably be gone.

"But it's here now." Rhett smiles and takes a seat on the ground.

One by one, we all drop to the cold grass in the middle of campus. Maverick goes into his coat pocket and brings out a bottle of Mad Dogg. "I came prepared."

It hits me, sitting here with my friends—people I can no longer imagine not being in my life—I found this amazing group of people in the hardest five months of my entire life when I needed them the most. And amidst my brother's friends. Who would have thought?

But, if I've learned anything since coming to Valley, it's that we can only really prepare for the small things. What to wear, what to bring on a trip, which direction to go. The rest is fate and luck. And I feel like the luckiest girl of all.

JUNE

Epilogue

GINNY

D o I look okay?" I smooth a hand down my dress and turn in the mirror. Heath's sitting on the bed waiting for me as patiently as one can while his girlfriend changes clothes five times.

"You look gorgeous." He stands and wraps his arms around me, meeting my eyes in our reflection. "You don't need to be nervous. You've already met my family."

"I know, but it's not just your family—there are a bunch of people here this weekend and I don't know any of them."

"You know me. Besides, I only know half of them myself." He brings his lips to mine in a quick kiss. "Come on, I promise I won't leave your side."

The hotel is huge and right on the beach in California where Nathan's fiancée Chloe is from. Later tonight, we have the rehearsal dinner and tomorrow they'll say I do.

Down in the lobby, Heath guides me to a long table where his brother Nathan sits with a group of guys. Nathan and Heath look a lot alike, same nose and same eyes. Heath's hair is darker, and his build is bigger, although Nathan is a little taller. Nathan stands when he sees us, and he and Heath hug.

"You guys made it," Nathan says and smiles at me over Heath's shoulder.

When they separate, Heath comes back to my side. "We got in about an hour ago."

"This is gonna be fun." Nathan looks around at all the people and grins.

"Are weddings allowed to be fun?" Heath asks, earning a playful glare from his brother. "We're going to grab a drink."

"Baby Payne!" one of the guys calls as we start to walk off. "Grab me one too." He holds up his empty glass. He has deliciously dark hair and a cocky smirk. He turns that smirk on me and I go stupid.

"Who is that?" I whisper as we get to the bar.

"Hey now, no creeping on my brother's friends."

"I wasn't creeping, but *damn*. Is he a model?"

"He is happily married, young lady."

"I wonder if his wife gives him hall passes."

Heath chuckles. "Well, your boyfriend does not."

I bite back a laugh as he pulls me into his side possessively. Heath and I grab a drink and head back to the table where I meet Nathan's friends, Joel, Wes, and Zeke.

Watching Nathan with his friends reminds me a lot of Heath and his. They have the same easy way about them with all the teasing and competitiveness I've come to love. When their wives and girlfriends join us, I sit next to Heath, his hand around the back of my chair, missing our friends and wondering what we'll look like in five or ten years when the whole group of us gets together. I hope it looks even half as happy as this.

Nathan and Chloe are the picture of excitement and love as she sits on the edge of his lap and absently plays with the hair at the nape of his neck. I don't think she's stopped smiling since she sat down.

Joel, the one I'm pretty sure could have a second career in modeling, looks at his wife Katrina like she's the center of his world. And she looks at him the same way. Every time he looks at me I blush, I can't help it, he's stupid hot.

Zeke and his oh so very pregnant wife Gabby are possibly the cutest couple I've ever seen. She's all big, blonde hair and tiny body except for her bump. Zeke's at least twice her size and keeps reaching over and touching her stomach. I don't even think he realizes he's doing it.

Wes, who I've met before, and his girlfriend Blair are currently in the hot seat. They're the only couple of the group that isn't married and their friends are poking at Wes to get on the ball. Blair doesn't seem to mind. She leans over and kisses Wes, and they share some sort of private exchange.

I'm fighting a yawn and Heath notices. He sits forward. "I think we're going to take a nap before the rehearsal. We were up at dark-thirty this morning to get here."

Heath takes my hand and we start toward our room.

"Don't be late," Nathan calls after him.

Heath rolls his eyes and yells back, "I know how to tell time and work an alarm."

I pull him to the elevator and up to our floor.

"How long do we have?" I ask, climbing into bed and grabbing my phone to set an alarm.

Heath takes the device out of my hands and places it on the

bedside table. He pulls his dress shirt out of his pants with a wicked glint in his eye.

"I thought we were napping," I say as I unbuckle his pants.

"We will, but first…" He shrugs out of his shirt and my hands slide up his abs, enjoying the way the muscle cords and dips. Yeah, I'm suddenly not tired either.

His body covers mine and he kisses me hard. He rolls us so I'm on top. Making quick work of undressing me, his hands come up to palm my breasts. They ache. My entire body does. That's the way it is with Heath. One touch is never just one touch. He touches me and I feel it in my soul. It's all foreplay, he said once and I think he was right. My body sings when he's near. I keep waiting for the newness to wear off, but the more time we spend together, the more convinced I am that what we have is a once in a lifetime type of love.

I guide him inside of me and we both groan. This… this feeling. It's completeness, it's connection, it's everything.

THE NEXT MORNING, I SHOWER AND GET READY TO MEET UP WITH the girls. Chloe and Nathan's mom, Lana, invited me to join them for hair and makeup.

"You're leaving now? It's barely noon," Heath protests, arms wrapped around my waist as I comb out my wet hair.

Last night's rehearsal dinner went late. I'm not sure how many people they invited, but with their family and friends and Nathan's teammates… there are a lot of guests here to watch Nathan and

Chloe exchange vows. In a whirlwind of excitement and drinks, I met a lot of them after the rehearsal dinner. We closed down the hotel bar and then continued to hang out on the outdoor patio for well into the early morning hours.

So, the only thing we've done this morning is lie in bed—not that I'm complaining. Spending all day in bed with Heath is one of my favorite activities.

"Yes, I'm leaving now. Don't make that face—I don't want to be late."

"Fine." Reluctantly, he loosens his grip. "You're lucky I didn't tell Chloe you're a better makeup artist than the one she hired."

My jaw drops. "I would maim you, Heath Payne. It's the biggest day of her life!" My pitch rises with the panic I feel just imagining it.

"Relax, baby doll. You're secret's safe with me." He drops a kiss on my lips. "I guess I should find Nathan and see what he needs from his best man."

I kiss him again quickly and make my way to Chloe's suite. It's intimidating walking into the chaos. Chloe and her friends are chatting excitedly and fawning over her dress which hangs in the corner.

Gabby spots me from the chair she's sitting in and waves. She and the other bridesmaids are wearing matching pink robes, but Gabby's is shorter where it hitches up to cover her baby bump.

"I would get up, but the longer I sit today, the less chance that I'll have cankles when I stand up next to the blushing bride."

"You look beautiful. You totally have the whole glow thing going on."

She rubs at her stomach. "Thank you."

"Do you know if you're having a boy or girl?"

"Girl." She winces. "And I think she's dribbling a basketball in there."

"Ginny, hey." Chloe hugs me tightly. "Let me introduce you to everyone and then you're first up for hair and makeup."

HEATH

THE GUYS ARE KICKED BACK IN NATHAN'S ROOM, A BOTTLE OF Jack on the table between them.

"Couldn't spring for something a little nicer?" I ask as I take a seat next to them and pour myself a glass.

"Old school, Baby Payne," Joel says. "It was this or Everclear, and I don't think Chloe would appreciate your brother passing out before the ceremony."

Nathan wears a sheepish smile as he tips back another small sip. A knock at the door gets him to his feet.

"Linc," Nathan calls as he holds the door wide and my boss walks in.

I stand to greet him as well with a hug. "Hey, I didn't know you were coming."

"Wouldn't miss it." He steps back and looks me over. "How've you been?"

"Good. Great."

"He met a girl," Nathan says as if that clarifies why everything is great. I guess it does.

"Man, I hand you over to Wally for weekly check-ins and I miss all the good gossip."

When I first started working with Lincoln and his sports coaching website, we talked weekly. I reported directly to him. But the busier he's gotten, the less frequent our calls have been. I'm also pretty certain that the only reason I was reporting to him was so he had an excuse to check in on me. I'd like to think he and Nathan have finally started to trust that I can take care of myself and are giving me more credit.

"Is Keira here too?" Nathan asks. "She killed it at the tournament last weekend."

"She is." He beams with pride talking about his pro-golfer wife.

The room becomes a back and forth of questions and cross conversations as everyone catches up. When Nathan gets up to get another bottle of liquor, I follow him.

"Hey, I have something for you."

"Yeah?" He abandons the bottle on the wet bar and takes the box I hold out for him.

"Wrapped it myself," I say as he pulls back the flaps of a battered box I re-used from my collection of care packages he's sent.

Grinning, he pulls the items from the box. Gum, breath mints, sunscreen, condoms, earplugs.

"What is all this?" he asks with a chuckle and holds up the earplugs.

"A little honeymoon care package from me to you. Those are for Chloe so when she's tired of your shit, she can tune you out."

"Thank you."

I take out the smaller gift from my pocket. "Your real present."

He tears off the white paper and a ghost of a smile pulls one side of his mouth. "Is this—"

"Yeah, it's the same cologne Dad wore. I was walking through the store and the scent just hit me. I don't expect you to wear it. I thought you might like to have a reminder… especially today."

His hug is unexpected and tight. It takes me a moment to return the gesture, but when I do, there's a feeling like Dad's really here with us, or at least looking down and watching.

THIRTY MINUTES BEFORE THE WEDDING IS SCHEDULED TO START, we put on our tuxes and prepare to head down.

"Yo, Heath, can you do me a favor?" Nathan approaches me, looking sharper than I can ever remember seeing him. "I need to give Chloe her wedding gift before the ceremony, but I'm not supposed to see her."

I take the present covered not in wrapping paper, but in college-ruled notebook paper with his writing all over it. I give it a little shake. "What is it?"

"It's not for you." He blushes and now I really want to know what's inside. "Can you get it to her or not?"

"Yeah, of course."

I find the girls' suite and knock. When it swings open, my heart squeezes in my chest. "Holy shit, babe."

"Heath." Ginny looks around. "What are you doing?"

I'm still staring slack-jawed. Listen, Ginny, on an average day, is a knockout. She's generally casual—not a lot of makeup, hair straight or pulled away from her face in a braid… she doesn't need all the extra stuff to be the hottest girl I've ever seen, but right now… hair in big waves, eyes lined with black, wearing a dress that pushes her boobs up and shoes that make her legs look twice as long…

"Heath?"

I shake my head. "Fuck, you look… fuck."

She giggles. "You look nice too. I've been waiting for this day." She runs a hand along the lapel of my jacket. "You in a tux is really something."

"Yeah?" I step into her. "I'm starting to see the appeal of weddings."

"What's that?"

"Open bar and a night of fun while I try to figure out how to sneak you away without anyone noticing."

"You're ridiculous."

"You're beautiful."

"Five-minute warning!" someone yells from inside the room.

"Can you give this to Chloe? I don't want to go in there. It looks like a bomb went off."

"Yeah, I'll see you down there."

She turns, but I catch her wrist and pull her back to me, taking her lips in a much quicker kiss than I'd like. Someday I'm gonna marry that girl, but today it's all about Nathan and Chloe.

The guys and I head down first. The hotel restaurant has a huge patio that extends out onto the beach and there are flowers everywhere. In pots, hanging from the doorway, lining the wall. It's nuts.

People are seated and waiting for the ceremony. The other groomsmen bring Chloe's mom and grandparents up the aisle.

"What do you say?" I hold out my arm for my mom. Her eyes are already glassy. She's for sure going to cry, probably in the first thirty seconds. She lets out a breath and flutters her lashes a few times as if she's trying to stop the tears.

Turning to Nathan, she regards us both. "I'm so proud of the both of you. If your dad were here, he'd give some speech about baseball or fishing that somehow related back to life, but since he's not, you're going to have to make do with the girl version."

"Which is?" Nathan asks, hands in his pockets.

"Just be happy. Life's too short." Her eyes are tear-filled again, but she smiles. "He loved you two more than anything and so do I."

Nathan leans forward and kisses her cheek. "I love you too, Mom."

She slips her arm in mine and lets out a long breath. "Okay, ready."

I guide her up the aisle and to the groom's side. Ginny's sitting two rows behind the family. I shoot her a wink as we pass. Kevin stands from his seat when we approach.

We shake hands, and he smiles at Mom. He's a good guy and I'm coming to enjoy having him around. If nothing else, I know he's been good for Mom.

Today is one of those happy days when I can practically read Mom and Nathan's thoughts, all of us wishing Dad was here for our own selfish reasons. It's moments like these that will always remind us our family looks different now.

She squeezes my arm and then slips hers out to take her seat next to Kevin.

"Mom, wait." Her brows raise as she looks to me expectantly.

"I love you." My chest aches with emotion. Fuck, maybe I'm

going to cry today, too.

Her eyes well with tears again and this time, one slips down her cheek. I've waited too long to say the words to her, but I mean them now in a way I didn't before. Acceptance, forgiveness, or maybe it just took me growing the fuck up. She hugs me tightly. I clear the lump from my throat and take my place at the front.

As the processional music starts and all eyes go to the back, mine go to Nathan, my mom, and then Ginny—my family. I couldn't imagine life without them. If that's not love, then I don't know what is. Maybe it's not supposed to mean the same thing to everyone or maybe it is and it's about finding someone whose meaning matches yours. I don't plan on giving it a lot more thought. It is what it is and that's good enough for me.

Ginny glances at me and it hits me in the gut, like it does every single time she's near. Our love matches, plain and simple, and it's the best thing to ever happen to me.

Life is short. Be happy and enjoy every moment.

The End

ABOUT THE AUTHOR

Rebecca Jenshak is A new adult romance author, caffeine-addict, and lover of all sports.

Be sure not to miss new releases and sales from Rebecca – sign up to receive her newsletter *www.subscribepage.com/rebeccajenshaknewsletter*

www.rebeccajenshak.com

Made in the USA
Las Vegas, NV
16 January 2023